Death by Chocolate Malted Milkshake

Center Point
Large Print

Also by Sarah Graves and available from
Center Point Large Print:

Winter at the Door
The Girls She Left Behind
Death by Chocolate Cherry Cheesecake

**This Large Print Book carries the
Seal of Approval of N.A.V.H.**

Death by Chocolate Malted Milkshake

Sarah Graves

CENTER POINT LARGE PRINT
THORNDIKE, MAINE

This Center Point Large Print edition
is published in the year 2019 by arrangement with
Kensington Publishing Corp.

The text of this Large Print edition is unabridged.
In other aspects, this book may vary
from the original edition.
Printed in the United States of America
on permanent paper.
Set in 16-point Times New Roman type.

ISBN: 978-1-64358-130-9

Library of Congress Cataloging-in-Publication Data

Names: Graves, Sarah, 1951– author.
Title: Death by chocolate malted milkshake / Sarah Graves.
Description: Large Print edition. | Thorndike, Maine : Center Point
    Large Print, 2019.
Identifiers: LCCN 2018058573 | ISBN 9781643581309 (hardcover :
    alk. paper)
Subjects: LCSH: Murder—Fiction. | Poisoning—Fiction. | Large type
    books. | Eastport (Me.)—Fiction. | GSAFD: Suspense fiction. |
    Mystery fiction. | Love stories.
Classification: LCC PS3557.R2897 D44 2019 | DDC 813/.54—dc23
LC record available at https://lccn.loc.gov/2018058573

Death by
Chocolate Malted
Milkshake

One

Flailing his arms wildly, Eastport, Maine's local bad boy Toby Moran flew out the front door of the Rubber Ducky Bar & Grille as if shoved hard from behind.

Or possibly he'd been kicked. Staggering, he snarled something ugly over his shoulder at the waterfront drinking establishment he'd been ejected from. Then he stumbled unsteadily through the gathering dusk toward the paved path overlooking the harbor and the fishing pier beyond.

I watched from my seat at one of the big, round tables by the front window in the Pickled Herring, on Water Street across from the Duck. Around me, the savory aromas of roasting, grilling, and sautéing mingled with whiffs of seawater drifting in through the open front door.

Outside, it was a lovely late-spring evening, the kind that often lured unwary visitors into buying old houses here. Right now, in fact, a pair of them strolled unsuspectingly, hand in hand on the other side of the Herring's window.

". . . architecturally unspoiled," I heard one of them saying in reverent tones as they went by.

"And so affordable!" the other agreed brightly.

Yeah, and there's a reason for both those things, I thought, sipping my Irish coffee and remembering the days when I, too, was as innocent as a little lamb. Back then I'd bought one of the big old houses here, then spent years fixing it up.

Not to mention nearly every penny that I'd possessed. But there'd been little choice, since the house—fourteen rooms, forty-eight old double-hung windows, eight fireplaces, and an ell, all covered with white clapboard and topped by a roof so full of holes that it could've doubled as a spaghetti strainer—showed every sign of being ready to fall down on my head.

Which it still might; old houses are sneaky, it turns out. But at the moment I had a different problem.

"I'm just not ready to throw in the towel yet," my friend Ellie White said. She pursed her lips determinedly around the straw in her tall drink.

Not ready to give up and close the little chocolate-themed bakery business we'd started together a little over a year earlier, she meant. It's what we'd been discussing before I got distracted by the action across the street; now I turned from the Rubber Ducky's flashing yellow neon sign and the shadowy path behind the place, under the building's metal fire escape stairway where Moran had gone.

"Ellie," I began. "I know it's hard. It is for me, too. I really hate the idea of closing the shop, but I'm not sure we have a choice."

The problem being that, as usual at the end of a long winter in downeast Maine, right now ready cash around here was extremely scarce, and that went double for our own bank account.

"But we could still squeak through with just one big order," she insisted, brushing a long curl of strawberry-blond hair back from her face.

Ellie had violet-blue eyes, thick, dark lashes, and a sprinkling of gold freckles on her nose, which like the rest of her was cute as a button. Ordinarily she was the jeans-and-T-shirt type, but for our dinner out tonight she wore black leggings, a bright red leotard top, and a smock-topped cotton dress with purple rickrack around the neckline, the dress itself a vibrant—some might even call it eye-popping—shade of pistachio green.

"I mean, couldn't we?" she implored.

The rest of her outfit included soft black ballet slippers with bright, multicolored fake jewels on their toes, feathered earrings, and a gauzy pink scarf with lots of sparkly stuff woven into it, to tie back her hair.

What can I say, she liked dressing up when we went out. "And we've even *got* the order," she added coaxingly. "A wedding cake with all the fixings . . ."

"Right, but we haven't been paid for it yet, or for any of the ingredients, either, and—"

I stopped as the fellow the Pickled Herring had hired for entertainment began tootling on his flute. For one thing it seemed rude to go on talking when he was playing, but also I could see that for now, at least, Ellie's mind was made up.

"Let's discuss it later," I said, while outside the big front window, evening thickened into night. Now I saw only my reflection in the glass: long, narrow face, a dimpled chin that has been fairly accused of jutting, deep-set eyes.

Atop it all, unruly tendrils of short, dark hair went wherever they wanted. Also, there was a new wrinkle just there by my right eye; oh, good, I thought sourly.

Still, my looks hadn't scared any small children so far, and I seemed to have made some good friends and even acquired a family, one way and another. At the large table in the restaurant with me and Ellie now, for example, were all the rest of my immediate kin and Ellie's, too. I'll tell you more about them later, but in my big old house alone we had four generations ranging from elderly to infant.

Which meant that the house could get hectic, and often did. But like I say, never mind that now:

"We just *can't* give up," Ellie repeated, mostly to herself. Then she sucked up some more of her drink, not even making a face, much less falling dramatically to the floor with both her hands clutched to her throat, coughing and gagging.

Which is what I would've been doing. Her beverage of choice was a mixture of Moxie, a Maine-made soft drink that tastes like some bitter, old-fashioned medicine, and Allen's Coffee Flavored Brandy, a beverage that many, if not most, downeast Mainers insist really *is* medicine.

Then, "Hey, Ellie?" I said.

From his high chair between my son Sam and his wife, Mika, their baby, Ephraim, waved his rattle at the window, grinning toothlessly. Ephraim liked flute music, he liked restaurants, and most of all, he liked being with other people. I looked again where he was gesturing, and—

"Ellie?" I ventured once more. The Rubber Ducky's murky yellow neon sign blinked on and off in the bar's front window: DUCK! DUCK! DUCK!

But she didn't hear me. "I mean, so we're out of cash," she was saying. "That's bad, and even with the wedding-cake money we'll still just barely be able to pay all our current bills, I know that, too." She turned to me. "But, Jake, the season is just beginning."

Tourist season, she meant, that brief period in the summer when people from away come to spend money here in Maine. Some even make it all the way to Eastport: three hours from Bangor, light-years (or so it seems) from anywhere else, and about as far downeast as you can get without crossing over into Canada.

But I wasn't thinking about the tourists, either. "Ellie," I persisted, "isn't that Andy Devine over there? Coming out of the Duck?"

The guy just now leaving the bar across the street was tall and broad-shouldered, wore a dark blue poplin jacket and slacks, and had wavy, coppery hair the color of a new penny. Under the streetlight he glanced around briefly, shrugging his jacket up, then strode off into the night much more steadily than Toby Moran had.

Same direction, though, toward the gloom behind the Duck. But by the time Ellie looked he was gone.

So back to our problem, which obviously she wanted to talk about now instead of later.

"Jake, we've got to do something," she said. "If we could just make it through the next month . . ."

But we couldn't. "Ellie, we've gone through our options."

And found out we didn't have any, I thought but didn't add; she knew.

"And we can't put our own money into the shop anymore, either," I said. "I'm tapped out. And so are you."

Sighing, she drank more Moxie with Allen's

brandy in it while, around us at the table, the rest of our party enjoyed less fraught conversations.

Well, less fraught for us, anyway. ". . . disabled the poor guy's impeller," said my husband, Wade Sorenson.

Wade's a big man, burly and built like a lumberjack with blond, brush-cut hair and pale eyes that are blue or gray depending upon the weather.

"Jeez," said Ellie's husband, George Valentine. He was a small, dark-haired fellow in his forties whose stubborn chin and banty-rooster way of carrying himself gave him a feisty appearance that he more than lived up to.

"The impeller, what a dirty trick," he said of the case of marine vandalism that Wade was telling him about.

I agreed with George, because an impeller is a boat's water pump and without one, the engine cooks to death. And for a lot of people in Eastport, where fishing for scallops, lobster, and shrimp is among the few good ways of making a living, no engine meant no boat, no job, and no income whatsoever, for the foreseeable future.

Which coincidentally was pretty much the situation that Ellie and I were facing, minus the watercraft.

"Ellie, the light bill and the insurance are already overdue," I said. What we needed was an impeller that pumped money.

"We've paid our suppliers, though, right?" she wanted to know.

Our sources for chocolate and our other baking ingredients, she meant, and for our rent.

Meanwhile, the rest of our party was readying to go, Wade digging out his wallet and the waiter looking pleased when he saw the tip.

"The small businesses like ours," Ellie went on as we got up, "none of them are getting stiffed, are they?"

The flute player on the stage finished up and set the flute in its case.

"No," I conceded. I knew this because it was my job to pay the bills. "Don't worry, we're still current with our local suppliers."

Because for one thing, we wouldn't have been able to hold our heads up around town if we weren't.

"But I'm not sure," I warned Ellie, "how long even that can continue."

Not long at all if something good doesn't happen, pronto, I added silently as we made our way to the door; I'd paid this month's rent with the last of what few crumbs I could scrape up out of our business checking account. But when next month's came due I had no idea how we would manage it, which was why I was arguing against getting that far.

On the sidewalk outside, my elderly father, Jacob Tiptree, gazed around happily, his stringy

14

gray ponytail snaking down his flannel-shirted back and his ruby ear stud glinting under the streetlamp. Nearby, Sam and Mika busied themselves with the baby, settling him into his car seat. Behind them, Bella Diamond—my housekeeper and also my dad's wife, and yes, I do know it's complicated—gave them pointers on how to do it.

Luckily, the young parents loved Bella to pieces and were good-natured, besides. Nearby, Wade and George still chatted animatedly together.

Sighing, I turned to Ellie again. She'd worked very hard at our little business, it was important to her, and the truth of the matter was that we weren't yet *completely* doomed. . . .

Not quite. "You're right," I said quietly to her. "That wedding job could save us. If everything went perfectly."

That is, it could bridge the gap between the poverty of winter and the relative prosperity of an island summer in Maine . . . if we could make it until then.

Ellie beamed at me. "Yes! Oh, I'm so glad you see that. I knew you would," she added confidingly.

"If it doesn't, though," I cautioned, "or if we have any other setbacks at all, our baking business is history."

"Mmm," she replied, gazing across the street past the fish pier and the boat basin to where a big white full moon spread its silvery reflection on the bay.

"Pretty," she murmured, and it was, too, with the lights from the little houses on the nearby island of Campobello shining steadily across the water and a bell buoy clanking faintly out there somewhere, familiar as an old friend.

But even then, something about the evening made me feel uneasy, as if despite the lovely Maine scenery and the reassuring presence of family and friends, something nasty was lurking.

Something dangerous, maybe even deadly. Something evil . . .

And as it turned out, I was absolutely right.

Soon after my friend Ellie White and I opened our small downtown bakery, The Chocolate Moose, we began offering chocolate milkshakes. Partly it was because no one else in Eastport was selling them, but mostly it was that Ellie had found a gorgeous old milkshake mixer at a local church sale and wanted to try it.

The mixer was shiny mint green with four stainless-steel spindles that you snapped the metal mixing containers onto. It was a vintage item, you could tell by the solid materials and good design, although the first time we flipped the "on" switch the ancient electrical cord caught fire, filling our kitchen with smoke.

But once we'd replaced that part and started

again with milk, chocolate, ice cream, and a secret ingredient that Ellie wouldn't even tell me about, the shakes that came out of that mixer were . . .

Well, they were spectacular. Thick and creamy with the rich, full-bodied flavor of top-quality chocolate, Moose Milks were served in a reinforced paper cup with a moose silhouette printed on it and came topped with chocolate sprinkles shaped like tiny antlers; almost at once, they became the fastest-selling item in our shop.

Which made it all the sadder when, the morning after our dinner out at the Pickled Herring, we learned that someone—Toby Moran, to be precise—had apparently been murdered with one of them.

Specifically, he'd been discovered at 3 a.m. on the walkway behind the Rubber Ducky, dead with a near-empty milkshake cup lying beside him and some of the remaining milkshake dripped down his shirt. The smell of insecticide rising from the cup and the body made it pretty clear what must have happened.

"It was nice of Bob Arnold to give us a heads-up," I remarked to Ellie a couple of hours after we'd heard the news.

Bob was Eastport's police chief as well as a family friend, and he'd come by the shop just as we were arriving.

"Yes, but it's still awful. Who would do such a

17

thing?" Ellie replied, meanwhile beating a lot of sugar into a lot of shortening.

We stood across from one another at the work table in our shop's back-room kitchen, each with our own task.

"I mean, not that he didn't have enemies," she added. "Moran, that is."

A short laugh escaped me. "That's putting it mildly."

Past the doorway to the shop's front room I could see through to the outdoor window boxes, where the petunias and geraniums we'd planted earlier in spring now bloomed cheerfully in the sunshine.

"That he earned," Ellie added. "The enemies, I mean. Because the fact is, Toby Moran was a son of a—"

She thumped the big wooden spoon energetically back into the sugar-and-shortening mixture she was laboring over. I'd already finished getting the shop ready for the day: switching on the credit card reader, turning the door sign to OPEN, filling and starting the coffee-maker, and so on.

Much to my surprise, I'd turned out to enjoy all these tasks a great deal, and I liked the shop itself very much, too.

Inside our bay-windowed and exposed-brick-walled storefront on Water Street we had a single glass-fronted display case, a trio of small cast-iron café tables with chairs, and a cash register, plus a pretty impressive little professional bakers' kitchen setup in the back part of the store.

And that milkshake mixer, of course, in its place of honor atop the display case. "You're right, he was no prize," I admitted. "What about not speaking ill of the dead, though?"

The kitchen contained a massive gas stove with two ovens, one normal-sized and one large enough to roast an ox. To one side of them stood a pair of sinks, one for dishes and one for hand washing as per health department requirements, and beyond that were shelves of baking ingredients: flour, sugar, cocoa powder, spices, and so on.

The rest of the floor space was mostly occupied by the butcher-block-topped worktable. Racks of pots and pans hung from pegboard on the walls, and a massive old wooden-paddled ceiling fan turned slowly overhead, under the high tin ceiling.

"I'm not speaking ill of the dead," said Ellie. "I'm speaking of when he was alive."

For her baking duties today she wore her strawberry-blond hair tied up into a pink hairnet. A white bibbed apron over a white cotton T-shirt, jeans, and leather moccasins made up the rest of her outfit.

She twisted the top off a jar of Marshmallow Fluff. "Dead, he's a lot less trouble. For one thing, it guarantees that this time he won't come back."

From the various reformatories, jails, and prisons that Moran had been sent to during his lifetime, she meant. Burglary, car theft, drug offenses, assault . . . if there'd been a poster child for bad behavior in Eastport, Moran would've been it.

His worst crimes, though, were . . . well, it was this way: Moran was the kind of guy who, despite his history, could still convince a woman that he'd turned over a new leaf for her. Then when she saw the error of her ways—either before he'd twisted her arm and/or blackened her eye, or afterward—he'd show up at her door late at night with a song in his heart and a loaded pistol in his hand, wanting her back.

Demanding her back. Sometimes he'd fire off the weapon a few times, other nights he'd just sit there staring balefully, but always he would return night after night, slipping off into the darkness just before the cops got there.

He'd done it to at least three Eastport women that we knew of, and probably more. "Can't argue with you about that," I conceded.

The less trouble now that he was dead part, that is. "I mean, for a guy who was only thirty years old . . ."

Cops from three towns had needed calling to his birthday bash at the Rubber Ducky not quite a year earlier, which was how I knew.

"He'd sure racked up a lot of bad deeds," I

20

finished as Ellie began beating Marshmallow Fluff into the sugar-and-shortening mixture.

The kitchen timer buzzed; together with the luscious aroma of Toll House cookies floating from the smaller of our two ovens, it told me that the early-morning's last batch of baking was complete.

The trick to these cookies, by the way, is to use a little less flour than the recipe calls for. Also, some recipes include cinnamon and salt, but shouldn't; the butter's salted already and the cinnamon, you should excuse my saying so, is an abomination.

I slid the cookie sheet out of the oven, set it on a rack at my end of the worktable, then with a thin spatula began transferring the cookies onto white paper doilies on a display case tray.

And then I hesitated. They *looked* lovely: golden brown, darker but not too dark around the edges, with plenty of chocolate morsels in them. But I couldn't be sure, unless . . .

Ellie glanced over suspiciously. "What are you doing?"

"Testing one," I mumbled, "to be sure it's okay." Oh, it was. It definitely was.

"We wouldn't want to be selling anything that wasn't, would we?" I added through a mouthful of chocolatey heaven.

"Surely not," said Ellie, unable to repress a smile. Going into business is a learning experience, they say, and one thing we learned right off the bat was that I had a sweet tooth the size of a Buick.

"I am," I said after licking the remaining melted chocolate off my fingertips, "our taste tester, after all."

Hey, it was a tough job, but somebody had to do it. Also, I saw it as payback for me having to deal with all those bills.

"Oh, indeed," Ellie retorted wryly, squinting at her measuring cup. "Fine, then. Just don't give yourself a stomachache."

Saying this, she walloped the remaining Marshmallow Fluff into the sugared shortening mixture. But then her voice went somber.

"I almost wish we hadn't used those antler-shaped sprinkles."

We'd been delighted to find them in a specialty baking supply catalog, but now they were how the fatal milkshake had been identified as one from The Chocolate Moose, along, of course, with the instantly recognizable paper cup with our antlered mascot on it.

Apparently Moran had drunk most of the milkshake before he died, which I thought posed its own problems. But I would wonder about that later, I decided as Ellie frowned down at the bowlful of sweet stuff she'd been working on.

Marshmallow Fluff was not a regular item on our ingredients list; personally, I'd rather eat lard than a fluffernutter, and Ellie thought the stuff was right up there with Spam straight out of the can.

But in this case it was required. "Now this frosting needs to get chilled," said Ellie.

I took the bowl, covered it with plastic wrap, and set it in the cooler alongside a half-dozen already-baked trays of Chocolate Cruller Muffins, Heavenly Devil's Food Cookies, and Criminally Good Fudge Drops. In fifteen minutes when the shop opened at 10 a.m., I'd have them all out in the display case with the cookies and we would be ready.

"There," I said, dusting my hands together. But my satisfaction was mingled with worry; as I slid open the glass door of the display case I couldn't help wondering how many more times I'd get to do it before we really were forced to quit.

A year earlier when we began, we'd hoped Ellie's grandmother's wonderful old baking recipes, Ellie's own skill at following them, and my ability to pinch a penny until Abe Lincoln screamed would carry us through any little deficiencies in our actual storekeeping experience.

But so far, all we'd been able to do was keep our heads above water—barely—especially in winter, when there just weren't enough customers around to pay the light bill, much less make any profit.

Still, we'd been friends for a long while and I

felt sure that much at least would continue; small comfort in the business world, maybe, but to me it was everything. Now while I swept a final time under the tables and straightened up the napkin dispensers, she began her next task of the day: putting together the bottom layer of a whoopie-pie wedding cake for what promised to be—in our remote little corner of the world, anyway—the wedding of the century.

Also, at least if Ellie was right, that cake was going to bring us the payday that would save our business, and the wedding was just five days away. So maybe things were looking up, I thought hopefully.

But just moments after I'd gotten the front door unlocked and the last of the Fudge Drops onto the tray in the display case, the little bell mounted over the shop door jingled and the bride-to-be walked in.

And she was crying, which could not be a good sign. "Oh, have you heard?" she managed. "Toby Moran's been murdered!"

"Yes, we have, you poor thing," I replied, hurrying to her.

I pressed a napkin into the hands of the wretchedly sobbing young Eastport kindergarten teacher, Sharon Sweetwater, and guided her to one of the small tables, then brought her a box of tissues and a glass of iced Perrier water with a lime slice in it.

"Here, drink some of this." I sat across from the distraught young woman while she obeyed me as best she could, given how hard she was still crying.

"Oh," Sharon breathed. Her eyes were still streaming and her shoulders hitched with lingering sobs.

With her dark curls clipped closely to her small, neat head, her wide green eyes framed by lashes black as ravens' wings, and cheeks that really did look as if the roses of spring were blooming in them, Sharon was just about the prettiest girl we'd ever seen.

The happiest, too, usually. But not now, of course. "The police came to my house a little while ago," she said. "They asked if they could come in, and they asked me a lot of questions."

She took another hitching breath. "A lot of very worrying questions, and I'm very upset, and I couldn't think of anyone else but you two that I wanted to talk to about it," she finished, the words coming out in a rush.

She sucked in a shaky breath. "Because I thought it was all over with," the words tumbled from her, "but now it'll all be brought up and hashed over again, and at the *worst* possible time, when the last thing I want is to remind anyone at all that I . . ."

That she'd been one of Moran's victims, she'd have added if she hadn't begun crying so hard again. Before meeting her current fiancé, she'd been one of Moran's girlfriends—everyone in Eastport knew it—and their inevitable breakup had, of course, come with his own special brand of terrifying harassment.

"Just like the others. He'd sit outside my house at night," she said. "Staring and glaring, and scaring me half to death."

"Ugh. In that awful car of his? And did he have the gun?" Ellie wanted to know.

Because naturally Toby'd had a gun; guys like him always did, and he'd made a show of it whenever he could. The car he drove was characteristic of him, too: a black Dodge Charger with dark-tinted windows, a hideously realistic skull-and-crossbones hood ornament, and a custom chrome grille like a mouthful of shiny metal teeth.

"Yes, that car. And the gun. It was a .22, he'd showed it to me before," Sharon said bleakly.

Of course he had. "So what the cops really wanted to know was if maybe you ended Moran's harassment by ending him?" I asked.

Which didn't quite make sense, partly because she'd already broken up with him long before and partly for another reason.

"Yes." Sharon nodded energetically again. "They didn't say so, exactly, but why else? They asked me a lot about whether was I still angry with him, that's for sure." Another shuddery breath. "And I said I was."

She'd made no secret of the fact that she despised him; probably every woman he'd ever met still did, some murderously so, maybe.

"And what made it worse was that I've got no alibi," she said. "I was home finishing up the crocheting on my wedding veil, all alone. So it's not like I couldn't have done it."

Only that she wouldn't have, since angry or not, here's the thing about Sharon: if you were a housefly—a large, thoroughly repulsive housefly, buzzing around annoyingly and making a complete nuisance of yourself—she wouldn't swat you. She'd trap you in a jelly jar, then fling you out into the fresh air and watch you fly.

"They were skeptical of me," Sharon added, meaning the police.

Which was most likely an understatement. She'd had a restraining order against Moran— it's what sent them to her so fast, probably, her name in some database or another—so while she might not yet be a no-kidding murder suspect, she was surely a person of interest.

Once more the little bell over the door tinkled; this time Jenna Waldrop waltzed in, all auburn ringlets and copper bracelets, wearing a pair of black slacks and a white cardigan with ruffles around the neckline.

Jenna was a kindergarten teacher, too, and in her twenties, but that was where any resemblance between her and Sharon Sweetwater ended.

Meanwhile the kindergarteners' school year, always abbreviated for the littlest children, had ended even earlier this year due to a roof leak, which was why neither young woman was at work.

"Sharon, are you okay?" Seeing her colleague looking distressed at the café table, Jenna plastered a look of concern onto her face.

But if her sympathy had been any more fake, her nose would've begun growing; Jenna was well-known around town for her strong sense of entitlement, as well as for the few scruples she had to go with it.

And according to local rumor, what Jenna felt recently that she deserved but hadn't gotten was Sharon's fiancé.

"Oh, I'm just ducky, Jenna, thanks for asking," replied Sharon. Then, with a daggerish glance, "Give my best to your mother."

Oof. Jenna's mother, Henrietta, was a well-known domestic terror of the daughter-dominating variety, and reminding Jenna of this was as cutting as any insult. Never mind Sharon's fiancé, Andy Devine; Jenna would've married a department-store mannequin if it got her away from Mrs. Waldrop.

"Yes. Well," Jenna said, digesting Sharon's remark while picking out a half-dozen chocolate macaroons from the display case. "I'm sorry about your friend." Biting the words off, she took the white paper bagful of macaroons Ellie handed to her and accepted her change.

"Friends, actually," she amended, turning to Sharon again. "Your *dead* friend, Toby Moran, and Andy Devine, too. Who the cops already think probably killed Toby," she added meanly.

She paused at the door. "I overheard them saying so just now in the diner where they were getting coffee, and d'you know what?" Her dark eyes narrowed in satisfaction. "Say what you want about the golden boy," she delivered her final thrust, "but I'll just bet they're right."

The golden boy . . . She flounced out. I turned to Sharon, now pressing a fresh tissue to her lips in a vain attempt to stifle her own sobs.

"I don't get it," said Ellie, looking puzzledly from me to Sharon and back. Jenna had a viperish tongue, and not getting Andy for herself had made her bitter. But still . . .

"What'd she mean by that last part?"

I stood there silently thinking about what it would take to get poison into a chocolate macaroon. Not the deadly substance that had killed Toby Moran, of course; *insecticide, they could smell it ten feet away,* police chief Bob Arnold had told us.

Just something that was thoroughly inconvenient. Outside, Jenna strode past the window and down the street.

"I mean, the very idea of Andy Devine being

29

a suspect," Ellie went on, "how could they possibly . . . ?"

Andy Devine, the most dashing young Coast Guard officer any of us had ever seen, resembled Great Britain's Prince Harry without the beard. Smart, funny, and a sure bet to be promoted in the not-too-distant future, the Maine Maritime Academy graduate-with-honors was an Eastport success story.

And now, at least if you believed Jenna, he was a murder suspect—a situation that promised to sink not only the upcoming wedding celebration, but also The Chocolate Moose.

"It's too bad Jenna can't come right out and complain about her mom," Ellie said. "She'd find a lot of sympathy if she did, I'll bet."

I nodded agreement. We'd sent Sharon up to my house to be cosseted and cared for by Bella Diamond; Sharon had no relatives here in town and her friends were mostly other teachers, all of whom were busy teaching the older students who were still in school right now.

"Jenna grew up with meanness, now she's mean, too," I said. "And doesn't know how to stop, maybe, she's been that way for so long."

Just then my daughter-in-law, Mika, arrived to tend the shop for the day. A talented violinist, my son Sam's beloved wife, and the mother of my fabulously wonderful grandson, Ephraim

Tchang-Tiptree, Mika had also turned out to be a competent pastry chef, fortunately for me and Ellie.

"Hello, hello," Mika greeted us smilingly, pulling back her shiny black hair and stuffing it into a hairnet like Ellie's.

"How's he doing?" I couldn't resist asking. The very idea of having a grandchild had once stuck in my craw; for one thing it meant I was no longer a teenager myself, as if I'd needed any more proof. Now, though, just the thought of him melted my insides into something much like the Marshmallow Fluff Ellie had been using.

"Oh, he's great." Mika pulled a white bibbed apron on over her blouse and capri pants. "Sam's taking him to the park this morning and then over to the health center for his six-month checkup."

She began polishing the display case with one hand and neatening the toothpicks in the ceramic jar on the cash register counter with the other.

"You two can go if you want," she added. "I'll be fine here."

Not that we needed toothpicks, usually. We just liked the way they looked in the jar. Thinking this, I peered again at the counter; it seemed different, somehow.

But before I could figure out why, Ellie came out of the kitchen with a sweater over her shoulders and her bag over her arm.

"Maybe you can figure out something with that

31

frosting," she told Mika, meaning the stuff still sitting in the cooler. "I'm starting to think I'll never get it the right consistency."

Because even a small whoopie pie slides sideways if the frosting is goopy, and for it to happen to a wedding cake would be disastrous. Assuming, I mean, that there was still going to *be* a wedding. . . .

On Water Street the breeze off the harbor was refreshing, the salt air tinctured with an invigorating mixture of seaweed and wood smoke. As we went by, Ellie brushed off the tops of the cast-iron café tables we'd set up on the sidewalk.

"Hello again, ladies," called a familiar voice. It was Eastport police chief Bob Arnold, slowing his squad car alongside us.

Bob had plump cheeks, thinning blond hair over a high, wide forehead, and pink rosebud lips that didn't look as if they belonged on a law enforcement professional. But what he lacked in appearances he more than made up for in the ability to wrangle evildoers.

And talk their secrets out of them, too, sometimes. "State boys been by to see you yet?" he wanted to know.

In Maine, only Portland and Bangor had their own murder squads; the rest got handled by the Maine State Police department's homicide investigation unit.

"Not yet," Ellie replied. "But I'll bet they will be. Wanting to know if we sold Toby Moran that milkshake, I imagine."

How he'd gotten it, complete with a Chocolate Moose cup and even the antler-shaped sprinkles, was still a mystery.

"But, Bob," Ellie went on, "is it true about Andy Devine, that the state police think he might've killed Toby?"

Static fritzed out of the squad car's radio. Something about a break-in somewhere made him grimace. When it was done, he answered. "Yeah, the two of 'em had a beef last night in the Duck, nearly came to fists before Moran got tossed out on his ear."

More static, then: "Bad blood between 'em anyway," Bob went on, " 'cause of Sharon. And," he added unhappily, "people saw Andy follow Toby onto the path *behind* the Duck, after Toby got eighty-sixed and Andy left on his own."

"Rats," I said, not mentioning that I'd seen him, too; as Wade would've said, Andy didn't need more weight on his anchor chain.

"That doesn't sound good," I added. "I wish we could help about the milkshake, at least, though. Maybe someone who really *hated* Moran came in and bought one?"

Ellie nodded disconsolately. "That's possible. But Mika was in the shop all day yesterday," she said.

I'd have been there myself, but my dad had had an eye doctor appointment, so I'd played chauffeur. He'd been saying for months that his recovery from a heart attack was complete enough for him to start driving again, and an eye exam was the first step.

And also the last, I earnestly hoped, but that was another story. Bob pulled over to let a pickup truck loaded with lobster traps pass by him, the big wire cratelike traps stacked high in the truck bed.

"So what's she said about it, anything?" Bob asked, meaning Mika.

"Not about Moran," I said. "I don't think she's heard about him yet. But last night at dinner she said she'd sold milkshakes all day."

It was a week after Memorial Day, and a few early-season tourists were already in town, but I doubted she'd recognized many of them.

"You can ask her yourself, though," I said. "What about you, have you heard anything else?"

"All Moran's friends are shut up tighter'n ticks," Bob said. "To hear them talk, the guy didn't have an enemy in the world."

"Hmph," said Ellie. Like me, I guessed, she'd decided not to say anything until we got the lay of the land figured out a little better.

Because for one thing, why would he drink something that stank of bug killer?

Another truck rattled by, this one loaded with

clam hods. Also in the truck bed were boots, clam rakes, shovels, and a lot of slat-sided crates full of empty beer bottles; clamming is thirsty work.

"Have they talked yet to any of Moran's old girlfriends?" Ellie asked. "I mean, besides Sharon?"

It never failed to surprise me how many of them there had been. But the idea that a truly terrible guy was just waiting for the right woman to reform him was as beguiling here in Eastport as it was anywhere else, apparently.

Bob grimaced wryly. "Oh, yeah. Been calling them all morning. Got 'em lined up to talk to, all this afternoon."

He sighed at the prospect. "I don't expect much, though. Seems they all were with people last night."

Drat; they had alibis, in other words. Not that I wished any of them ill, but it wasn't their wedding that Ellie and I were relying on to save our business.

Just then an old station wagon packed with mooring chains rumbled by, its registration sticker out of date and its weight-challenged rear end shooting sparks from the vehicle's dragging muffler.

Bob gave it the hairy eyeball and let his own car creep forward. I could see him planning a chat with the driver.

But right now, he was chatting with me. "Meanwhile, I know what you two are probably thinking of, and I want you to stay out of this whole thing, you understand?"

Ellie and I glanced at each other. Bob could be forgiven for his suspicion that we might snoop into Toby Moran's murder, especially because one of our own milkshakes had been the weapon, it looked like.

Besides, we'd meddled in local mayhem before. There was the time, for instance, that another young man had met his maker and my own ex-husband (now deceased, but at the time he'd been an awful pain in the tail) had ended up as the main suspect.

And although there'd been plenty of things I'd have liked seeing him get nailed for—during our marriage he hadn't seemed to know the difference between me and a piñata, for instance—murder wasn't one of them. So Ellie and I had pursued the real killer, and the killer had pursued us right back, with near-fatal results.

Now Bob eyed me warningly. "I mean it, Jake. Besides the state cops all swarming around here investigating, with this big wedding coming up we'll have plenty of extra people in town, lots arriving in the next few days."

He hadn't thought yet about the fact that, if things stayed as they were, there wouldn't be a wedding. And considering how insistent he was

36

about our not snooping, I figured I wouldn't remind him.

What he hadn't done, though, was explicitly *forbid* us to do any snooping. . . . Down the street, the loaded station wagon went over a bump in the pavement. More sparks flew, as did chunks of the ramshackle vehicle's rotting undercarriage.

Bob winced. "So I've got lots of aggravation already. That radio call was about a copper theft out near the airport."

By this he meant someone had broken into an unoccupied house and stripped the pipes out of it; you could do this, I'd learned, with pliers and a pipe cutter, and it didn't take long. The next step would be to sell the stolen pipes to an unscrupulous scrap-metal dealer.

And yes, it was a dirty trick. But the people who did it didn't care; they just wanted the money. So now Bob had to deal with it.

"Which means I don't need any more trouble," Bob finished, then took off after the station wagon whose driver had apparently decided he didn't need that raggedy old muffler anyway, and sped off without most of it.

"Ohh," breathed Ellie when Bob had gone. "I wish he hadn't said anything about the wedding. I'm already nervous enough about it."

"Me too," I said, not adding that what I was nervous about was mostly whether or not it would still happen at all. Thinking this, I walked with Ellie up Water Street past the art gallery, the coffee shop, the pharmacy, the water company, and Wadsworth's Hardware Store.

"Don't worry about the cake, anyway," I said as we reached the corner. "Mika will get that part of things under control; she's good at that stuff."

She was, too, but privately in this case I wasn't as confident as I sounded. Making a whoopie-pie wedding cake was challenging enough; the real difficulty in doing it successfully, though, was still getting the thing to stand upright.

"The whole problem with it," said Ellie, "is still that darned frosting."

Too soft and the thing leaned sideways; too stiff and it stuck to your teeth. And I wasn't sure even our beloved Mika could find a happy medium between the two.

"I mean, assuming the cake we end up needing isn't one with a hacksaw baked into it, so Andy can break himself out of jail," Ellie added bleakly.

Which from what I'd heard so far was also a real possibility; it seemed Andy Devine had the motive as well as the opportunity.

"All those state cops need now is to find out he'd gotten hold of one of our milkshakes, somehow, and presto, instant murder suspect," she said.

I couldn't disagree with that, either, and on that

sorry note we turned up Key Street toward my old house: white clapboards, three tall redbrick chimneys, two porches, and those forty-eight old wooden windows, each with its own pair of dark-green wooden shutters.

On the back porch we made our way past a stroller, two bicycles, a mop bucket with a mop standing in it, and a bunch of fishing poles rigged up and bristling with multiply-hooked mackerel jigs.

From inside the screen door floated the tantalizing aroma of hot apple pie. I opened the door and a plastic rattle flew past my head.

"Gah!" said Ephraim, grinning at me from his playpen in the middle of the bright, spotless kitchen.

"Gah, yourself," I said as he hurled another toy; he knew I was a reliable retriever.

Then, with the faint sound of alarm bells already ringing in my head, I peered around. With its tall, bare windows, pine beadboard cabinets, and an antique fireplace hearth on which our modern propane stove now stood, my kitchen also held a large butcher-block table, a trio of potted pink geraniums that Bella had raised from cuttings over the previous winter, and an antique soapstone sink perched on four white metal supports as thick as piano legs.

What *wasn't* in the kitchen was Sharon Sweetwater.

"Blrgh!" commented Ephraim. I'd been nervous about having a baby in the house—colic, diapers—but this one was at least easy in the daytime, if not at night. Today he wore a yellow knit onesie with ducks printed on it, plus a grin with a spit bubble in it.

"Flrfl!" he enthused, while at the stove, my housekeeper-slash-stepmother, Bella Diamond, stood frowning over the pie.

"Bella, where's Sharon? She said she was coming here."

"I don't know. I haven't seen her." She frowned harder, peering down at the pie crust. "I think I might have burned this."

Small and wiry with large grape-green eyes, frizzy henna-dyed hair, and a bony, buck-toothed face beautifully softened by its owner's possession of the kindest heart imaginable, Bella was our resident household goddess.

"Better let me test it," I said, whereupon she cut me a generous slice, and one for Ellie, too.

"Where's Dad?" I asked, digging in. "And are you sure you haven't heard from Sharon at all?"

Bella had begun as my part-time employee, since when I first bought the old house I'd been too busy repairing it to have any time to clean it. Only later had she moved in and married my dad.

"I said I don't know about her," Bella replied with a touch of asperity. "I'm sure I can't keep an eye on everyone around here; it's a full-time job just trying to keep track of your father."

Uh-oh. I didn't like the sound of that. Since regaining his health he'd seemed devoted to the project of letting us know he could do whatever he pleased, whenever it pleased him.

Which, of course, didn't please Bella one bit, especially since lately what he liked was either unsafe, illegal, or—most often—both. He was a big fan of homemade fireworks, for instance, a hobby he'd been pursuing—sometimes even professionally—all his life.

That is, if by "homemade fireworks" you actually mean small bombs, but that's another whole story.

"Right now," said Bella, "he's at the health center getting a complete physical."

I put down my fork. Since his heart attack, he'd been getting checked out every month by his own doctor, a cardiologist in Bangor.

"Why?" I asked, suddenly anxious. "Has something happened?"

He was the youngest old man I'd ever met: big-hearted, broad-minded, and as wide-eyed at all the many wonders of the world as his great-grandson, Ephraim.

But he was still an elderly guy, with all the potential for sudden, irreversible disaster that phrase really can't help but imply, and he'd had one heart attack already.

"Now that his eyes have checked out he's even more set on driving again," said Bella, her tone conveying what she thought about that.

He'd given up his license after he'd gotten ill, saying he didn't want to be the kind of old fart who drove through a store window.

But now, I gathered, he wanted to be the kind of old fart who'd changed his mind.

"I guess the eye doctor must not've discouraged him," said Ellie, scraping up the last bits of pie.

I guess not, too . . . unfortunately. Just then the phone rang, and Bella hurried to answer while I smeared some pie juice onto my finger and offered it to Ephraim.

"What do you think, buddy?" I asked him. "D'you know where Sharon Sweetwater might be? Because she's making me nervous."

I mean, of course, she could've changed her mind and gone somewhere else. But—

"Glrk," Ephraim pronounced, sniffing interestedly, then latched on to my pie-smeared fingertip so hard with his baby mouth that it was a wonder my whole hand didn't go down his throat.

Removing my finger, I glanced to make sure it still had flesh attached, which miraculously it did, just as our German shepherd, Max, wandered into the kitchen. Large, long-haired, and with big black toenailed feet so huge and furry they could've doubled as dust mops, the dog ambled over to the playpen and stuck his snout through the bars.

I jumped up again; the kid didn't have teeth yet, but Max did, and in the nose-bopping department little Ephraim was already a champ. But before I could get there, tiny fingers had already found Max's ear.

"Ohh," the baby breathed, touching the dog's soft ear leather with a look of wonderment.

"Umph," said Max, his whiskey-colored eyes quizzical. Then he withdrew very slowly and gently, lowering himself to the floor by the playpen with a sigh of doggy contentment.

From the phone alcove I heard Bella's voice rise in inquiry. "She *what? Where?* But, Marienbad, *why* is she—"

Well, at least it wasn't about my father. But then I realized who it almost certainly *was* about.

"Ellie," I said warningly. She'd put our pie plates in the sink and was rinsing them; Bella was the type of housekeeper who if there was a dust mote within range, that dust mote was history.

And so were you, if you didn't rinse your plate. Now she returned from the phone alcove, looking annoyed.

"That was Marienbad," she reported. "From the Rubber Duck."

Marienbad Jones—named after the film, of

course, and no, I have no idea why her parents thought that was a good idea—was the Duck's owner and usual bartender.

Crossing her ropy arms exasperatedly over her flat chest, Bella went on. "Sharon Sweetwater is in there. All upset, Marienbad says, and drinking hard. Marienbad wants you two to come and get the girl, says she's going to fall off the bar stool if somebody doesn't."

Bella took a breath. "Sharon will, I mean, not Marienbad."

Ellie sighed. We'd meant to spend a few hours here testing more whoopie-pie fillings, looking for one that could glue big wedding cake layers together securely while also not cementing your molars together permanently.

But Marienbad must have seen Sharon sobbing her way into our shop, earlier, and on the basis of that flimsy connection had decided to call us, now that the prospective bride needed rescuing from herself.

Two

My name is Jacobia Tiptree, and when I first came to Maine I was leaving behind a husband so mind-bendingly atrocious that my marriage license should have had a skull and crossbones stamped on it.

Victor—that was his name, appropriately— thought fidelity was a savings and loan outfit. At the big-city teaching hospital where he was a brain surgeon—it was the perfect job for him, messing with people's heads—he was known for his habit of sweeping young student nurses off their feet and into his nearby secret bachelor apartment.

Not in that order, of course, and at the time I didn't know about the bachelor apartment, either. Not that I could have done much if I had, being by then so vastly pregnant that it was all I could do just to waddle across a room, gasping.

Then after Sam was born the whole twenty-four-hour-a-day baby-care routine kicked in, trapping me in our Manhattan apartment. Sirens and car horns from twenty stories below drifted up to me like faint signs of life from a distant planet, and taking the garbage down the hall to the chute felt like an exotic trip.

Meanwhile, Victor bought a sports car and began commuting in it to another hospital, this one in Connecticut. I'd say he had admitting privileges there, but the man never admitted to anything in his life, so I won't, and somehow we went on.

Years earlier, however, I'd wrangled a freakish talent for large numbers into a career as a money manager for the kind of people whose cash arrived packed into fancy briefcases, carried by stone-faced men whose expensive jackets didn't quite hide their shoulder holsters.

So after Sam started school, I went back to work, and for a while I was one of the few people on Earth who could: (a) guide your average dim-bulb mobster through a thicket of tax rules so thorny that he would surely be ensnared by them otherwise, and (b) keep her mouth shut about it.

That last part being crucial. One peep out of me and I'd have found myself in a barrel at the bottom of the East River. Instead I salted away some decent money over the course of the next few years.

Not millions; crime didn't pay *that* well. But by the time I began finding bits of unfamiliar black lingerie in my bed—

Sam, meanwhile, had begun running with a crowd of boys whose idea of fun included riding the tops of speeding subway cars while high on better pharmaceuticals than even Victor's patients had access to—

By then I not only had some decent money saved, I had a plan, and step one of it was getting the hell out of Dodge.

And oh, boy, did I ever: on the day when it all finally blew up irrevocably, I got a sulky, recalcitrant Sam into the car by explaining to him very sincerely that if he didn't make it snappy, I'd run him over with the damned vehicle. He knew I wouldn't really do it, of course, but I was desperate and the look on my face when I said it must've been awful, because in response he hopped in silently and speedily, even fastening his seat belt without my having to nag him about it.

All the way up the east coast, I kept him quiet with Funyuns and McDonald's, a combination that made the car smell like fast-food purgatory. But since it was getting me out of hell, I didn't complain, especially when a few days later we reached what looked like heaven: Eastport, Maine, a remote island fishing village with a population of about 1200, lay at the end of a long, curving causeway six miles from the mainland. The island itself, seven miles long and two miles wide, smelled like sea salt, chamomile, and blooming beach roses, and when we got there even Sam looked around and pronounced it "bitchin'."

Walking up and down the little streets full of picturesque old wooden houses, we fantasized living in one of them, although, of course, we couldn't afford to; as I said, I hadn't saved *that* much money. As we strolled, Sam peered wide-eyed at bikes and skateboards scattered on the lawns where the kids had left them when they ran in for supper.

"Won't they get stolen?" he asked, and when I told him I didn't expect so he looked thoughtful. Later we discovered Eastport's harbor and the boats bobbing in it, and for him I think right then was when it got decided, even before I found out that one of those old houses cost about a tenth of what I had been expecting it would.

So we were staying, come hell or high water, both of which we promptly encountered. The house we chose—two centuries old, full of ramshackle charm and with a half-dozen working fireplaces, but at the time no operable furnace—had a few defects I wasn't told about at the time of sale.

For instance, that quirky little dip in the roof beam wasn't a feature. Also, the house leaked; not just the roof, but all the drafty, 200-year-old wooden windows as well.

And don't even get me started on the cellar, a dirt-floored, cobwebby horror so chronically full of water you could've run a trout farm down there. By that time, a taunting refrain had begun repeating itself in my head: *Move to Maine, they said. It'll be fun, they said.*

But we persevered, or I did; Sam took to it as if he'd always been here, buying himself a slicker and some high boots to go with the black oilcloth squall hat he'd acquired at the marine store.

Meanwhile, I bought plywood, plaster, tools, Band-Aids . . .

But that's all in the past. Now, with Sam grown and married, my own life squared away, and the house rehabilitated (by which I mean no longer openly plotting to collapse onto us), I'd needed a new challenge.

Which turned out to be The Chocolate Moose. It was Ellie's idea, but I ended up loving the place: creating delicious chocolate treats and selling them to locals and tourists was right up my alley.

For one thing, it rarely involved guys wearing shoulder holsters; also, a mistake wouldn't earn me a one-way river trip. After a while I got so I could even look at a bag of concrete mix without breaking out in cold chills; funny how those old memories can stick with you.

But running the Moose was turning out to be stressful, too, I reflected as Ellie and I hustled back downtown to the Rubber Duck on the morning after Toby Moran was murdered.

"Why'd Sharon hit the Duck instead of coming up to your house like she said she would?" Ellie wondered aloud.

Sharon had been so distraught and without other immediate resources, I hadn't known where to send her but to my own place. But I should've known she wouldn't go; it wasn't as if we were close pals.

"I don't know." I said. "Marienbad told Bella that Sharon was crying too hard to talk. And," I added, "drinking too fast."

Probably that was why. Bella would've given her a whisky or even several if she asked but Sharon didn't know that. Crossing the street by the cheerfully spouting fountain that was once a public horse trough, we quick-stepped toward the Duck.

"Anyway, you gather her up and I'll pay," I told Ellie when we got there. From what Marienbad had described, it sounded as if Sharon might've run up a sizable bar tab.

Despite the ghastliness of her day so far, I couldn't imagine what else besides too much liquor would have her weeping into a bowl of the Rubber Ducky's habitually stale peanuts at this hour of the morning. Or at any time, actually; in Eastport the young teacher was a well-known paragon of all kinds of virtue.

Except maybe not right this minute, I decided as we pushed open the Duck's front door and a billow of stale beer fumes hit me in the face. At the bar, a man his forties wearing a shirt-tie-and-vest combo over a pair of brown corduroy slacks stared down into an empty glass.

"Hi, Norman," I said, but he didn't look over at me. Norm McHale was a veterinarian, or he had been until he lost his license; turned out he'd been embezzling heavily from the animal hospital he'd worked at, a crime the licensing board thought worth suspending him over.

Now he was waiting for an upcoming licensure hearing, to see if he'd get it back. I looked past him to the small wooden table where Sharon sat, drinking. Or she had been; Marienbad had cut her off.

"Have you heard what they've done?" Sharon cried when she caught sight of us.

She was still wearing the white slacks and pale-pink embroidered T-shirt with a lacy white cotton cardigan thrown over her shoulders, just as she had been when we talked with her in the Moose earlier.

But the outfit didn't look sweetly spiffy anymore, and neither did she. Glancing around the Duck's interior—low, whitewashed ceiling, a long row of windows overlooking the boat basin, masses of paper lanterns in bright colors hanging from the dark, heavy beams overhead—she pounded the table with her fist.

". . . not *fair.* How could they *think* such a—"

"Thanks for coming down," said Marienbad Jones, a handsome, big-mouthed brunette who resembled a '40s pinup model and had more smarts than your average supercomputer.

"No problem," I told her. For her barkeeping duties today, she wore denim shorts and a midriff-baring red halter top with big white polka dots on it, and if you thought her outfit made her vulnerable to any unwanted advances from customers, you'd have thought wrong.

Because remember that housefly that Sharon wouldn't have swatted? Splat was its middle name here in the Ducky, and that went double for grabby patrons. Anyway . . .

"I figured I'd better get her out of here," the bar owner went on. "She's done for, and the lunch crowd is due in soon."

"Okay," I told Marienbad, not particularly well pleased to be nominated the drunk rescuer of last resort. Still, this was Sharon we were talking about here, and probably she hadn't realized how that much Bristol Cream Sherry would affect her.

But I did, and it wasn't going to be pretty. "I hear you had a little excitement here last night," I added, meanwhile sizing up the project of moving Sharon.

Marienbad grimaced. "That jerk. I don't see why he couldn't leave well enough alone."

A couple of regulars wandered in looking thirsty and she drew them both draft beers, then went on. "You'd think Sharon was the love of his life or something, the way he wouldn't just give up on her and move on."

52

She looked sour. "It's not like he couldn't find anyone else, he always managed to have a girlfriend."

Sharon had said so, too, that Moran was a charmer when he wanted to be. And we all knew his history; just not every single little bit of it, which coincidentally was the amount I thought might come in handy to us now that Andy was under suspicion.

"So who was the girl before Sharon?" Ellie asked casually.

"Carrie Allen," said Marienbad. "And she didn't get out of it so easily, either, come to think of it. From what I heard, before she got rid of him he'd broken her nose."

"Sharon says he harassed her pretty badly," Ellie put in. "I can't help wondering if that's what Toby and Andy Devine got into it about last night."

Marienbad nodded grimly. "That's what it was, all right. Norm can tell you, he was here, and . . . oh, Jenna Waldrop was here."

The bar owner shook her head. "Poor Jenna, if I were her I'd want a drink, too. That mother of hers . . . but now that I think of it," she frowned, "maybe Jenna left earlier? I'm not sure."

More customers came in; Marienbad went back behind the bar to serve them. While she was there I looked around some more, noting the emergency exit at the far end of the room.

It was new. I brought Ellie's attention to it. "So we're not the only ones," she said, sounding vindicated.

Six months earlier, we'd taken a lot of guff for putting our own emergency door in; it wasn't even our building, people said. But with our landlord's happy approval, George had volunteered the labor and afterward we felt better, knowing we could get out in an emergency; now lots of the businesses downtown were doing it.

"Goes right out onto that fire escape there," Ellie commented approvingly of the metal structure outside the windows.

I quietly thanked my stars we hadn't needed one of those; the cost would've been exotic.

Then Marienbad returned. "So, you going to take her with you?"

"Yeah, we'll take her. Let's get her under the arms," I told Ellie, and together we hoisted Sharon, guiding her past the rest room doors and the old phone booth toward the exit.

On the way we passed a supply closet whose open door revealed paper towels, hand soap, a mop bucket, and a clutter of what looked like very large mousetraps.

"Rats," said Marienbad darkly, seeing my raised eyebrows. "On a waterfront like this there are always . . ."

"Oooh," Sharon moaned wretchedly, so we left

the topic of vermin for another day and urged her forward some more. But we'd only gotten to the stairway that led to Marienbad's living quarters upstairs when the inebriated young teacher's legs went out from under her and we had to let her down onto a chair.

"Oh," she gasped shudderingly. "Oh, I'm so sorry."

Her hand reached out blindly; Ellie put a wad of tissues into it. "But have you heard?" Sharon demanded again after a long blow. "Have you heard what those awful homicide investigators have done now?"

She sat up, blinking owlishly at us. "Jenna was right! I was on my way to your house when I saw Andy getting into a state police car with two officers."

Norm glanced over at us, then went back to staring into his shot glass. "They arrested him," Sharon went on, "they must've! Oh, what are we going to do?"

Well, the first thing we did was get her out of the tavern and across the street, then down the sidewalk and back into our own shop. People stared as we went by, and I happened to know that one of them—*Quelle horreur!*—was an Eastport School Board member.

But we just kept hustling her along, supporting her when her legs went rubbery and muttering a hasty "she doesn't feel so well" to each curious person we encountered. The bell over the shop door tinkled sweetly as we muscled her inside and lowered her into a café chair.

Mika came out from the back, wiping her hands on a towel and looking puzzled as I pulled the shade in the bay window and turned the sign in the door to CLOSED. Catching sight of Sharon, she wrung out a cold cloth for the girl's forehead and poured her a glass of water.

Then, once Sharon had stopped sobbing and hiccupping and begun sipping, we got the whole story out of her.

I'd known something more must be coming. But when it did, it was even worse than I'd feared.

Eastport, Maine, is home to the easternmost Coast Guard station in the United States. The big white building with its red tiled roof and green lawn sloping down to black iron gates is well positioned to watch over the harbor, the bay, and the entire sector from Jonesport to the Canadian border.

Everything from massive freighters to the piddliest of rowboats comes under the Coast Guard's supervision, which you may resent a great deal when they are boarding your fishing boat, hassling you about life jackets and flares, and wanting to know whether or not your radio is working properly.

But you will like them a lot when you are sinking. That big orange Zodiac inflatable they zip around in will pluck you out of the water so fast, you'll hardly know you got wet.

Well, except for the shivering, of course; right now, the water temperature off our shores was about 50°F. But back to Sharon again, and to her fiancé—or as Jenna had called him, the golden boy.

The Coast Guard is a military organization, so, of course, it has officers, and in Eastport the most well-known of them was Andy Devine. Smart, level-headed, and as reliable as the dawn, he had a string of glowing references and commendations from peers and superiors alike.

As a result, it was likely he'd be promoted again by the end of the year if nothing got in his way. But now it seemed something had.

"Ohh," Sharon moaned again, putting her neatly manicured fingertips to her temples.

She hadn't drunk as much sherry as I'd feared. Four small glasses were all it had taken to turn on the waterworks.

So at least she wasn't stomach-sick; bending solicitously to the girl, Mika, who before moving here and marrying Sam had been a nurse, assessed the situation.

"Fluids and fresh air," was her unhesitating prescription. "Some caffeine, possibly, and maybe a sugar boost."

She placed a white paper bag into my hands. A sweet smell rose from it.

"No peeking," she admonished me, her dark eyes twinkling. "Take this with you."

Still at the café table, Sharon sat up straight and used the cold cloth we'd given her on her face and hands. So she was recovering, I saw with relief. But she still looked like half the blood had been let out of her.

"My car's out front," Ellie reminded me, so we guided Sharon into it, got her settled beside Ellie, who was driving, and took off.

Whereupon the whole story finally came out. "Okay, so you know about Toby and the milkshake, right?" Sharon wanted to know first of all.

We confirmed that we did. "And we know about the poison, and that it was in a Chocolate Moose cup," I added. "With sprinkles."

I sat in the backseat with the bag of sweets Mika had given me, plus a thermos of coffee I'd liberated from the carafe in the shop.

Ellie turned left, past the high school and the ball field. "Why not tell us something," she suggested, "that we *don't* know."

Because we were both up for hearing the story, all right, but not for hauling the words out of the young woman one by one.

Sharon caught our drift. "Okay, so here's the thing," she said. "I didn't just date Toby Moran.

I borrowed money from him. Not that it was a loan at the time," she amended, "he said it was a gift. But then he wanted it back."

She sucked in a shaky breath. "And before you say it, I know. It was stupid. *I* was stupid. I needed it to finish up some courses to get my teaching license, and I thought—yeah. What an idiot I was."

She half-turned to face me. "Please don't laugh. I knew almost right away what a mistake it was. A few thousand dollars . . . it might not be that much to some people, but to me it was. And he held it over me, of course. It was bad enough at the time, not being able to tell anyone I was dating him at all, and you know how hard it is to keep a secret around here."

Right, having the town know she was seeing a guy like Moran wouldn't have done much for her kindergarten-teaching career here in Eastport, would it? And putting money into the mix would've just made it all sound that much worse.

So she was right, the whole situation had been a mistake on her part, one she was suffering for now. But . . .

"I'm not laughing," I said. No way was I going to tell her that I knew just how she felt. The less anyone here in Eastport knew about my romantic history, the better.

But my late ex-husband, Victor, had been a mistake, too, and even though I knew very well who'd been the villain that time around (hint: not me), I still felt guilty about it all.

"So what did he say about the money when you broke up with him?" I asked.

As I recalled, that had been about six months ago according to the town's gossip wire, which was where it ended up because, of course, people found out about the relationship eventually and then followed it avidly.

"Oh, he went nuts," Sharon replied.

"Surprise, surprise," Ellie murmured. She'd been driving while we talked; now she angled the car down a sandy track leading toward the water, pulled into a grassy parking spot, and stopped.

"Let's get out," she suggested, so we did, making our way past heaps of driftwood and patches of sea lavender to the beach.

Protected from wind on each side by granite outcroppings, the narrow strip of small stones mingled with bits of beach glass gleamed freshly, lapped by wavelets that had already crept as high as they would go with the tide.

Three weathered wooden Adirondack chairs were lined up just above the high-water line; we settled in them. "I mean, he took it well at first," Sharon went on when we'd arranged ourselves.

"But then he must've figured out that I really meant it, that his jealousy and his anger and his threats . . . well, that they were all just too much and I was ending it with him. Permanently."

"What about the money?" Ellie wanted to know. "Did he demand it back right away?"

"No," Sharon said. "I think he figured it gave him some sort of leverage over me, that it was a way to get me back to him."

Her black curls fluttered prettily in the breeze off the water as she spoke, and her face, turned up into the pale spring sunshine, was regaining some of its color. But then her look darkened.

"Once he saw I wouldn't cooperate, though, he started stalking me. Following me, lurking everywhere, texting and phoning. One time he started yelling at me in the grocery store, and another day he grabbed me as I was leaving school. By the wrist, pulling me toward his car."

Her cheeks reddened as she remembered. "It was awful, some of the parents saw and called the security guard, and he shooed Toby away."

I passed her the thermos and she took a long swallow from it; the amount of sherry she'd drunk had been a stroke of luck, as it turned out, not hurting her seriously but loosening her up so she could talk about this.

Because those flushed cheeks of hers, I realized now, weren't pink with embarrassment over having to be rescued out of the Duck.

They were burning with an earlier shame. "What a stupid mistake," she repeated, "getting involved with him at all."

"Oh, stop," I admonished her. The retreating

wavelets made faint slopping sounds against the stones as the tide went out. "That's what they're good at, these guys, they fake it until they trap you."

I ought to know, I thought as I watched the birds skittering at the water's edge, cheeping softly while scanning the shallows for edibles.

"I'm sure he was lovely all the while he was luring you in," Ellie said. "Like the spider and the fly."

"I guess." Sharon seemed to be getting her wind back.

"But once I did end it with him, he got so bad I finally had to tell Bob Arnold." She turned to me, her look earnest.

"I was afraid to go out of the house. I even borrowed the money from Andy to pay Toby, finally, but that didn't stop it, either."

So that's how Andy learned about Toby Moran, I guessed at once, and at my look, Sharon's answering glance said I was right.

"Uh-huh, and you can imagine how *he* reacted," the young teacher said. "He was furious, it was all I could do to keep him from—"

She stopped suddenly. Then, "And I won't even tell you what all was in the awful text messages Toby would send me. Disgusting."

She shuddered, pulling the lacy white sweater closer around her shoulders, although at nearly noon the day was getting warm.

"And Bob took care of it?" Ellie asked.

Sharon nodded emphatically. "Oh, yes. I don't know what he said to Toby, but whatever it was stopped the nonsense. Until . . ."

Ah, yes, the inevitable "until." And now I was pretty sure also that I knew until what. "Until he found out you were getting married."

She glanced gratefully at me. "Yes. I didn't tell him, but how could he not find out? With all that's going on about it around here, you'd think we were Prince Charles and Diana."

She had a point. A pretty, popular, young teacher and a dashing young Coast Guard officer . . . in Eastport, you could hardly get any more royal than that. Ellie took the white paper bakery bag that Mika had given me and opened it.

"Oh!" she said, pleased, pulling out a Toll House cookie and then two more, handing one to each of us.

But the sweet taste of the chocolate did nothing to squelch the sour suspicion growing steadily in me.

"So what did he do then? Toby Moran, when he found out about the wedding, I mean?" Because, of course, it hadn't really been about money.

Sharon looked uncomfortable. "Well," she began slowly.

I glanced past her at Ellie, who returned my look; both of us hoped very much that everything was going to turn out all right for Sharon and Andy.

But we also hoped they would turn out to be all right for us, and at the moment neither of those things was looking likely.

Sharon bit her lip. Then said, "He sent me some photographs. E-mailed them to me."

Uh-oh. A gull swooped down at the clutter of little birds on the beach, scattering them.

"What kind of photographs?" Ellie inquired gently, as if this wasn't already obvious.

Because when your nutball ex-boyfriend's got a mean streak as wide as a superhighway, nowadays you can pretty well be assured that any photographs he sends you—especially on the occasion of your marriage to somebody else—won't be G-rated.

And with her next remark, Sharon confirmed this. Only there was a twist. . . .

"Bad ones," she admitted. "Lingerie, and . . . poses. Not obscene, but shocking enough if they're of your kid's teacher, you know?"

She sat up straight. "The thing is, though, they're not really me. As near as I can tell they're of models, pictures he got on the internet, advertising for lacy underwear and so on. And then he got other pictures of my face, normal ones, and put them together."

"Like with Photoshop or something?" Ellie asked. Her little girl was a budding computer nerd, so she knew about such things.

Sharon nodded hard. "Yes, some program that

lets you move parts of photographs around and combine them. Not that he was good at it."

She sucked in a breath of fresh, salt air, blew it out again. "They're *amateurish*. No one who looked at them for more than a minute would think that they're really me. But the effect is still . . ."

Uh-huh, like a handful of mud smeared on everyone's idea of her, and right before her wedding, too. "Can you just imagine," she went on, "what all my students' parents must've thought?"

It was the second time she'd mentioned this, and now it hit me. "Wait a minute, how'd they get to see the pictures?"

I crumpled the white paper bag, then shoved it into my satchel under the glinting eye of the seagull that was watching for crumbs.

"Because he sent them to the parents of every student in my class," she replied. "I don't know how he got their e-mail addresses; he must've worked hard compiling the list. But he did it."

"And then Andy found out about it?" Because that had to be it.

Her lips tightened. "Yes. First the principal came to me and showed me what some of the mothers had brought in."

"Printouts of the pictures?" Ellie tossed a cookie piece at the seagull, which snatched it up greedily and flapped away.

"Yes, and I've never been so humiliated in my life," Sharon said. "I couldn't even promise it wouldn't happen again, of course, because how in the world could I possibly control what Toby might do?"

I could think of one way. And the cops already had, it seemed.

"And while I was in the middle of trying to talk with the principal, Andy was outside sitting in his car, waiting for me. He'd come to pick me up after work, you see, we were going to Bangor to pick out our—"

It didn't matter what they'd been going to pick out. This whole story was giving me the heebie-jeebies.

"But he got tired of waiting," I interrupted. "And this was when, just recently that all this happened?"

Sharon nodded, finishing up her cookie. "Few days ago."

There wasn't much coffee left in the thermos. To give myself a minute to think, I swallowed what remained and screwed on the cap.

"Everyone up there likes Andy," I said. At the school, I meant, but it was the same all over town.

"While he was waiting he figured he'd get buzzed in himself and say hello to everyone, I suppose."

It was the kind of thing he would do. "Yes," Sharon confirmed. "And I was upset when I came out of the principal's office, so he wanted to know why."

She turned to me. "We tell each other everything," she added.

Yeah, maybe, I thought. "That's when Andy learned Toby was still harassing you? And you didn't end up going to Bangor, after all."

We got up and made our way toward the car, up the weedy slope past the sea lavender and the driftwood.

"Yes, it was, and no, we didn't," said Sharon. "We didn't feel like it anymore, so Andy just took me home."

She glanced puzzledly at me. "But how'd you know that?"

"Oh, just a feeling." A feeling that now I knew Andy had already been very upset with Toby even before their argument in the Duck; the one, I mean, right before Toby had his arguing days ended for good.

But I decided not to say so; Sharon already felt bad enough about it all. Instead Ellie got behind the wheel and we started back toward downtown. Mika would want to be getting home to check on the baby, and Ellie and I had things to talk about by ourselves.

"But them arresting him was a mistake," Sharon said, "I'm sure it was. Andy hasn't even seen Toby since he found out about the—what?"

She'd caught sight of my expression. "Might as well tell her," said Ellie.

Yep. There was no avoiding it now, really, or not without a lot of conversational gymnastics that I didn't feel up for.

And she'd find out sooner or later. "Listen, Sharon, what did Andy say he was going to do last night?"

She blinked puzzledly. "He said he was going home to study for a class he's taking. For his promotion, he has to pass some technical examinations."

She turned again to where I sat in the backseat. "What do you mean, though, what he *said* he'd be doing. Of course he—"

I took a deep breath. "Sharon. You were home last night, but I wasn't. I was in the Pickled Herring with my family."

"So?" Sharon demanded a little shakily; by now she knew something bad was coming, too.

"So . . ." I replied, then described what happened: first Toby getting tossed out of the Rubber Duck, and then a little later Andy Devine coming out and going the way Toby had gone, into the shadows on the path overlooking the boat basin and the harbor.

By now we were back on Water Street, where a few early-season tourists in hats and windbreakers strolled in the sunshine. Ellie pulled into a parking space outside the Moose.

Sharon looked aghast as we got out. "He *lied* to me? Andy lied about where he was going? Oh, no, you must've made a—"

Outside our shop, someone had tossed aside an emptied Chocolate Moose milkshake cup. The moose depicted on it had a wide, toothy smile, googly eyes, and a big brown cartoonishly exaggerated moose snoot.

Plus the antlers, of course. Only on this cup, someone had scribbled out the moose face with black magic marker and replaced it with the word *POISON!*

"No." Ellie spoke firmly. She'd spied the cup, too; I saw her eyes narrowing at it. "No mistake," she went on to Sharon, snatching up the offending bit of litter.

"But probably he didn't lie, you know, most likely he just got done studying and decided to change his plans."

It seemed that word about the probable murder method had gotten around town. She stuffed the cup into her satchel.

"But," she went on, "the fact is, he was downtown last night and he did see Toby, whether you knew it or not."

"But that doesn't mean anything!" Sharon exclaimed. "Just because he saw him . . ."

"Right," I said. "Not to us. For one thing, we know that if Andy wanted to do something to

69

someone, he's the kind of stand-up guy who would do it in plain sight."

Seriously, and speaking of vintage cartoon characters, you never met anybody more like Dudley Do-Right in your life than Andy Devine.

"But the state police don't know that about him," Ellie went on in gentle agreement, "so to them he's just a guy with a motive."

Up and down the street, storekeepers swept sidewalks and washed windows in preparation for the imminent tourist rush. Eastport had become a legitimate sightseeing destination in recent years; the few visitors who were here now were only a preview.

"A motive?" Sharon repeated. "But . . . oh, no." She looked stricken. "You mean the cops think Andy killed Toby Moran on account of me?"

Her voice rose. "But what'll happen to him?" she demanded. "Do you think . . . do you mean we might have to cancel the wedding?"

It was a question upon which the whole future of the Moose depended, as well as her own. But there was no way to know the answer for sure, and anyway, just then out of the corner of my eye I spied my father.

Ye gods . . . He was driving a brand-new, bright red pickup truck, and right behind him was Bob Arnold's squad car with its siren whoop-whooping and its cherry beacon whirling.

My dad pulled over. The grin on his face was

wider than the one on the Moose's mascot, and if his eyes had been twinkling any brighter you could've used them for a pair of headlights.

"Hello, ladies," he greeted us cheerfully, his gnarled, liver-spotted hands resting on the steering wheel as if they belonged there.

Which as far as he was concerned, obviously they did. But I didn't agree and neither did Bob Arnold seem to as he got out of his squad car and approached us.

"Okay, Jacob, let's see some paperwork. License, registration, insurance card, you know the drill," he told my dad skeptically.

And you could've knocked me over with one of the éclairs that Mika was just then putting into our shop's display window when my dad pulled out his brand-new driver's license and his truck registration and temporary insurance card, none of which I'd known he had.

Heck, I hadn't even known he'd bought the truck. "How'd he do that?" I mouthed incredulously at Ellie, but she just shook her head, shrugging.

"Everything all right?" my dad asked Eastport's police chief, smiling like a cat that had swallowed a whole flock of canaries.

Bob stood frowning over the paperwork my dad had given him. Then he handed it back; reluctantly, but he did it. He had no other choice.

"Yes, Jacob, I believe it is." He paused once more, seeming at a loss for what else to say.

I knew what I wanted to say, starting with all the profanities I hadn't used since the last time my dad pulled a wild-hair stunt like this. But first . . .

Bob's rosebud lips pursed. "Your temporary license plate needs to be visible," he advised my father. "Yours is kind of folded down there in the rear plate holder, that's why I pulled you over."

"I'll go fix that little difficulty right now," my dad said, just as Bob's phone trilled.

"Darn," he frowned at it. "Burglary, out at the lake. Gotta go." He drove off in his squad car while my dad was still climbing down out of the new truck's cab.

He wore a blue chambray work shirt, jeans, and leather sandals on his knobby feet. As usual his long gray hair was tied back in a leather thong; a ruby stud gleamed in his earlobe. The blood-red stone had been my mother's; I had the twin to it in my own ear.

Crouching to smooth and straighten the temporary license plate on the truck, he caught sight of me again and winked.

Ellie took Sharon into the Moose while I talked to my father.

"Dad," I said, struggling to keep my temper.

"Look, I realize you've been feeling a little confined lately. But—"

Between all the medicines he'd been taking and the doctor visits he'd been enduring since his cardiac event last year, "confined" was probably not the right word for it.

Imprisoned, maybe. Or *entombed;* he'd been complaining about it for months. Now he dusted his hands together.

"Between you and your stepmother, if I were any more confined I'd be wearing an orange jumpsuit."

The twinkle in his eyes flared. "Walkin' along the highway with the rest of the work detail, digging out culverts, pickin' up trash."

He sucked in a breath. "Stabbin' it with a stick, there, the bags and the plastic soda cups. Which at this point I might not even mind, you see, if it just got me out of the damned house!"

"Dad," I began, but he wasn't having any; this outburst had been a long time coming.

"The heart attack I had was a bad one, but it wasn't fatal, all right? I'm an old man," he added grumblingly, "not a dead one."

Seized by the sort of wisdom that comes over me only rarely, I let him go on.

" 'Jacob, don't do too much,' " he mimicked. " 'Let me lift that for you. Jacob, take your forty million pills, now, or you'll keel over.' "

His bushy eyebrows bristled at me. "Listen, this

business of me being the household invalid—it can't go on."

Then he stopped, his kind, old eyes crinkling as his temper cooled. "I know you mean well, and I love you for it. And your stepmother, too."

The part about the forty million pills hit me especially hard. I'd been setting out his medications every morning for a year now, and watching to make sure he took them, too, I'm embarrassed to say.

And driving him everywhere, anytime he wanted, but that wasn't the same as just taking off in your own pickup truck and coming home when you pleased, was it?

No, it certainly wasn't. "Jacobia, listen to me," he said gently. "People don't turn into infants when they get old, all right?"

I swallowed hard, wondering when being a good daughter had turned into . . . well. The truth was that I really didn't want to think too deeply about what it had turned into.

But if my dad had to go out and buy a pickup truck to escape it, then I wanted it to stop, too. "I see," I murmured shamefacedly.

He wasn't finished with me, though. "Eye test," he recited, "and a new driver's license, written *and* road tests. *All,*" he emphasized, "passed with flying colors."

He tucked his driver's license back into his old leather wallet. It crossed my mind to wonder how he'd even gotten to the Motor Vehicle Department until I recalled that he'd visited Walmart with the Senior Center group a week earlier.

I guessed he'd managed to play hooky from them somehow. Thinking about how good at it he'd probably been, I couldn't help smiling.

He saw it. "All I need," he added, relenting a little, "is to get out now and then. On my own," he added before I could reply.

The money to buy the truck wasn't a problem; he had enough. It was the prospect of him driving alone in the vehicle that bothered me.

"I don't want you getting into troubles you can't get out of," I said, which the minute the words left my mouth I knew was ridiculous.

He'd been in trouble all his life, since before I was born. It was why he had money to live on now; his homemade explosives hobby had become, back in the 1960s, a profitable, if entirely illegal, business, and not all his gains had been lost when that old world came crashing down on him.

Starting with the death of my mother. Behind him the door of The Chocolate Moose flew open and Sharon stepped out, tucking her cell phone back into her bag as she peered up and down the street.

Then I spotted another familiar figure. The tall man in the navy sweatshirt and khakis hurried down the sidewalk toward us.

Or rather, he hurried toward Sharon; from the look of him, you'd have thought there was no one else in the world.

"Jacobia," my dad said, but I couldn't take my eyes off the pair. It was like pieces of a jigsaw puzzle fitting perfectly together when the man bent to wrap his arms around Sharon.

"Jacobia," my dad repeated. "I'm doing this, all right?"

The truck, he meant, and he wasn't asking permission. He'd been down but not out, and now he'd recovered, was his message to me.

Or he had as far as he was concerned, at least; as recovered as he could get.

"Okay, Dad," I conceded, since clearly there was no arguing with him.

Nor did I want to try prying the truck out of his hands; not now, anyway. Maybe when the novelty of the thing had worn off a little, not that I was feeling a whole lot of optimism about that, either.

My dad hopped into his shiny new vehicle and backed out. I saluted him in farewell, hoping this really was the Jacob Tiptree we all remembered, fully healed after his illness and now once more, as Bella would've put it, as independent as a hog on ice.

The red truck cruised away down the street. Behind the wheel, my father gazed around happily, lord of all he surveyed. You could tell that in the back-in-the-saddle department, he felt no doubt.

But I did. On the sidewalk, the big, redheaded guy set Sharon carefully back down on her feet and beamed at her. It was Andy Devine, of course, but how?

"Man am I glad to see you," he was telling Sharon as I walked over to them.

Her eyes shone with joyous relief but narrowed as she reached up to touch the Band-Aid over his right eyebrow.

"Andy, the police . . . did they *hit* you?"

A bit of black suture material stuck out from under the Band-Aid. Whatever had happened to him, he'd needed stitches for it; recently, too.

"Oh, no," he brushed off her concern, "that's just . . . but never mind, it's got nothing to do with what's happened. I mean, you are not going to *believe* what—"

"We've heard," I told him, hustling them both back into the shop. "Come with me, now, the two of you."

Inside, the old paddle-bladed overhead fans turned slowly under the high, pressed-tin ceiling, stirring warm air that was richly sweet with the aroma of baking chocolate. Emerging from the kitchen, Mika slid a tray of really lovely-looking almond-chocolate biscotti into the glass-fronted display case.

Meanwhile, at Sharon's anxious insistence, Andy's story poured out of him: he had not in fact been arrested, just questioned intensively and told to remain available.

"They think I did it, though. I could tell they think I poisoned that little son of a . . ."

"Andy, how *could* they?" she cried. But then I saw it hit her, the memory of me telling her I'd seen him coming out of the tavern when he had told her he'd be home.

He must have seen it, too, the question on her face. "I was in the Duck last night," he confessed. "I got done studying; you'd said you wanted the night to yourself . . ."

Crocheting, I recalled. "And you had words with Toby Moran?" I put in. "In the Ducky, you and he argued about something?"

He looked down at his freckled hands, clasped atop the café table. "Yeah. You know Toby, he can't leave anything well enough alone. Couldn't, I mean," he amended.

A pair of customers came in, bought Fudge Drops and Toll House cookies, and went out again. No milkshakes, though, and when I angled my head queryingly at the pretty green Mixmaster on the counter, Mika shook her head.

"But after a little while he did leave me alone and got rowdy with someone else, and Marienbad tossed him out," Andy went on. "Not much later, I headed home, too."

"By way of the harbor path," I said. "Where Toby had gone. I saw him, and you as well," I added, and Andy looked guilty, suddenly.

"Yeah, but I didn't see him down there. Either he'd gone on ahead of me or he was passed out in the bushes, somewhere."

The passed-out-in-the bushes part was possible, I supposed. "And your forehead?" I asked gently. "Was that also a part of your argument with Toby in the Rubber Ducky, him slugging you?"

He frowned. "No, there was no fistfight; you know how Marienbad is about that." A pause, then, "It happened back at the station, I walked into the corner of my locker door," he added, touching the spot gingerly.

He was tall enough for that to be true. Just not clumsy enough, I thought. Putting his hand atop Sharon's, he changed the subject.

"About the cops, though. I mean, this thing's making me pretty nervous. I've been in on disciplinary hearings before, you know? Just not in the hot seat myself."

Of course not. He was the golden boy. "So I know the voice, the look," he went on, glancing at me in appeal. "Those cops think they've got their guy."

Because of Sharon being harassed by Toby, of course; then the argument in the Rubber Duck . . . but no, Andy hadn't told the cops he wanted an attorney, he said when I asked. Why should he, when he'd done nothing wrong? It would only make him look guilty.

I didn't answer on account of having already said all my allotted swear words for the day. Instead, "Wait," I told him, and he did.

Then in swift succession I sent Sharon home— "And no detours into the Duck this time," I called sharply after her—and relieved Mika of her shop duty for today, after making sure Ellie was both free and willing to hold down the fort for a little while.

"Also, I'm borrowing your car," I told her, and in reply she nodded enthusiastically at me, no more believing Andy Devine's story about last night than I did.

"All right, now, damn it," I told Andy as I pulled out of the parking spot in front of The Chocolate Moose.

Beside me in the passenger seat he looked as miserable as a kid being grounded, his hands in his lap and the eyes behind his pale blond eyelashes downcast.

His whole demeanor, in fact, clued me in on how best to approach this. "You know," I remarked, "I've got a son only a few years younger than you."

More like a dozen years, actually, but never mind, it wasn't my accuracy being questioned at the moment, it was Andy's.

"So I know what a lie sounds like," I went on, gunning Ellie's little sedan up Water Street past the big granite post office building on the corner. Beyond that lay the breakwater parking lot, the boat ramp, and Rosie's Hot Dog Stand.

"But I'm not—" Andy began as we passed them.

"Oh, can it," I cut him off. Uphill between the Coast Guard's iron-fenced lawn, the street narrowed and curved between small wooden houses overlooking the water.

"I'd like to help you, Andy, I really would."

No kidding; his fortunes and Sharon's, I was now very sorry to realize, were inextricably linked to mine and Ellie's.

"But I don't quite yet know how," I went on, "and I don't get why you keep shooting yourself in the foot about the whole thing, either," I added.

I mean, really, he wasn't stupid, was he? I wouldn't have thought so, but . . .

Sighing, he took a biscotti from the bag Ellie had handed us as we went out and bit into it, his clean white teeth making quick work of the crunchy goodie.

Personally I thought he was in way too much trouble to be eating anything but the kind of energy bars the Tibetan Sherpas feed to you in the hours before an Everest attempt. And this much, at least, he seemed to understand.

That he needed help, I mean. Just maybe not how much.

Or from whom. "Seems to me what I've got to do now is figure out how to handle this *being arrested* stuff," he said.

Then, turning earnestly to me. "Because there must be a right way to go about it, you know, the proper steps you're supposed to take."

Controlling my temper, I reminded him that there were people who did know how to handle such things, and that these people were called *lawyers*.

"Also, you should have a talk with your commanding officer," I went on, "but not until after you consult with your own lawyer first."

I had no experience of how the military handled this sort of situation, but a little attorney-client privilege never hurt anything that I'd ever heard of.

Thinking sourly about how delighted said attorney was going to be when he found out that Andy had already spoken at length to the cops, I gave the accused young Coast Guard officer the number of a defense lawyer that I had confidence in.

Then, after reaching the end of Water Street and the high bluff looking out over the bay from the gravel turnaround there, I took a calculated risk.

First, I reminded him that by his own admission and Sharon's, he'd had the motive and opportunity to kill Toby Moran. Now all the cops needed for an arrest was to figure out a plausible method.

"And you have had access to our shop, Andy; you're in and out of there all the time," I finished. "You could've gotten the milkshake."

Finally, I declared that if he wasn't 100% truthful with me right that minute, Ellie and I wouldn't bake the whoopie-pie wedding cake that Sharon had her heart set on.

"But that's okay. You can get yourself a nice sheet cake from the IGA," I added mercilessly.

He groaned as my shot hit home. "Oh, man, she really wants that cake. Her folks from away are all big fans of whoopie pies, and—"

"Then spill it," I insisted, whereupon he did . . . sort of.

"Yeah, well," he began a little embarrassedly as he gave in. "The thing was, it was Friday night, you know? Nobody around the station, and after I'd been studying a while I just decided to take a break."

"You said that already. What else?"

Out on the water over the bluff at the end of the turnaround, the waves were the deep, dark indigo of new, unwashed blue jeans. He gazed glumly at them.

"So I walked down to the Rubber Ducky," he replied. "I figured a lot of the guys from the station would probably be in there."

He turned to me. "But they weren't, they'd moved on to the Happy Crab."

I understood: the Duck had cheap beer, but the Crab had a pool table and a flat-screen TV the size of a highway billboard.

"But Toby was there," Andy went on ruefully, "in the Ducky, all boozed up and running his big mouth as usual."

"And you were already mad at him, weren't you? Because she'd told you about the pictures of her with her face stuck onto a lot of lingerie models' racy advertising photographs."

Talking about it was a relief to him, I could tell from the way his shoulders relaxed and his face smoothed. But now at the memory of encountering Moran, anger furrowed his forehead.

"Yeah," he nodded. "Yeah, and in the bar I overheard him yapping about them, too, and what he was saying wasn't very nice."

I could imagine, and I could imagine Andy's reaction, as well. "So you confronted him." Because naturally he would have.

"And he backed down," I guessed further. "Then he got into it with somebody else, though, did he? And Marienbad tossed him out?"

That's when I'd seen Toby fly through the Duck's front door, out onto the street. "But afterward, outside—"

Here came the tough part. Andy had lied about

it before, I wasn't sure why. But if at first you don't succeed, et cetera. So . . .

"You didn't know he'd be there, either," I said. "In the shadows behind the Duck. You were walking home on a pleasant spring evening, that's all, not looking for any trouble."

I took a breath. "But he was there, and . . . he jumped you?"

Andy's hand went reflexively to his forehead. It must've been quite a punch, I thought, to open a gash that had needed stitches.

The pale blond hairs on the backs of his fingers gleamed as he touched them. "Uh-huh," he admitted. "Got me a good one, Toby did."

But, of course, Andy hadn't been carrying a poisoned milkshake, ready to somehow force it on Toby Moran. That was a crazy idea, Andy said indignantly; he wouldn't poison somebody for revenge.

And yes, he had told the cops all of this, he declared. He just hadn't wanted Sharon to find out about it because he thought it would scare her.

Which probably he was right about; I'd have been scared, too. Except for the method, which still had to be nailed down, from the cops' point of view it all couldn't have been neater if it had come in an envelope marked: "Contents: One Murder Conviction."

"What happened, then?" I asked. "After he slugged you?"

And naturally he'd told the cops all of it; heck, if he'd had a third foot he'd have probably stuck that one in his mouth, too.

Now at my question he looked regretful. "I took a swing back at him. He'd surprised me, you know? I did it before I could think."

He shook his head, remembering. "But it didn't connect. He was already half-passed-out drunk, so he just staggered backward and sat down in the bushes. When I left him, he was trying to get up again."

"And the stitches?" I asked. "Who put those in?"

Was there a medical record of all this, I meant; it seemed like a simple question. But when he heard it, for the first time Andy's chin thrust out stubbornly.

"I'd rather not say."

I glanced at him in surprise, but he didn't relent, just stared out the front windshield as we made our way back toward town.

By this time it was just past two-thirty, when the high school let out and the teenagers began flooding downtown; as we arrived, a line was already forming outside the Moose.

As I'd noticed earlier, nobody else in town was touching our milkshakes now. In Eastport, the gossip wire is so fast and accurate that if you catch a cold at one end of the island, twenty minutes later someone's making hot lemonade and getting out the Kleenex for you at the other end.

But teenagers all know for a fact that they're immortal and anyway, they'd have drunk liquid uranium if we put enough chocolate in it; through the shop's front window I saw Ellie running the milkshake mixer.

"I've got to go back inside now," I told Andy, pulling the car back into its parking spot out front.

On the sidewalk, I confronted him a final time. "I mean it," I said. "You need an attorney."

Maybe a good lawyer could pound some sense into his head. Because while Sharon seemed properly worried by what might happen next, for a guy who was a hairsbreadth from being a murder suspect, Andy himself appeared oddly unmoved.

Concerned, naturally. But far from frightened. Once I'd pressed him about it, he'd very calmly related what had happened the night of the murder; accurately, too, I was guessing.

Well, except for whatever it was that he was still lying about, of course.

Three

"Okay, so here's an idea," said Ellie a couple of hours after I'd sent Andy on his way.

She turned the key in the shop door's lock as we went out.

"We make each cake layer in sections, in square cake tins, and we lay the sections like tiles for the base and then the same for each of the layers."

I shrugged my sweater up onto my shoulders and slung my satchel over one arm while clutching our bank deposit in the other hand.

"That way," she said, "we won't need such sticky frosting, so—"

It was by no means a large bank deposit, but it would cover the light bill so the power didn't get cut off.

"Aren't wedding cakes supposed to be round?" I asked as she drove us up Washington Street toward the bank. Not only did we not have a big deposit today, we hadn't had one last week, either.

Or the week before that. "So we'll have to trim the corners, and then what'll we do with all the parts we cut off?" I continued.

But she wasn't listening. Instead, "Oh, look!" she exclaimed.

In the grassy vacant lot behind the massive old granite-block post office building, the farmer's market was setting up for the first event of the year. This early in the season, it would feature pansies and peas, new potatoes the size of babies' fists, and the last of the garlic.

"It'll make a lot of waste," I said, meaning the cake, as Ellie selected pale-green lettuces, tender scallions, and a bunch of parsley I thought would go beautifully over those infant potatoes. She must have thought so, too, because she also bought a lot of those, and some garlic for the butter sauce.

"Trimming the cake layers that way," I clarified. "To make them round, for a wedding cake. Will create—"

Ellie sighed deeply, acknowledging my remark, and if she'd seen the deposit slip I'd filled out she'd have sighed even more. But . . .

"Buy some pansies, Jake." She waved at the table offering bunches of newly picked blooms, their winsome purple-and-yellow faces so fresh and pretty that I couldn't resist.

The overalls-clad woman at the table took my money and wrapped wax paper around the stems, and I bought a bar of homemade goat's milk soap, too, the grapefruit-and-honey variety that Bella liked so much.

No doubt she also could use some cheering up, or she'd be needing some soon; my dad was still out in his new pickup truck, I imagined, but he'd have to face the music sooner or later.

"I'm dreading when Bella finds out about that truck," I said.

"You don't think your dad already told her about it?" Ellie asked as we got back into her car and started up Washington Street again.

I shook my head as we passed the Eastport Arts Center and, across the street, Spinney's Garage with a jungle of geraniums in its window.

"If my dad had told Bella about the new truck he bought without consulting her, we'd have heard the explosion already," I said, only half-jokingly.

"Actually, though," I added, "I expect he's getting home right around now. He gets hungry this time of day." Then, "But, Ellie, there's something very weird about what Andy Devine told me."

I'd been mulling it over. "Those stitches in his forehead," I went on.

We passed the IGA, a hair salon called the Mousse Island Clipper, and the convenience store. "He admits Toby slugged him. Even says he took a swing, himself."

"So?" Ellie pulled carefully into the bank's ATM lane, where the night deposit slot was. I handed her our envelope.

"So," I replied, "there's no medic at the Coast Guard station. Coasties go to the clinic here in town just like everybody else."

I knew because I'd seen them and talked with them in the waiting room while accompanying my dad to his many appointments over the past twelve months. And the clinic, I also happened to know, was closed in the evenings.

Ellie looked puzzled, meanwhile lining the car up opposite the deposit slot with military precision. "So who did put those stitches in?" she asked.

Then she glanced into our deposit envelope, and her look changed to one of horror. "Jake, how do we only have—?"

A sigh escaped me; throughout the previous winter we'd bumped hopefully along toward spring when we thought sales would surely pick up, and in fact they already had, a little bit.

Just not enough, and not soon enough. Now with the amount we'd spent on ingredients for that dratted wedding cake—not to mention the other toothsome goodies we'd promised for the wedding reception—we were flat broke.

I explained all this. "Once they've paid, of course," I added, "we'll have money again. Some, anyway."

If they paid, I added silently; if all this murder stuff didn't put the wedding entirely off the rails.

"We should've asked for a deposit," I said.

Any other time, we would have. But Sharon, a school teacher, was nearly as broke as we were, and at the time Andy had been out on a Coast

Guard cutter, training new enlistees how not to fall overboard and drown.

"I'd feel terrible asking for money now, though," I added.

Sharon had told us that most of Andy Devine's paycheck supported distant family members, and we knew her own went for food, the roof over her head, and the clothes on her back, as well as a lot of school supplies for her less-well-off kindergarteners.

"They've been saving for this wedding practically forever," I added as Ellie dropped our deposit envelope into the slot, then eased forward out of the lane.

"D'you think he did it, though?" she added.

We headed toward my house, past the ball field, where the Little League moms were mowing and trimming, then past the Community Center, where long tables and metal folding chairs were being hauled in for tonight's combination bingo game and baked bean supper.

Which I always think is a potentially very funny combination, but never mind. "No," I said. "If he had, he wouldn't have been so sneaky about it."

He'd had, I was sure, plenty of weapons training; the Coast Guard was, after all, a military organization at heart. And from the rapidness with which he had ascended his career ladder I gathered there was also a spine under all that good-heartedness he displayed.

Maybe a temper, too, although I'd seen no evidence of that; the opposite, actually.

"So why not just say who stitched his forehead up?" she wondered aloud.

That was my question, as well. Or one of them. "Maybe he's protecting someone? But if that's true, then who? And why?"

We turned onto Key Street, where the maple trees unfurled sticky green leaves. Daffodils flashed yellow, and behind white picket fences the tight purple clumps of lilac blooms were beginning to open.

Over it all hung the sweet smell of saltwater, but the sight of my driveway and what was in it wasn't sweet; not even a little bit.

Rather, what *wasn't* in it: no red pickup truck.

All our other vehicles were there: my husband Wade's old pickup, Sam and Mika's little Toyota sedan, my own car, an elderly Rav 4, and the vintage Ford Galaxy that Bella had been driving.

Vintage in the sense that it was old and beat-up, that is, with enough silver duct tape holding it together to build a whole new car. But that wasn't the point.

The point was, my dad hadn't come home. That or he'd been there and taken off again, which was worse. Ellie glanced alertly at me.

"Not ready to go inside yet?"

"How'd you guess?" My stiffened shoulders

and anxious expression must have clued her in. Besides . . .

"Look," I said. "If Andy did kill Toby Moran, or Sharon did—"

Tellingly, Ellie didn't contradict that last part.

"—then there's not going to be a wedding, so there won't need to be a cake."

Which solved one problem, all right. But it didn't solve our bigger difficulty.

"And I don't know about you, but I just don't have the heart to ask either one of them for that money."

The fairly hefty sum that we'd already spent on the ingredients, I meant. Ellie was already backing out of the driveway again. I could only hope that Bella hadn't noticed our arrival.

But probably she was already so angry at my father's absence, she couldn't see straight; it was yet another of the good news/bad news situations I seemed prone to lately.

"Me neither," said Ellie, meaning the money we didn't want to request. "And if they didn't do it, but the police decide that one of them *did* . . ."

"Correct. Then it's the same; no wedding, no cake." And no more Chocolate Moose, either, I added silently, not having the heart to say it aloud.

"The only scenario that gets us paid in time for us to stay in business," I went on, "is if they

94

didn't. And if we can prove that they didn't. Kill Moran, that is."

By showing, I meant, that somebody else had. Ellie kept driving—back down Key Street, turn right on Water Street, straight out to the island's end and then via tight, twisty lanes, narrow alleys, and long driveways all the way around the island, and back nearly to where we'd started from.

Half a block from downtown she pulled to the curb, up against a lot of rosebushes grown nearly together across an old brick path.

She'd been silent a while. But now: "I've been thinking the same. The finding-out part, I mean. It's why I brought us here."

And that in a nutshell was my friend Ellie White. Brave, smart, and utterly undaunted by any situation we'd ever confronted so far . . . If I could've saved The Chocolate Moose for her by feeding myself to lions, I'd have done it in a heartbeat.

We got out and made our way down the flagstone path leading to a cottage; a *tiny* cottage, with a low, arched front door half-hidden by more roses and a small, round window just beside the door so the occupant could peer out.

Halfway there, a white pea-graveled side path led invitingly downhill to a large, barnlike structure with a lot of chicken-wire-reinforced windows and a brand-new green metal gambrel-arched roof.

"Hmm," I said, pausing where the side path branched off.

Norm was a car collector, I happened to know, or had been when he was working steady and could afford to be. The barn was where he kept his cars; that's why the windows were all reinforced.

Which meant there was probably a lock on the door, too. Ellie squinted questioningly at me. "No reason at all," I said in reply to her look, then sprinted down the path toward the barn.

As I'd said, I had no reason to think Andy Devine's troubles had anything to do with Norm's car barn. But I was curious, and here we were, and it's not like me having a look through one of those windows was going to hurt anything, was it?

No, it certainly wasn't. But it didn't help anything, either, as far as I could tell.

Making our way down the path, we glimpsed a rat skittering away into the rocks heaped by the water's edge, but it wanted nothing to do with us, so that part was all right. When we got to the barn, though, I couldn't see much, and what I could make out had nothing to do with Andy Devine or Toby Moran.

"What's in there?" Ellie asked as I pressed my face to the wire-reinforced window. Inside the barn, dusty shafts of sunlight slanted down from the higher panes, raising the visibility inside the large, mostly empty space from nil to minimal.

"Looks like he's got six of them left," I replied.

I recognized a vintage Fiat, an old Alfa Romeo sedan, and a cute little MG two-seater in dark British Green. The rest were covered with tarps.

I stepped down from the cinder block I'd been perched on. Norm had owned eight cars; I knew because he'd had them in the Fourth of July parade the previous summer. Now I theorized aloud that being out of work for a while might've meant he'd had to sell a couple of them.

"And we care about that because . . . ?" Ellie wanted to know as we made our way back uphill again.

I shrugged. "We don't, I guess. You just never know when a little background info will come in handy, that's all."

Also, I'm very nosy, I might have added, but she already knew that. We reached the house, built on a bluff overlooking the water.

"What a great spot," said Ellie, smiling as she breathed in the perfume of the roses all around us. "Quiet, private, and yet it's just a couple of blocks from downtown, and with a water view, too."

I agreed. With its burnished brass nameplate on the massive old wooden door, the rough cedar-shingled roof and mossy wooden gutters that looked as if they'd been there for centuries, the cottage was the kind of place that an elf from a storybook might live in, or a hobbit.

Or a disgraced veterinarian.

I wasn't sure anyone would be home, but after a moment scuffling sounds came from inside. After eyeing us coldly through the porthole-type window by the front door, Norman McHale let us in.

Grudgingly, but he did it. And I gathered he didn't spend the entirety of his mornings in the Rubber Ducky, either, as I'd feared when I saw him earlier; having no work and not knowing if or when he'd get his career back must've been wearing on him.

"Sit down," he told us, sweeping stacks of books and magazines from a couple of dusty chairs and waving us to them.

He stood over us, his long-fingered hands rubbing themselves together uneasily. I got the sense he didn't often have visitors. Then without asking, he put tiny glasses of liqueur on a tray and set it down for us.

I took one as Ellie began: "So, Norman . . ."

The room was small and low-ceilinged, made even more cramped-feeling by the heavy, dark-upholstered furniture and the bookcases lining the walls. A hissing propane heater glowed in the brick hearth at one end of the chamber, while a massive, ornate dining room set with eight chairs and a mirrored breakfront crowded the other.

In a plain black frame over the mantel hung Norman's veterinary degree. Someone had taken the parchment from the frame, scribbled out the elaborate, curlicued script on it with a thick black magic marker, then put the degree back into the frame and hung it.

By a roofing nail, it looked like, and was that an orange rubber band that he'd used in place of picture-hanging wire?

Ellie went on. "Norm, did you stitch up Andy Devine's forehead last night, by any chance?"

His dark, shaggy eyebrows twitched in annoyance. "No. Why, who says I did, and why do you want to know, anyway?"

I sat, managing not to cough at the dust plume puffing up from the upholstered chair beneath me. Surgical cleanliness had departed from his routine, apparently.

"Anyway, I don't talk about my patients," he added, suddenly sounding nervous. "Animal *or* human, not that I have any—"

I pounced. "So you did work on him, then." And before he could reply, "See, if you did, I've got no problem with that whatsoever."

Norm looked unpersuaded.

"And I understand that getting your name involved in a murder investigation, even trivially, might not be so good for your license reinstatement prospects," I added.

Still no reaction. Have I mentioned that Ellie is very smart?

"But if you say you didn't," I went on, "then I'll have to go on poking around trying to find out who did and if it turns out to be you, after all, who knows what I might have to do with the information?"

He caught my drift, his dark eyes flickering at me from under those massive eyebrows; really, they were remarkable.

"I see. So this is blackmail, then?" he demanded coldly.

I shrugged, fingering the smeary little glass he'd poured the liqueur into. "Nope, just me pointing out consequences. But, come on, Norman, you know us. We're not here to jam you up."

Ellie picked up one of the books Norm had moved. *Directory of Rural Veterinary Clinics*," she read from the cover.

I raised an eyebrow. "Planning a move, are you? Maybe find a place way out in some other boondocks where they haven't heard of you, and start your career all over again?"

Norm hiked the wine-colored dressing gown he'd changed into up over his narrow shoulders. It was a silk, elaborately brocaded number that should've gone with embroidered slippers and a pipe.

Snifter of brandy, maybe, late in the evening with the radio on, soft music tinkling out into the night. But it was early afternoon and I was willing to bet he'd be wearing that dressing gown all day.

He gave in suddenly, putting his liqueur glass down on the room's cluttered mantel. "All right, all right. So what if I did stitch him up? The Devine kid, I mean, what difference does it make if I—"

"He won't say so, Norm. Protecting you, maybe. But now he's in custody over Toby Moran's murder, and any secret he tries keeping from the cops could be the thing that sinks him."

I paused for breath. "And that'll sink his wedding, and *that* will sink Ellie and me. In a way," I added as he peered curiously at me, "that you don't need to know the details of, only that it's true."

Ellie chimed in. "Seriously, Norman. We're not trying to hurt anybody, including you. But if you did treat him, we need to know what he told you. Otherwise . . ."

"Otherwise he's done for, or probably he is, anyway, and by some logical connections too boring to go into right now, we are, as well."

To illustrate all this, she drew her finger dramatically across her throat. It wasn't the gesture I'd have chosen, but he brightened at it. Boring as his life was nowadays, I got the sense that even an imitation throat-cutting was better than the usual tedium.

"I see." He seized his liqueur glass again and sat across from me on a dusty velvet settee, brushing away a cat.

They were everywhere in the room, I saw as my eyes grew used to the clutter. On shelves, under chairs . . .

"In that case," he pronounced, "it seems that I have no choice. Do no harm and all that, right?"

He tossed back the liqueur. "All right. Short and sweet. He came over late, didn't call, knocked and I let him in. I'd just gotten in, myself, actually."

The timing sounded right. "What did he say?"

Norman rolled his eyes. "The standard line of head-bump sufferers everywhere, when they don't want to tell the real story."

He picked up my liqueur glass from the coffee table between us and drained it, too. "Said he walked into the corner of a locker door at the Coast Guard station."

Same story as he'd told us. "You believed him?" queried Ellie.

Norm snorted. "Please. For one thing, it wasn't that kind of a wound. This wasn't a gouge; it was the kind of split you get from a punch, not from a sharp corner of something."

A cat stepped into his lap; he stroked it automatically as he spoke. "Bit by bit, though, I got it out of him. He'd been accosted by a rowdy fellow who had a grudge against him. Toby Moran."

"I don't understand. Why wouldn't he want anyone to know that?"

Norman nodded agreement. "My thought precisely. Why not just go up to the emergency room in Calais, get your stitches from a pro?"

The bitterness in his tone made me reply. "You're a pro, Norman," I told him gently.

He looked mollified. "Be that as it may." The cat got up, walked away with its tail switching, then came back as Norm went on.

"He said the guy jumped him from behind on the street outside the Rubber Ducky. Sucker-punched him; Devine hit back by reflex, he said, but he missed."

Ellie glanced at me as Norman sipped liqueur and went on. "Thing is, he said, he's at a tricky point in his career, and if his superiors knew he'd been in a fight—even one that he hadn't initiated and never even landed a punch in—it could derail an important promotion that he was up for."

This did make sense; Ellie and I glanced at each other. "He's changed his story, today," I said, and Norm looked interested.

"He told us a little while ago that it happened behind the Duck. That's where the body was found, too," I said. "I don't see why he'd have told you otherwise, unless . . ."

Norman peered wisely at us from beneath his shaggy eyebrows. "Unless the truth is that our friend Mr. Devine never got jumped at all. That maybe instead Devine followed his victim into the shadows behind the buildings, but didn't want to say so."

"And since he never thought that you'd be talking to anyone about it—"

"Exactly," Norm replied approvingly to me. "This morning, he's realized his new story makes more sense and has felt free to change it, not thinking I'd ever contradict him."

But Ellie shook her head. "I don't know, Norman. That path overlooking the harbor leads straight back to the Coast Guard station. Andy had a perfectly good reason for being there last night, no evil motives required."

She picked her own little liqueur glass up, sipped from it, and blinked, putting it down carefully again. I'd smelled mine, and next to this stuff, Allen's Brandy was flavored sugar water.

"So he didn't have to lie about it in the first place, or if he did have a reason to, we still don't know it," she said.

"Yet," I added, annoyed, because why couldn't people just tell the whole truth in the first place? Why did Ellie and I have to go around dragging it out of them, when we had a wedding cake to figure out how to bake?

104

If we did. Turning my mind from the looming spectacle of our imminent financial destruction, I drank, then got up and poured myself more of the liqueur, which turned out to be dandelion wine—delicious, and with a kick to it.

Coughing at the second dose, I managed, "Good heavens, Norman, how long did you age this, anyway?"

The burnt-orange-colored liquid was like a cross between rocket fuel and something that has been sitting in an oaken cask for half a century or so.

He looked pleased, nodding and tenting his fingers. "Oh, about two years." Digging a battered Moleskine from the mess he'd moved from the coffee table, he added, "I'll put you on my list for a bottle of the next batch, shall I?"

His deep-set eyelids lowered and raised slowly. "Meanwhile, to get back to the point."

He wrapped the ribbon around the Moleskine. "Your friend's head injury was superficial, bleeding freely when he came to the door and asked me to administer first aid."

"Which you did," I said as Norman nodded again. "Did he say anything else about what happened?"

By now, the mid-afternoon sun sent hazy shafts between the parlor's drawn curtains, lighting up more of the room's jumbled furnishings: an antique mirror, a tarnished silver samovar, a chandelier whose myriad crystal pendants were heavily swathed in cobwebs.

From the front hallway, a large green parrot squawked; we'd passed it on our way in here. Norm still looked reluctant. Finally: "I'm still a good veterinary surgeon, you know. I mean—"

He regarded his fingers, which were slim and well-kept, tipped by clean, short-clipped nails. "I still have something to offer. But first I'll need my license re-instated."

He looked up at us. "And you're right, I don't imagine stitching up the split forehead of an accused murderer—which, by the way, constitutes practicing *human* medicine *without* a license—will do my argument much good when I go before the board again."

I got up. Ellie too. He put his glass down. "I want my life back, you know? But if the board turns me down, makes my suspension a permanent thing, it will all be over."

He crossed the worn Persian carpet and paused by the ornate carved mantel, fingering the grimy samovar perched on it as wistfully as if it held memories instead of dead tea leaves.

"I didn't believe the door story and I told him so," said Norm. "I advised him to make a police report about it."

Remembering this, he let a small smile curve his lips, softening his bitter expression. "Big kid," he recalled of Andy Devine. "Strong, too, you could tell he's not just some overbuilt gym rat."

"He didn't even say anything about going to the police?" Ellie asked.

She picked up a cat and cradled it like an infant, which it obviously enjoyed; I swear that woman is so *sympatico* with all kinds of animals, she could make a pet out of a vampire bat.

"Prutt," the cat uttered; Norm's look softened further.

Then his eyes narrowed calculatingly as he plucked up a pair of fingernail clippers from the coffee table. "Just hold him like that for a sec, will you?"

He approached the animal. "Here I'm a veterinarian and even I can never get him to let me—"

Sensing trouble, the cat stiffened, then sprang from Ellie's arms with a betrayed-sounding yowl and streaked from the room.

Norman looked philosophical. "Oh, well," he said, dropping the clippers into his dressing-gown pocket. "Maybe I'll just sedate him and do it that way."

He followed us to the hall. "It doesn't matter much, though, he's got most of the stuffing out of the furniture with those sharp claws, already."

"Norman." I stood by the front door. Between the dust and the cat dander and the smell of cabbage cooking in the too-warm cottage, I was dying to get outside. "Norm, darn it all, what more did Andy Devine *say?* About the police, or anything else?"

"Oh! Right." He opened the door. From outside, the cool fresh air and soft perfume of the rosebushes beckoned.

"What he said was that I shouldn't worry about it. Because—"

From another room came the unmistakable sound of a cat scratching in a sandbox. I stepped hastily through the doorway and Ellie joined me.

"Andy said that I shouldn't worry about it because the important thing was, his assailant wouldn't be hurting anyone ever again," Norm McHale told us flatly.

Ever again . . .

And then he closed the door on us.

Ordinarily, one or both of us would return to The Chocolate Moose in the evening, to get started on tomorrow's baking. But neither Ellie nor I felt very enthusiastic about that idea today, so we decided to get it over with right now and not have to come back.

"I'll get started in the kitchen," said Ellie, "and you do the necessary out here, okay?"

"Fine with me," I said, and began straightening up the shop area.

In the glass-fronted display case only a few lonely cake fragments and cookie crumbs remained. Nothing wrong with our product, in other words. It was our shaky business model that was nailing our hides to the wall, as my father would've put it.

The thought reminded me that I hadn't seen him since earlier in the day. Now, checking my phone, I found three urgent text messages from Bella, inquiring about him.

"She seems to think I can just drop everything and go out looking for him," I groused irritably, dampening a paper towel with Windex to wipe off the display case's glass front.

In the kitchen, the exhaust fan went on, the cooler door clicked shut, and then the pan rack rattled as she got sauce pots and mixing bowls down from it.

"Maybe you should," she said.

I blinked. Our baking for tomorrow included chocolate-frosted pistachio logs, a raspberry jam-filled fudge layer cake, and a flat chocolate wafer cookie, frosted like the pistachio logs but with a sliver of white chocolate stuck into the top.

A lot of work, in other words. She came to the door. Behind her one of the fluorescent overhead lights buzzed, flickering. I put it on my mental to-buy list—that is, if we ever had money again, which I doubted we would.

"I said, maybe you should go." Her tone was resolute.

I followed her back out into the kitchen. The makings of the wafer cookies were assembled on our work table: flour, sugar, butter, eggs, a little salt and some leavening, and the cocoa powder.

"Bella would appreciate it," she added. She'd tied a white apron on over her T-shirt and jeans, and popped a hairnet on.

Overhead, the big old paddle-bladed fan turned slowly. "And it's not going to make any difference to us, after all," she added. "I'm just doing this baking because I don't know what else to do."

I understood. Things looked dreadful for Andy Devine, and what he'd said to Norm about Toby Moran never hurting anyone again made it all seem even worse.

And his imminent downfall now meant ours was nearly certain. But I still didn't want to leave Ellie alone; there was too much work in front of her, for one thing, and for another, she looked too sad.

She measured out the sugar. Then she softened some butter in a mixing bowl in the microwave and slid the bowl across the table to me along with a wooden spoon.

Perched on a stool, I began working the sugar into the butter; I didn't know what else to do, either. While I creamed the mixture in the bowl, my phone buzzed with another incoming text: Any news?

It was Bella again, and this time I wasn't going to reply. I was certain that my dad was fine, just off the radar for a little while, and although I found it almost as annoying as Bella did, that also was probably a good sign.

He was, I told myself, a stubborn old coot enjoying his newly regained independence, and he'd come home when he was done feeling his oats.

At least somebody was having fun. "Ellie," I said.

She looked very glum. The butter and sugar mixture was done; I set it aside and began shelling nuts for the pistachio log.

"Ellie, I know it's disappointing." I tried consoling her.

She shrugged, sifting cocoa powder and flour together. "I'm not disappointed," she declared unconvincingly. "It'll be fine. Once we've closed the place, sold off all the equipment, and so on—"

She stopped, sighing heavily, then got eggs from the cooler and cracked them into the butter and sugar mixture along with some vanilla extract.

Real vanilla extract, that is, not the imitation stuff. It had been Ellie's vision from the start to do everything the old-fashioned way, with genuine ingredients. She wouldn't even use an egg that she hadn't gathered from the hens in the fenced area behind her house.

At least she hadn't insisted on churning the butter and refining the sugar. "And as for me, I'll find something else to do," she said.

A pistachio flew from between my fingers and plinked against her mixing bowl. She managed a shaky smile.

"After all, it's not the end of the world if . . . if . . ."

I got up, put my arm around her shoulders, and handed her a tissue. "Oh, honey," I said as she gave it a long blow.

And then, of course, she had to wash her hands, and while she was at it I made her wash her face and comb her hair, and when she'd finished all that I fixed her a cold cloth to press against her eyes.

"There, now," I said, sitting her down at one of the café tables out front. "Better?"

I'd been busy, too; now I set a tall glass in front of her.

She bit her lip, not looking up. "Jake, this bakery's not a hobby for me. It was supposed to be the way I helped make money for my family."

I'd known that. "Not that I think you don't care just as much as I do," she added hastily.

She knew I was as committed to our business as anyone could be: late nights, early mornings, whatever it took. But the fact was that my husband Wade Sorenson had one of the most secure jobs in the world, as a harbor pilot for Eastport's port authority.

And Ellie's didn't. "George is over in Bangor again," she said. "Living in a trailer with other men during the week, putting up a new medical center building. Comes home on weekends."

"Or when it rains, or snows, or the wind blows too hard, or the materials don't get delivered on time so they can't work," I said.

Freelance construction, even skilled work of the type that George did, was not exactly a secure occupation. Income rose in summer and dropped in winter; jobs came and went.

Ellie noticed the glass I'd brought her. "What is that?" She sniffed curiously. "Is that a milkshake?"

She'd been in the washroom. "Maybe. Taste it and see."

I already had; tasted it, that is. And, after all, how can you go wrong with milk, ice cream, and chocolate syrup?

So I was pretty sure it would pass muster, especially since in one of our cupboards I'd located what I was fairly certain was Ellie's hidden stash of her secret ingredient.

We'd been out of the little packets that Ellie packaged the stuff in so as to avoid revealing its nature. But I'd found the can it came in, with the original label plus a set of helpful instructions printed on the side: how much to use, and so on.

Also, I swear that vintage milkshake mixer was so gorgeous—bright stainless steel, shiny mint-green Bakelite, an Art Deco shape like the front of an old-fashioned streamliner locomotive . . .

Well, you could pour dry plaster mix and turpentine into the stainless-steel mixer cup, I felt sure, and come up with something delicious.

"Go on, have some," I urged her. I'd poured a bit for myself, as well; now to encourage her I stuck in a fountain straw and took an eye-openingly delicious swallow of the cold, sweet mixture.

"Oh, good heavens," I sighed, as cautiously she followed suit. Then, "Well?" I waited for her reaction. "What do you think?"

I was a little nervous about it, honestly. "Did I get it anywhere near right?"

In reply she frowned thoughtfully, her eyes still sparkling liquidly with her earlier tears.

"Jake," she declared, "that's the most delicious chocolate malted milkshake I've ever tasted in my life."

She drank some more of it, looking brighter and cheerier by the minute. It made me think they should stock this stuff in ambulances right along with the heart medications and IV fluids.

"But . . ." She tapped the glass with a clean, clear-polished index fingertip. Never mind chickens; Ellie could keep elephants and still have an intact manicure, she was that meticulous.

"Sweet, creamy, malty. And just thick enough," she pronounced, and kept tasting. "But there's something else in it, I think. Something . . . new." She eyed me quizzically. "Isn't there? Something . . ."

So I was caught. "Yes, I put in some vanilla extract. A couple of drops, that's all."

Her eyebrows rose minutely; she sipped once more. "Not enough to overpower. Just enough to . . . complexify."

She set the glass down. "It's an improvement. It really is. Way to go, Jake, you've really done it. I think that now our Moose Milks are perfect."

I straightened proudly; coming from Ellie, this was high praise. But then her expression crumpled.

"Too bad we're not going to be open long enough to rehabilitate their reputation," she said. "Because in time, people would stop being scared of them and start buying them again, don't you think?"

I did think so. But time was what we didn't have. We wouldn't even be baking for tomorrow except that we already had the ingredients and we didn't want to waste them.

"Rent," I said quietly. "And insurance," I added, since the moment you let it lapse, someone would trip over a pastry crumb or something and you'd be on the hook for the equivalent of a heart transplant.

Which we also couldn't afford. "Licenses and permits," I added, "and the payments on that new stove."

I waved toward the double-oven cooking appliance that we'd bought the previous summer, back when the new-business stars were still in our eyes and at least some of our original startup money was in the checking account. Now if we didn't manage to sell the stove, the balance would come out of my credit card.

It was a little detail I hadn't told Ellie at the time, and I didn't mention it now, either; she already felt awful. In fact . . .

I peered closely at her; *really* awful. "Ellie. Come on, now. Is there something you're not telling me?"

She buried her face in her hands. "Oh, Jake," she blurted through them, "if we have to close the shop, I'll have to . . . I'll have to move away from Eastport!"

"What? But I thought as long as George was working—"

His presence at the Pickled Herring had been a treat. But he'd gone straight back to the job site afterward.

"We're okay money-wise as long as he keeps at it," she went on, dabbing at her eyes with a paper napkin.

My cell phone vibrated in my pocket again. I ignored it. Bella would just have to wait.

"But he can't, Jake," Ellie said. "It's killing him being over there all the time, away from us, and the drive's awful—"

Between here and Bangor lay a hundred and twenty miles of bad road. No interstate; you either wanted to get there or you didn't.

"Lee's growing up without him," she said, "and as for me—"

She bit her lip. Then, "It's just really lonely, you know? I tell myself that I've got to be a grownup about it, but—"

A picture of us all at the Herring popped into my head. George's daughter had stuck to him like a happy barnacle, a situation he'd clearly enjoyed, and Ellie had been delighted, too.

But when we all went home together afterward, my family *had* gone home, while George had a dark, three-hour drive back to a shared house trailer with dirty socks and fast-food bags all over the place.

"It's no way for him to live, either," Ellie said sadly.

Outside, the long, spring afternoon was fading, a thin white moon rising over the harbor, where the fishing boats still puttered.

"Bunking with roughnecks," said Ellie, "showering in a locker room. And the food . . ."

She straightened. "I haven't wanted to say it, but if we do have to close the Moose I'll be talking to George about . . . about . . ."

Uh-oh, the waterworks were threatening again and neither of us wanted that. Besides . . .

"You mean you haven't? Told him we might be—"

"Flat broke?" she suggested. "In over our heads? Up you-know-what creek without a—?" She laughed a little wildly. "Jake, you know how he is, he thinks I can do no wrong. That I've got the golden touch, or something."

More napkins, more dabbing. She sucked in a shuddery breath. "And he's been working so hard, and he's so happy when he is here, I didn't have the heart to . . ."

She drank a little more of the milkshake. "Well, I might not have exactly filled him in on the precise details," she finished.

"So not only are you broke, you're alone with that information. And if you can't get things back on track, you think you'll have to . . ." I could barely bring myself to say the words. "To move away from Eastport. Sell your house, start all over again somewhere else."

She nodded again. But: "Not just *think*. We do have to. If we want to live together as a family anymore, in any way that actually counts. Because there's not enough work here for him, Jake, there just isn't."

She looked helplessly at me. "I don't know how I'll even bear it. I've lived here all my life. I know everyone, and everyone knows me."

A final sigh lifted her shoulders and subsided. "So that," she finished sorrowfully, "is why I've been so stubborn about the shop."

I got up from the cast-iron café table that I'd bought with the rest of them and the matching chairs, too, at a garage sale back when we still thought The Chocolate Moose was going to be sensational.

And it was, too; a sensational failure. To keep our little bake shop alive, we'd done everything short of opening an artery.

But it hadn't worked. Outside, the soft, golden glow of late afternoon deepened to blue. *Ellie leaving . . .*

What would I do without her? She'd cushioned my landing when I first got here, popping over with doughnuts and fresh gossip back when I was so new in Eastport, I barely understood her downeast accent.

"Flippahs," she'd say, meaning my son's swim fins. Or "hah-bah," which was where the boats came in, of course. And when my hideous ex-husband ended up coming here to die in my guest bedroom—hey, it's a long story, and I'll tell it to you some other time—Ellie came every day to visit with him and read to him, even though she despised him.

And I don't know about you, but I think that a woman who will sit reading Dickens every day to a guy whom she loathes just because he is on his deathbed is a woman worth doing things for.

"Ellie," I said, standing by the front window gazing out.

Down in the boat basin, a ramshackle old scallop trawler motored unhesitatingly into the narrow space between the finger piers, pivoted in a tight one-eighty, and slotted itself against the dock.

Meanwhile, a different mental picture replaced the one of my ex-husband, his eyes closed while Ellie read *Great Expectations*.

"Ellie, were you watching when Toby Moran got thrown out of the Duck?"

The flailing arms, the angry grimace; I could still see his denim jacket flapping and his boot-cleats glinting as he staggered away.

Ellie nodded. And as usual, she was thinking the same way I was.

"He didn't look sober enough to throw a punch, did he? Much less connect with one."

But that's not what Andy had said. "I've thought all along there was something odd about that," she said. "About all of it, really."

"Makes you wonder, doesn't it?" I agreed. "I mean, if there's more about Toby that we might want to know. And it's not as if there's more here we need to do right now," I said.

We did still have to bake all those cookies; besides eliminating waste, everything we sold meant more cash on hand and fewer debts outstanding, eventually. But it wouldn't be the first time we'd pulled an all-nighter to get the display case stocked.

"The police have already gone through Moran's house," said Ellie. "I saw them there bagging things and taking them away early this morning, when I was on my way here."

Moran had a place in an old sea captain's mansion that had been turned into apartments, down the street from where Ellie lived. "But when I passed by later, they were gone," she added.

"Huh. So anyone else who took a look around wouldn't be messing things up for the cops. In the evidence department, I mean," I added.

Ellie frowned. "Let me just check that, though." She got out her cell phone and pressed the speed dial button just as my own phone buzzed again.

Bella, of course. "Oh, brother," I breathed in exasperation.

I typed on the tiny keyboard, pressed send. "It's about my dad again," I said. "He's still not home and it's driving her nuts. So I told her we'd have a look for him," I added apologetically.

"Fine. Gives us a good reason not to rush right home, ourselves."

Her daughter, Lee, was away at a school choir concert and the bus wouldn't be back until late.

"She's got a violin concert coming up soon,

too, doesn't she?" I asked. The kid had more events on her schedule than most adults around here.

"Oh, thanks for reminding me," Ellie responded, checking the calendar on her phone, "you're right, it's the day after tomorrow."

She tucked the device away. "But what's this about your dad?"

"He's behaving like a teenager," I said, snatching my sweater off a hook as we went out.

"But you do think he's okay?" she asked, waiting while I locked the door behind us.

Outside it was nearly evening, the shop's OPEN banners all taken in and the parking spaces in front of them vacant. In a month we'd be so full of tourists that there'd barely be room to move, but right now the town felt as still as a held breath.

In the east, the first few stars began twinkling. I dropped the shop keys into my bag.

"Ellie, I don't know that he is," I answered. "Okay, I mean. But he's an adult, and he's made it clear he doesn't want me checking up on him. So I'll look around, but I'm not going on an all-out hunt for him."

The phone vibrated again. I shut it off without looking at it.

"He's not a child, and he's not stupid," I said as we set off on foot through the gathering evening; for this errand, we both knew the quieter our approach was, the better.

Besides, it was lovely out here, cool and fresh with a hint of soft, damp fog. "And he's not an invalid anymore, either," I added.

The little downtown business district thinned as we left the harbor area behind, striding uphill past the Coast Guard station, the marine store, and Rosie's Hot Dog Stand.

"He'll show up," I said, "when he gets hungry."

Or I hoped he would. As we walked, the big old houses looming on both sides of the street sent warm light from their curtained windows onto the lawns; dinner smells and the sound of TVs drifted from their front doors.

"You did call Bob Arnold?" I asked. She'd started to, but . . .

Ellie shook her head. "I changed my mind. Toby had a landlady, so we'll just ask her to tell us for sure whether the state police have been through his room yet or not."

It did seem like a better plan; no sense alerting Bob that we were on snoop patrol, since if he didn't know, he couldn't stop us.

Soon we reached Ellie's house, a small, well-kept bungalow set back from the sidewalk and surrounded by a hedge of beach roses. The yard lamp lit the garden plot and the chicken coops; beyond, the other houses lay much farther apart and the sidewalk ended, leaving only the road's gravel shoulder.

Still we continued, between fields and thickets of saplings; on the water to the north, the moon's reflection lay silvery as mercury.

"Here we are," Ellie whispered at last.

A shape loomed up suddenly in the moonlit darkness, a jumble of sharp angles and tall, peaked roofs, narrow windows, and treacherous-looking balconies.

It was an old sea-captain's mansion with a widow's walk and a cupola, the perfect place if you happened to like chains rattling and sheeted figures wafting around hauntingly.

"Yeesh," I said. All it needed was bats flapping around it. The windows were dark, and there was no porch light.

"Who lived here besides Toby, the Addams Family?"

In the gloom I made out a yardful of weeds, ragged draperies sagging at the windows, and a house-number bracket dangling crookedly by one nail on the half-open front door.

Wait a minute, the half-open front door? "Ellie, is anyone else living here?" I whispered. A landlady wouldn't leave a door open.

Just looking at the place made the hairs stand up on my arms. And it didn't help that right now someone else was looking at it, too, only they were doing it from the inside.

"I told you," Ellie whispered. "The landlady lives here. But—"

The flashlight's beam flared again behind one of the upstairs windows.

"Her name's Mrs. Starne," whispered Ellie. The flashlight up there flickered some more. "Oh, I hope she's all right."

She marched away from me, up the weed-choked gravel path leading to the house. Tripping over tangles of bittersweet vines and shoving through clumps of birch saplings carelessly sprouting in the path, I managed to keep her in sight.

"Ellie, wait!"

She stopped, and I saw the set of her shoulders in the moonlight, her head high and her fists clenched combatively. "There's somebody in there, and I want to know who," she said, staring at the house.

The flashlight glimmered upstairs yet again. She stomped up the front steps and shoved the heavy oaken door the rest of the way open.

"Hello? Mrs. Starne, are you in here? Are you okay?"

She stepped into the dark front hallway. In the yellowish glow of a single bare hanging lightbulb I glimpsed an ornate staircase, strips of peeling wallpaper, and what appeared to be a moth-eaten stuffed owl perched on a chair back.

Then: "Help!" quavered a frightened old voice from somewhere deep in the house. "Help, somebody!"

Ellie found a light switch. A weak glow showed threadbare rugs, antique furniture, and a hanging planter with a dead philodendron leaf dangling from it. We rushed past all of it toward where the voice had come from, into a dim-lit kitchen.

"Oh!" gasped an elderly lady from the straight chair she'd been tied to. Around her, the kitchen was like an old, sepia-toned photo from the 1890s: wood-burning cookstove, a half-barrel full of kindling, and an age-battered, cast-iron sink standing next to the gas-fired hot water heater.

"Foolish girls, get me out of here!" Mrs. Starne spat. Tiny and white-haired, wearing a shapeless housedress, she was so goggle-eyed with fury that I thought she might be about to have a stroke.

"Hurry!" she demanded, glaring at me while I hastened to comply. I yanked at the clothes-line binding her to the chair, then found a knife in a drawer and sliced away the rope.

She sprang up, grabbing at the glass of water Ellie brought to her. "Oh," the landlady fumed inarticulately. "Oh, that rotten . . ."

"Who, Mrs. Starne, who did this to you?" Good heavens, but I was irked; the very idea, tying up a helpless old woman—

"Are they still in the house?" I asked, but just then a shout came from the front hall, where Ellie had gone.

"Jake, come quick, they're getting . . ."

Away. Of course, I realized, whoever had been up there was now deciding to vamoose. Footsteps thudded down the stairs as I hurried back out to the hall, but before I got there Ellie cried out again.

"Oh, no, you don't, you—" Then the front door slammed hard and shoes thumped across the porch.

"Ellie, are you okay?" I found her peering out into the darkness, where faint crunching sounds on the gravel path moved hurriedly away.

"We'll call Bob Arnold," I said, pulling my phone out.

"No." Mrs. Starne's voice came harshly from behind me. Turning, I found her in the hall wearing a pair of rolled-down white stockings, that blue flowered housedress, and fuzzy slippers.

She had a little gunmetal-gray pistol in her hand. "Don't call anyone," she snapped. "I don't want the police."

Her eyes were as pale and shiny as silver bullets, her lips pressed tightly together like thin slices of liver. "If that bastard shows up here again, I'll save them the trouble."

It struck me that having her out here shooting people might not be Bob's idea of preventing trouble. But never mind.

"Did you see who it was?" I asked.

"No," Mrs. Starne retorted. "He grabbed me from behind, tied me before I could blink."

She was waving her little gun around in a way I found nervous-making in the extreme. "But if he comes back here again—"

"He won't have to." Ellie sounded discouraged. "Whoever it was had a bundle in his arms when he went by. Jake, I think he's beaten us to the . . ."

"Right, but for what?" This being to me the big question, right up there with whether or not Mrs. Starne was going to accidentally put a bullet in my head.

"Have the state cops been here?" I asked the landlady. If I hadn't been sure before that I wanted to see Moran's room, I was now.

"Because if they have, we'd like to go up there and take a peek, ourselves," I added.

Besides, I was eager to put distance—not to mention a ceiling and some sturdy floorboards—between me and that weapon.

The landlady's glare was so cold, you could've used it to freeze fish. But she told us the room had already been examined, and that she'd been told she could go ahead and clean it.

"Going to need a fire hose for the job," she grumbled.

Then she followed us up the massive old staircase with the gun still gripped in her hand; not what I'd been hoping for. Still, we got to the landing and the hall beyond it without suffering any gunshot wounds, and found Moran's door.

It had been kicked open. Inside, a rumpled bed and a dresser with its drawers yanked out stood opposite an antique washstand with a razor and a can of Barbasol perched on it.

Magazines lay scattered across the floor amidst a clutter of dirty socks. A closet's narrow door gaped open; all the hangers had been yanked down. A shelf above was similarly swept clean.

Ellie was examining something on the small, flimsy-looking desk by the window. "Jake, look at these."

A laptop cord lay on the desk, but no laptop; I guessed that the police investigators had taken it. Stepping aside, she revealed a big manila envelope whose contents she'd already removed.

"Good heavens," I breathed. From the envelope, Ellie had pulled a bunch of photographs, either the same ones that Moran had sent around to embarrass Sharon Sweetwater or ones very like them.

And they were worse than Sharon had said. "Oh, dear," Ellie murmured. "That's quite a costume he's got her wearing."

"Yeah. Expensive, too, I'll bet. Probably the black boots and the little whip with the tassels on it cost extra."

I turned the photos facedown on the desk. Also in the envelope was a list of local names and addresses, written in a whimsical mix of capital and lowercase letters and including e-mail addresses.

The names were of Sharon's student's parents, I guessed; I tucked the whole mess back into the envelope.

"Well, at least now we know what Andy was so mad about. I mean, *specifically* what he—"

"Right. And these aren't going to make him seem any *less* guilty, are they? Even though, I mean, look at them, Jake, they're obviously Photoshopped."

I shoved the envelope into my pocket. Ellie was right; it didn't matter that the photos were faked, that by the miracle of modern computers Sharon's head appeared to have been clumsily glued onto each model's body by a kid wielding a pair of blunt scissors and a bottle of Elmer's.

What mattered was that their mere existence might be enough to make a boyfriend blow a gasket, and that Moran had not only made them—or had someone make them for him, maybe—he'd tried hurting Sharon by mailing them to her students' parents.

I said as much to Ellie. "Moran doesn't seem like the kind of guy who'd know how to alter digital photographs, though."

The magazines scattered about his room were of two types: the kind that were about hunting or fishing, and the kind that were about cars. Nothing in the room suggested any other interests or skills.

"What I'm wondering," I went on, "is why the cops didn't take them."

We looked at each other. Then, "Because the pictures weren't here when the cops were," we said, both of us speaking at the same time.

Ellie looked thoughtful. "Someone printed them out and put them here for the police to find, but too late? The cops had already . . ."

"Uh-huh. To help build the case against Andy, maybe."

Something twined around my ankle; my heart leapt into my throat. But it was only a gray cat, agitating to be picked up.

"Scat," I told it, unpersuaded by its ratty-looking fur and notched ear. Then I noticed the dead mouse in its mouth.

"Eek," I added as the cat dropped the mouse's stiffening corpse on my foot. I kicked it away with a shudder and it landed at the back of the room's tiny closet, whereupon the cat leapt after it, grabbed it again, and vanished.

"Huh?" I said, then realized there must be a hole of some sort back there.

"Ugh," I muttered, crawling through a clutter of old socks, dust clumps, and fallen plaster bits. Also, there was a book lying back there as if tossed when someone was finished with it: *Photo Editing for Dummies*.

Well, they had the right audience, all right. And it answered my earlier question, too, about

Moran's minimal picture-faking abilities; even he, I imagined, might be able to follow simple instructions.

"Hand me the flashlight."

Ellie reached cautiously back to where I crouched. I shone the light at the rear floorboards of the closet, finding one dislodged just enough to make a hole that a cat could slither through.

Also, once the board was lifted away entirely, that you could slide a shoe box into. I pulled the top off and stared at what was inside.

It was a gun. Small, ugly, and obviously very cheap, the weapon was a .22 pistol with a black plastic grip.

"Here's the gun he used to wave around," I said. I'd been wondering about it. I plucked it from the shoebox and slid back out of the closet, then dropped it into my bag.

"We'll give it to Bob Arnold along with the pictures," I said as Ellie and I went back downstairs, where we found Mrs. Starne bustling irritably around the cavernous old kitchen.

A bottle of vodka and a glass stood on the kitchen table. No sign of the weapon she'd been brandishing, though—probably she kept it in her apron pocket along with her brass knuckles, I thought uncharitably—and when we called good night she didn't answer.

"I can see why there aren't any other tenants,"

said Ellie as we made our way down the path outside. By now it was full dark, with the silvery moon shrunk to dime size in the blue-black sky.

"It's like the rooming house from hell," I agreed, glancing back.

Mrs. Starne's ramshackle old dwelling stood sharply against the night sky like a silhouette jaggedly cut from construction paper, its peaked roofs and gables jutting ominously this way and that.

"Brr," said Ellie, shivering as she followed my gaze; the place had all the vintage charm of a mausoleum. A breeze sprang up, setting the half-fledged birch leaves whispering stealthily in the darkness.

Suddenly it occurred to me that whoever had tied up Mrs. Starne might not have gone far away; that, in fact, he could be out here with us right now.

As we made our way out to the street, a shadow moved back there among the birches. But it was only a deer, its eyes reflecting yellow.

I quickened my step. A few blocks away in town, the houses were closer together and there were people around. But way out here at the north end of the island we might as well have been on the surface of that silvery moon instead of hurrying along beneath it.

We walked on silently for a while. Then, "You know," I began, meaning to bring up the murder method. Because let's face it, how *would* you get a cup of insecticide-laced poison into a victim?

Smelly insecticide . . . so maybe it wasn't. Maybe what killed Moran was something else instead, I theorized to myself, and the intensely smelly stuff was only to cover the real method. But before I could suggest this, headlights appeared. *Bright* ones, bouncing up and down as the vehicle approached; winter had long gone by, but the frost heaves it left behind on our little island's roads hadn't.

"Oh," Ellie said as the truck went by. A *recognizable* truck: bright red paint, shiny new hubcaps, still with the temporary license plate in its holder on the rear bumper.

My dad's truck . . . Its brake lights flashed on, cherry red in the darkness. I thought he must've seen us and was stopping for us.

Bella would be glad, I had time to think before the brake lights flashed once more.

Then suddenly the red truck swerved wildly across the roadway, its headlights illuminating a particularly dense stand of those birch saplings just before the truck crashed into them.

Four

"Cyanide," said Wade, "would do the kind of thing you're talking about." He pulled off one of his work boots while he began answering the question I'd just asked him.

Because the trouble was, I still couldn't think of why Toby Moran would swallow a milkshake that reeked of insect poison. Even if you were drunk, you'd have to notice it, it was so powerfully aromatic.

So maybe it was something else that had killed him: something deadly, fast-acting, and not quite as stinky as insecticide? Maybe the bug-killer was just a cover-up, added after the fact?

The thought begged another question, though: if it *was* a cover-up, why bother with it at all, especially when an autopsy would reveal the real method, eventually? But hey, one thing at a time:

"Cyanide is crazy-dangerous, but it used to be common," said Wade. "Farmers used it against coyotes and wolves, and you could go into a feed store and buy pre-made baits for rats and other vermin."

We'd been home for half an hour; he'd picked us up right near the accident site.

"The trouble with cyanide is that kids and pets might get a hold of it," Wade continued.

My dad seemed fine: walking, talking, not bleeding, and nothing obviously broken, and he'd forbidden us from calling an ambulance. Bob Arnold had shown up, of course, but even he had seemed pretty mellow about it all once he knew no one was hurt.

Mellow about the crash, that is; not about what Ellie and I had been doing just previous to it, and what we'd found. Because, of course, I'd told him and endured his reaction, then got scolded and shooed impatiently away so he could deal with Mrs. Starne.

Well, part of what we'd found. He'd have to call the state cops back to look over Moran's place again, he told me, not sounding happy about this.

"And cyanide doesn't smell like insecticide, so someone who doesn't suspect what it is could get injured or killed by it pretty easily," Wade added to me now.

He pulled his other work boot off, sitting in the rocker by the woodstove in our big old kitchen. "And that in a nutshell is why it's not that easy to get the stuff," he said.

Asleep in his playpen, little Ephraim shifted and found his mouth with his thumb. I pulled his fleece blanket up over him.

"The USDA was using baited spring traps

for a while; they'd put a capsule in there and fix it so that when the animal went for the bait, they got a mouthful of cyanide instead," Wade continued.

He pulled his other boot off. "Too many people around to do that anymore, though, too. Big ranches out west, maybe, but not where a youngster or somebody's dog might find it and mess with it."

My thoughts strayed back to my dad, who insisted that a deer had jumped suddenly out in front of him and he'd swerved to avoid it.

Which I believed, but Bella didn't. "Old fool," she muttered.

Standing at the sink, she used a toothpick to jab at nonexistent bits of grime behind the faucet mount. If I'd let her, she'd have been on her knees scrubbing the kitchen floor with a fingernail brush.

"So," continued Wade, "if you did want some, first of all I believe you'd need a permit to buy the spring-trap capsules."

He took another pull of his Sam Adams. "That is, if they're even legal for private citizens to possess anymore at all. As for where to get any . . ."

The baby stirred, cooed, and fell asleep again. Bella glanced up from getting that kitchen sink so clean you could've done bone marrow transplants in it, and her gaze softened.

She was a tough old bird, but she'd have walked through brimstone for little Ephraim.

". . . I wouldn't know that, either," Wade finished simply.

"Hello?" Ellie came in, her arms loaded with baking ingredients. Crossing the kitchen, she deposited her burden on the table across from Wade, who reached for the bag of chocolate chips.

"Oh, no, you don't." She swept them out of his reach. "We need those." But in their place she offered him a biscotti, which he seemed to think was a decent substitute.

The shower went off upstairs. I could hear my dad moving around up there. Bella's henna-red hair was in pin curls with a green bandana tied over them, a festive-looking combination that contrasted sharply with her steely gaze.

He'd just about scared the life out of her, and the bruise on his forehead when he got home didn't help any. Wade crunched one of the biscotti and tucked another into his pocket.

Then he skedaddled off to the workshop, where he repaired guns in his spare time; a determined pacifist at least where his in-laws were concerned, he wanted no part of this.

Ellie caught the drift, too, and while I reported to her what Wade had said she swept ingredients back into her bag and hoisted it.

Let's get out of here, her expression conveyed,

and I couldn't have agreed more. Outside, she stopped to use her phone while I waited in the side yard; then a few minutes later we were back in her car on our way out of town, on the causeway headed for the mainland.

The sky was milky with stars, and on either side of the narrow roadbed the water stretched away pale and metallic-looking. As we drove, I told Ellie the rest of what I'd gleaned from Wade.

"Huh. That's interesting, she said. Then: "I'd thought we could work in your kitchen and talk at the same time," she added, not commenting yet on the info I'd just given her.

She'd want to think about it first, I supposed.

"No point trying to talk anymore about cyanide with Bella there, though," she added astutely.

"You've got that right." My housekeeper-slash-mother-in-law was a fussbudget at all times, but now she was really angry. "Wouldn't want to give her any ideas," I said.

Not seriously, but still; you knew Bella was really mad when even Wade thought it was safer not to be around her.

We passed through Pleasant Point, the native American village just off the causeway, where streets full of small redbrick houses as well as some newer, clapboard-sided ones clustered around a community center, a firehouse, a church, and a school, plus tribal government buildings.

"Um, so where are we going *instead* of doing our baking?" I asked Ellie finally.

We'd reached Route 1 on the mainland. Around us tall fir trees with tops shaped like arrowheads loomed dark against the night sky.

Ellie turned left. "Boyden Lake." It was a body of fresh water not much bigger than a very large pond, deep in the woods.

She turned left again. "A friend of mine who lives out here might know something about those cyanide capsules," she added.

So she had been thinking about it, and not ruling it out the way I had, either. And it was still early enough in the evening to visit someone, only seven-thirty by the car's dashboard clock.

"Because your idea about the insecticide maybe not being the real murder method," she went on, "is a good one."

"It might not even have been poison that did it at all," I agreed, "and the obviously-smelly insecticide was just a cover for whatever really . . .

She glanced sideways at me. "No need to go that far, Jake. Like you thought at first, some other poison is what seems likeliest, especially since there were no stab wounds, bullet holes, or other—"

Right, no other obvious openings that would've

let Toby Moran's life leak out of him like water out of a sieve.

"So what *are* you suggesting?" I asked, still not quite getting it.

"I'm saying that if you had a good poison, one like cyanide that's not so easy to get and that Toby Moran *would* swallow, but you used it before thinking the whole thing through really clearly, that then afterwards you might want to cover the fact that you'd used it."

She took a breath. "Cover it just temporarily with, say, squirts of insecticide, to give yourself a little time to cover the rest of your tracks, too," she finished evenly.

I had to think about this for a moment. Then: "Ohh," I breathed. "You mean cover up *how* you got it, because whoever you got it *from* would be able to say . . ."

She nodded tightly. I'd thought she seemed a little anxious to go once she'd heard about Wade's thoughts on the matter; about cyanide, specifically. And from there her mind had jumped to—

"You think the killer might've gotten cyanide from your friend?" I asked.

Another nod, tight-lipped. "It's possible."

"And you think now maybe the killer has realized, too late, that once the autopsy results come in—"

Which of course they would, but like Ellie said,

maybe the killer hadn't thought quite enough about that before doing the deed—

"That whoever he – or she – got the cyanide from would probably be talking about it once the results were made public," I finished.

And *that* would end up being a bright red neon arrow pointing straight at the killer, wouldn't it?

"But, Ellie," I began, because this was still all very far-fetched and full of loose ends, not to mention theoretical in the extreme.

Also, we did still have to do all our baking for tomorrow, on top of which if a miracle happened and we somehow managed to clear Andy Devine, we'd be needing a wedding cake, as well.

But that too was getting to seem less likely by the minute, and meanwhile Ellie was very determined, I could tell.

For one thing, she was pushing the speed limit, which for Ellie was the equivalent of pedal-to-the-metal and to heck with the consequences; most times, she was a *very* conservative driver.

And for another . . . "She's a very nice elderly lady," Ellie said, "and we're going out to the lake right now to check on her *and* find out what she has to say about all this, and that's that."

"Check on her? But . . . ?"

Then I realized the rest of it: that on the theory

of better late than never, our killer might've decided to *do* something about that whole tracks-covering business.

Something . . . unpleasant. Ellie pressed the accelerator harder, which couldn't help reminding me—speed, vehicles, et cetera—of my dad.

Not happily. I said as much to Ellie, then went on: "What's wrong with him, anyway?" I fretted. "It's just not like him to be so . . . so . . ."

"Non-compliant?" Ellie peered into the darkness ahead for skunks, porcupines, or God forbid, a real moose. "Unable to be bossed around for another minute or his head will explode?"

I turned, stung. "Ellie, this whole past year we've been nothing but helpful to him. We've supervised his pills and overseen his therapy and engineered his diet and made sure he got . . ."

I stopped. She was nodding, one blond tendril bobbing up and down over her forehead. "Yep, you sure have."

An old railroad trestle crossed the gap between two high bluffs over a grassy salt marsh. In the moonlight, the cattails in the marsh stood motionless as if at attention.

At a fork in the road, we turned right. "You decide what he eats, what he wears, where he goes," said Ellie. "What he drives and whether or not he does. Which I gather that's the part Bella didn't like even a little bit? His driving, I mean?"

We were on Lake Road, passing between old farmsteads with cedar fence posts sagging under tangles of bittersweet. NO HUNTING signs peppered with rusting bullet holes hung on the fence posts.

"You," she pointed out, "wouldn't like being told to give up driving."

"That's . . ." *Different,* I was about to finish.

But it wasn't. Through the moonlit trees in the unkempt woodlots on either side of the road, the rank smell of mud from the nearby lake floated richly along with the trilling voices of singing frogs.

Also, the hum of mosquitoes. I rolled the car window up, wanting to forget what Ellie had just said. But I couldn't.

"So that's how it seems?" Oh, of course, it did. Even I knew it; I just hadn't wanted to see it. "That we've been *bullying* him?"

She squinted through the windshield. "The driveway we want is a little difficult to . . . okay, there it is." She turned, bumping onto a dirt track. Then as we juddered along, "Not at first, no," she answered my question finally. "I mean, at first it was you guys or a rehab hospital, wasn't it? And I'm sure he wouldn't have wanted that."

Nor would the rehab hospital. A mental snapshot of my dad in a powered wheelchair, plowing through a crowd of bathrobed invalids and frantic nurses in a wild bid to escape, flitted through my head.

I shuddered inwardly; it was a vivid mental picture, but not an unrealistic one.

"Now, though," Ellie went on, then fell silent. Ahead, light gleamed through the trees as the road narrowed and curved sharply.

She pulled into a turnaround and stopped, switching the ignition off. In the sudden silence those frogs sounded as if they were getting ready to attack.

The mosquitoes, too. "Don't worry," she said, misunderstanding my anxious look. "The cottage is right through there on the other side of those trees."

That wasn't what I was worried about. Or the frogs, either. I did have concerns about a shadowy figure I'd just glimpsed by the side of the road, though, crouched among the bushes as we went by.

Or . . . had I? "Ellie?" I said. Out here, it was hard to be sure; shapes slipping through the woods might be imaginary, or they might belong to the large and varied downeast Maine wildlife community: the ones I mentioned earlier plus possums, wolverines, even bears.

Or they might be people, which when I am in the woods late at night I'll take my chances with the wolverines, thanks very much.

As I thought about this, meanwhile swatting at

a pesky mosquito that had made it into the car, a sudden peal of wild laughter floated through the forest's darkness.

The *pitch* darkness, because the tree branches stretching overhead now blocked out the moon. Until your eyes adjusted, the only way you'd know your hand was in front of your face was if you punched yourself.

Which was what I felt like doing, for being dumb enough to come out here at all.

"Ellie, why couldn't we have done this in daylight?" I demanded as we got out of the car. This was all going to be a goose-chase, I now felt sure. "Or just called your friend on the phone?"

That laugh, again; a loon out on the lake, I realized, and why its call had to mimic the mad cry of a ghost who is wandering around swinging its own severed head like a lantern, I had no idea.

But it did. Also, that shape I'd glimpsed—or hadn't glimpsed, I still wasn't sure—went on bothering me.

"Seriously. Remind me why we're out here, again?"

In the dark woods, I meant, near a lake, on a dirt road—from what I could see by the wavering gleam of Ellie's flashlight, the road had narrowed to a ragged path—approaching a cottage.

A *supposed* cottage. So far, all I'd seen was a

few lights that might be windows and that shape shrinking suddenly away from our headlights. . . . "Ellie?"

She strode confidently ahead. "Because . . . listen, Jake, what Wade said about the traps just now, the ones with bait and a spring-loaded cyanide capsule? It reminded me . . ."

A low spot on the path turned my ankle. Recovering, I tripped hard over a rock. Somewhere nearby, the hum of a billion bloodthirsty mosquitoes busily sharpening their stabbers grew louder.

Or . . . wait a minute, that wasn't mosquitoes. "Ellie?" I said, louder this time, because suddenly it wasn't dark out here anymore.

Seemingly out of nowhere, a single bright light was roaring down the path we were on, straight at us. "Ellie, jump!"

I grabbed her shoulders and leapt sideways, carrying us both into a thorny thicket as what turned out to be a motorcycle howled past.

Its visored and helmeted rider, crouched over the handlebars, glanced back. But Ellie's flashlight had hit a rock and gone out.

So maybe the rider didn't see us. At any rate he didn't come back, the bike's roar dropping to a whine before fading away entirely.

"Oof," said Ellie, sitting up. "Are you okay?"

"Yup." Actually, I was seeing stars; that rock and my noggin had also met suddenly as I dove out of the bike's way, and apparently my brain cells hadn't enjoyed the experience.

Also, my ears were ringing. But there was no point telling Ellie this, since for one thing there was nothing she could do about it, and for another she'd already gotten up and was marching away again, into the darkness. "Great," she said. "I'm glad you're not hurt. And to answer your question, I did call her," she said over her shoulder as she moved away from me.

"I called, and I let the phone ring and ring," she went on as I hurried to catch up. "But there was . . ."

I knew what must be coming. *Brrr . . .*

". . . no answer," Ellie finished.

"There it is." Ellie pointed ahead to where the cottage lights peeped through the evergreens surrounding it.

As we approached, the gleam from its windows showed its general shape, low and log-built with a deck running around the two sides of the building.

"Hello?" Ellie called anxiously, looking around.

A motion-sensing yard light snapped on as we entered the cottage clearing. The dooryard featured a fish-cleaning table with silvery scales clinging to it and a chopping block made from the flat-topped stump of a big old tree, with an ax stuck into it.

"She usually comes right out to greet visitors," Ellie said worriedly.

A pair of solar panels on the shed roof fed electrical wires to the house. There was an outdoor shower, too, and an elegant little cedar-sided building that I was pretty sure must be a sauna.

"Who lives here, anyway?" I asked, thinking that the number of people who knew something about cyanide *and* enjoyed elegant saunas must be fairly small.

Ellie peered around, frowning. The uncurtained windows in the cottage showed no movement inside. "One of my most favorite old high school teachers, Sallie Blaine, moved here when she retired."

"Does she not have a car?" No vehicles were in evidence.

"Nope," said Ellie. "Never has had. She has a bicycle, she rides that three seasons of the year, and she has friends. They adore her and they take her places when she needs them to. She's . . . unusual."

I tried to imagine living way out here in the boonies with no car, and couldn't; "unusual," I gathered, was putting it mildly.

Downhill past the cottage, moonlit water gleamed. Then came that maniac cry again: ha-ha-ha-*HA!*

Ellie stepped up onto the deck to peer inside. "Hello?" she called again.

My hammering heart rate dropped from a fast rat-a-tat to a more tolerable thud-thud-thud. But it rocketed once more when Ellie touched the cottage's door tentatively, and it drifted open.

"Miss Blaine?" she ventured through the gap.

No answer, and call me a pessimist, but by now I wasn't expecting any. "Ellie!" I whispered loudly at her. "Ellie, don't—"

Too late; she'd already gone in. I hurried to follow, cursing the mosquitoes that by now were feasting on every exposed part of me, and on some that I hadn't known were exposed.

"Jake!" Ellie's voice came from inside. With a shuddering swipe at whatever had just brushed past my face—that thing about bats only eating insects is a myth, I'll have you know—I bounded up onto the deck and rushed inside, slamming the door behind me.

"Ellie, where are you?" I stopped in the tiled entry. The cottage's interior was on the open plan, one big room with low-beamed ceilings, pine paneling, and a fireplace whose huge stone-slab mantel occupied one whole wall.

Small, low-wattage lamps stood on burl-topped tables, casting a warm glow everywhere. Something savory simmered in a cast-iron kettle on the potbellied stove in the kitchen area.

"Ellie?" I moved cautiously into the big room.

A radio played: the New York Yankees were beating the Red Sox 3-0. In the Dutch oven at the back of the woodstove some biscuits were burning; I used pot holders to remove them and set them on a trivet.

A glass of sparkling wine stood on the counter, fresh bubbles still in it. Now I could hear Ellie moving around upstairs and every so often her unhappy voice, calling her old teacher's name again.

But the owner of this particular clean, well-lighted place was nowhere in evidence, and considering what we'd encountered on the way in here, I had a bad feeling about that.

Picking up a flashlight from a table by the back door, I stepped outside again, onto the deck. This felt reasonably safe; probably the bats that had dive-bombed me earlier were still hovering around the front door, chattering amongst themselves about how tender and tasty my throat had looked while hungrily awaiting my return.

Downhill in the moonlight, the lake's bright surface lay flat as glass. At the far end, a radio tower's red light blinked monotonously, its reflected gleam like a blood drop spreading on the water each time it flashed.

"Anyone here?" I called down the slope, then pulled my phone out. Bob Arnold was on my speed dial, and so was Wade; I'd call Wade first, I decided. But before ruining my night vision with the screen's glare, I'd just have a quick glance off the wooden dock that stuck out twenty feet or so from the shore.

By the flashlight's yellow glow I found my way there on a gravel path. A pair of kayaks floated by the dock, each with a DayGlo orange life jacket stuffed into its cockpit.

A metal ladder fixed to the dock led down into the water. "Miss Blaine, are you here?"

Something floated alongside one of the kayaks, low and loglike. But no log I'd ever seen wore a quilted down vest.

"Ellie!" As I leaned down off the dock to grab the body that was floating there, I saw the tears in the vest's front, three small ones and a larger one with dark, wet stuff welling up out of it.

Blood . . . I may have uttered an expletive or three. "Miss Blaine?"

Her face stared blankly upward, ghost-white under the moon. But she was breathing; the down vest was buoyant, I realized, and she was barefoot, which was also a stroke of luck. If she'd been wearing the hiking boots I'd seen by the back door, she'd have sunk out of sight.

Ellie hurried out onto the dock. Except for the cottage behind us, it was dark all the way around the lake. If there were any other dwellings here they were unoccupied this early in the summer.

Then she went briefly back into the house, returning swiftly and very unhappily. "Land line's disabled."

She made a snipping motion with her fingers. "Must've been done soon after I tried calling her a little while ago. And there are still no bars on my cell."

Mine, either; more expletives from me. Out here in the boondocks, the bears didn't need cell phone service, or so the phone companies—excuse me, the *telecommunications giants*—must've thought when they were skimping on cell towers. But . . .

"Miss Blaine has a computer, though," said Ellie, "and it's got an internet connection, so I e-mailed Bob Arnold on it. And Sam and Wade, too, telling them where we are and asking for help."

I found a thready pulse in Miss Blaine's limp wrist. "Great. Three cheers for satellite connections."

Or whatever it was. At the moment, I didn't care; I just wished Miss Blaine had had her phone service set up on it, too. "So if anyone checks their e-mail, we'll be all set."

But Sam was asleep; Mika as well, probably, since lately they both spent their wee hours tending the baby. Wade would've finished in the workshop and settled into the ball game by now, and Bella thought e-mail had been invented purely to terrify her, and only dealt with it under protest.

So she wouldn't be checking it. Meanwhile,

Miss Blaine needed to be taken to the hospital right this minute, if not sooner. But at the moment I couldn't even think of how to get her back up to the cottage, until . . .

Squinting around, Ellie spied a tarp stretched over a stack of stovewood. Hurriedly we dragged it down onto the dock, where we got Miss Blaine onto it.

Then we lugged, hoisted, and hauled our waterlogged burden until we had her inside, and got that cold, wet vest and sweatshirt off her.

"Ouch." Ellie frowned down at the ugly wound in her old teacher's exposed shoulder, then went rummaging in the kitchen drawers, where she found gauze squares and adhesive tape, and went to work.

"Not that it's going to help much," she said when she was done. "But I think the bleeding has at least slowed down."

Right, it had. But even though Miss Blaine was clearly a sturdy person—even pale as she was now, she had the tanned, weathered skin of somebody who bicycled in all weather just as Ellie had said, and that stovewood hadn't gotten split by itself, either—she remained unconscious.

"Ellie, we're going to have to get her to the emergency room ourselves," I said, and she agreed.

So we searched around outside some more and at last found a little red wagon by the larger woodpile stacked out front. Miss Blaine had used the wagon for bringing her fireplace logs inside, apparently, but now we laid a half sheet of plywood from the tool shed atop it.

Also, there was a length of clothesline in the pantry; we used that to secure her body to the plywood sheet. When we were done, it looked like we were transporting a corpse.

Which I sure hoped we weren't going to be doing. "Oh, this is just ghastly," said Ellie as we set off, me out in front holding the flashlight and pulling the wagon, Ellie trotting alongside watching in case the body on the plywood began slipping off.

"What's ghastly is these mosquitoes," I retorted, gritting my teeth. They'd descended en masse, but with flashlight in one hand and a wagon handle in the other, there wasn't much I could do about them.

Then with a *whush-whush* of heavy wings, something larger than a bat swooped out of the darkness. An owl, but not a stuffed one, this time . . .

I lurched sideways, the wagon jolted over a bump, and Ellie scrambled to right it while overhead the moon played hide-and-seek among the treetops.

Miss Blaine moaned. It was the first sound we'd heard out of her. But when we stopped to check, we found it wasn't for a good reason.

The bleeding had resumed. "Try the phone again," I told Ellie while I pressed more gauze squares to the wound.

But there was still no signal. "Only a little ways to the car," Ellie encouraged as we slogged forward once more. "And look at it this way, if she's moaning, she's breathing."

Which was cold comfort. Also, Miss Blaine wasn't fat by any means, but she was definitely a sturdy woman, so while I didn't begrudge the effort it took to pull her, I wasn't at all sure how long I could keep on making it.

Already my shoulder muscles felt like hot matches were being pressed into them, and if my neck got any stiffer I'd need to unkink it with a meat-tenderizing mallet. But despite all this, and with the added motivation provided by those mosquitoes, at last we reached the turn-around where we'd left the car.

"Okay," I said, opening the vehicle's rear passenger door . . . which seemed unusually low to the ground, suddenly.

Ellie groaned, aiming her flashlight. "Oh, no! Jake, it's a flat tire."

Correction: it was all four of them. "And Lee's going to be home before long, too, I've got to—"

The caps to the valve stems lay in the gravel, one by each tire; I guessed we should be grateful that the tires hadn't been slashed but instead merely deflated by hand.

I mean, depending on your definition of *merely* . . . "Someone wanted to slow us down," I said.

"Motorcycle guy, maybe," Ellie agreed.

"I hope he's not still around here somewhere," I said.

Oh, did I ever. Because so far tonight we had an elderly woman wounded, our car deliberately disabled, and all three of us stuck out here in what old Eastporters called the puckerbrush, with no way to call for help.

Except for e-mail, which I doubted was going to do the tiniest bit of good. And the night was still young, so there was plenty of time for even worse things to happen.

"Okay," I sighed. "I guess we'll just have to drive on the rims."

The dirt road was bumpy and studded with rocks, barely fit for a car to drive on at all, much less on flats. The tires wouldn't survive it, the rims would be ruined, and the rest of the car wouldn't exactly enjoy the experience, either.

Still, I was disappointed when Ellie turned the key and nothing happened, if by disappointed you also mean startled and beginning to be really scared, now. Somehow it just hadn't yet dawned on me that we could be in serious, possibly even fatal, trouble.

Or fatal for Miss Blaine, anyway. My mind

wasn't letting me go any further down that path; I mean, toward the notion that it could also end up being fatal for us. But if the phrase "at the mercy" were in the dictionary, it was clear by now that our photographs would be lined up right there next to the definition.

I got out again and lifted the car's hood. Under it was a mass of engine parts, few of which I could even name, much less tell if they were in working condition.

I was pretty sure all those wires and hoses were supposed to be connected to one another, though, not just flopping around loose.

Ellie peered over my shoulder. "Wow, somebody was thorough."

"Yeah." A whole lot of red, yellow, and green wires had been yanked out entirely; from where, I couldn't tell.

Meanwhile, in the trees all around us, *things* rustled: small cries, scufflings, and faint crackling that sounded like tiny bones breaking . . .

It was just deer and possums out there, probably, and possibly a moose; not carnivores, in other words. But I'd have felt a lot better about them if I could see them.

Fortunately, though, by then I wasn't just scared; I was also pissed off. Ellie, too; I could tell by the grim set of her jaw.

But neither one of us felt like leaving the other one alone here with Miss Blaine to run out to the lightly-traveled road for help that probably wouldn't be there. And neither of us wanted to *be* alone here, either; better we should stick together.

"All right, then," Ellie uttered, knowing as well as I did what we had to do next and not liking it, either.

Bumpy as the dirt road had been on Goodyears, the hard rubber wheels on that little red wagon with Miss Blaine secured onto it would make the rock-strewn surface ridiculous. Still, we put our backs into it, and thirty or so nervous, frustrating, and laborious minutes later, we'd dragged the wagon out onto the main road.

"Oh, my heavens," Ellie breathed exhaustedly.

"No kidding," I agreed. The smooth, freshly laid blacktop with the bright yellow stripe running down the middle of it gleamed in the moonlight while we stood catching our breaths.

The silence was so complete here, it was as if a glass jar had been dropped down over us. And no one had leapt out at us or otherwise harmed us, so of course, we were glad for that. No motorcycle-riding stranger had appeared now that we'd reached the main road, either.

But we were still way the hell out here with a badly wounded woman lying between us and still without cell phone service.

All we needed now was banjos, I thought sourly, and then I did hear something briefly; not banjos, though. I squinted up and down the road: nothing. So maybe I'd been mistaken.

"Please," Miss Blaine murmured faintly, her pale hand lifting and falling again pathetically.

At least she wasn't dead, I thought, feeling a cold rush of hardheaded practicality. By then I was so tired and angry, all possible tender sentiment had evaporated right out of me.

We would get her to medical help in good time or we would not, I thought, and that, as Bella would say, was the long and short of it. Ellie looked heartbroken, though, no doubt thinking the same.

"You know her well?" I asked as somewhere far in the distance that sort of grumbling sound I'd heard moments earlier began again.

"When I was in high school," Ellie replied. "She was our gym teacher and, Jake, she was so great. I owe Miss Blaine big-time."

She looked up from where she'd crouched by the teacher's side as the sound in the distance grew louder, a low *boom-badaboomboomboom.*

"Maybe we should start walking. The road's smoother here, at any rate. And if someone comes along, they'll help us," she said.

That part was true. People in Eastport have been known to lend strangers their cars, or take boats out in the darkness to find idiots lost in kayaks because, as they always tell their rescuers afterward, "We do this all the time in Florida."

160

Go kayaking alone at night, they meant, whereupon the rescuers, of course, don't grab Florida maps and shove them . . . well. Said idiots not carrying GPS locators, either, or even life jackets, never mind such a silly thing as a working signal flare.

Because, you know, Florida. But back to our predicament.

"All right," I gave in reluctantly to Ellie. "You go, though, and I'll stay here with her."

Because it was like I said before: we'd get help or we wouldn't. Meanwhile, Miss Blaine was unconscious again now, and I feared it was from loss of blood.

"You're right. She should be kept still." Ellie bounced up and down on the Keds she wore, readying herself.

"Be careful," I said, trying not to show how nervous I was. In a few moments I'd be alone with a dying woman. Or, anyway, I hoped I'd be alone, and, of course, the dying part worried me, too. With any luck she wouldn't manage to complete the process before help arrived.

But I had no idea how badly she'd really been hurt. All I knew was, she didn't look good.

At least the unidentifiable grumbling sound from somewhere down the road had stopped. "I wish we were at home baking a whoopie-pie wedding cake," I said, trying to smile.

"Me too. See you soon." Ellie squared her

shoulders. "I won't be that long. But if someone comes along before I get back . . ."

"Right," I replied stoutly. "Don't worry." I was doing enough of that for both of us. "If help arrives, I'll—"

Take it, I'd have finished. But instead the distant grumbling sound returned, got louder, and then was very loud indeed as from around a curve in the road a yellow light appeared.

A flashlight, I thought, but when the glow swelled to a bright orb and the rumbling rose to a roar, I knew it had to be a headlight. Another *motorcycle* headlight . . .

Really? I had time to think; then the bike pulled over. The figure on it propped the kickstand and pulled his helmet off.

From beneath it came short red-gold hair, freckles, a face as mild and harmless-appearing as an infant's. . . . It was Andy Devine.

"Goodness," murmured Ellie as he crossed the blacktop toward us, wearing a black leather jacket, black gloves, and boots so heavy and sturdy-looking that they could've qualified as deadly weapons.

"What an interesting coincidence," Ellie added under her breath.

"No kidding." If the hairs on the back of my neck had had hairs of their own, they'd have been bristling, too.

Because as far as I'm concerned, coincidence

is right up there with the Tooth Fairy, benevolent dictatorships, and the even-halfway-edible all-you-can-eat buffet in the believability department.

But I didn't say anything more about it; she already knew, not that *that* was going to do either one of us any good. And then . . .

Then I remembered the gun.

The weapon I'd taken from Moran's place and then forgotten all about was still in my bag; I drew it out, not making a big deal of it, but not hiding it at all, either.

Andy Devine saw it at once, and the look on his face changed. "Hey, hey," he said, stopping short, his hands coming up in what I'd have interpreted as a warding-off gesture.

That is if I'd believed in it, or in anything else about the way he was presenting himself right now. Suddenly the idea of us clearing him of a murder charge didn't seem like such a slam dunk anymore, not that it ever really had.

Because with him looming over us in the moonlight on a remote road in backwoods Maine, the charge didn't seem quite so preposterous as it had, either.

On the contrary: he was big, he was not pleased that I had the gun, and he wanted it. Like, *now.*

Holding out one hand, he took a step. "I don't know what's going on, but that doesn't look safe. How about if you just give me the . . ."

"Get your phone out," I said. I just love being patronized. I love it a whole bunch.

I held the gun level. I might not've been a crack shot, but my husband was, and he'd taught me a little bit.

How not to drop the thing, for instance. "Check your phone," I told him. "See if you've got any bars."

Different phone brands use different networks, I'd discovered. And some get better reception than others; it's the point of the whole "Can you hear me now?" ad campaign.

Devine obeyed, his brush-cut hair a curious orangey pink in the moonlight. And as I'd hoped, he had a cell phone signal.

"Okay, it works. Now what?"

Ellie knelt by Miss Blaine again. "She's breathing. That's all, though. Call 911, get an ambulance out here," she told Devine.

He looked vexed. "Look, are you sure you don't want me to—"

I took a step toward him, raising Toby Moran's cheap little pistol. I hadn't even checked to see if it was loaded, or if it was so junky that instead of firing, it would explode in my hand.

But it shut Andy Devine up very effectively, and at the moment that was function enough for me; he worked the phone again hastily.

"Good," I said, not bothering to sound friendly.

Because maybe some other cyclist had done

all the bad deeds we'd experienced in the last hour or so. Maybe Devine's being here right now really was what my son, Sam, would've called a coinky-dink.

But I was cold, tired, hungry, scared, hurting in every possible extremity, and thoroughly annoyed, not to mention worried about Miss Blaine.

So I didn't care. I could apologize later if I felt like it.

Or not.

"What in the world are we going to do now?" asked Ellie the next morning.

It was 5 a.m. The sun wasn't even up yet. So my answer would've been "go back to bed" if we hadn't still had all that work to do.

The Chocolate Moose opened promptly at ten, so by then there would have to be brownies and éclairs, pinwheels and chocolate snickerdoodles, and . . .

"Chocolate croissants," mused Bella Diamond dreamily. She plucked a bit of semisweet from the table in Ellie's kitchen and devoured it.

We'd started the croissant batter two days earlier; now the long strip of much-rolled-and-folded dough lay on the worktable, waiting to be cut into perfect triangles with the aid of a carpenter's T square.

"Oh, I can hardly wait," said Bella. She loved a good croissant, and ours were light and flaky with a solid punch of rich, taste-bud-bedazzling . . .

Well, you know. If chocolate were discovered now, it would be regulated as a drug, I think; certainly it improved Bella's mood.

Short-acting, though. Her look darkened. "Something has still got to be done about that father of yours," she said. "And it's got to be soon."

We'd spread all our ingredients out in Ellie's kitchen. We could have done it at my house, but Mika liked having the kitchen to herself in the early mornings, so she could feed Ephraim and get their day started in peace.

So here we were. "I really can't abide wondering which way he'll try to kill himself next," my stepmother went on.

Ellie's kitchen was low ceilinged, pine paneled, and equipped with an antique fireplace so wide and tall you could walk right into it. A cast-iron kettle hung from an old hook set into the brick.

But the room's other end boasted an enormous chest freezer, a side-by-side refrigerator, a restaurant-sized dishwasher, and a gas stove with double ovens and a plumbed-in pot filler that Ellie joked could double as a fire extinguisher.

George had bought it all at a discount from one of the building contractors he worked for and put it all in himself. Now Ellie got the wire egg basket from the refrigerator.

"How, though?" she asked Bella. "To stop him, without—"

Bella poured flour into the sifter, then measured in the baking soda and salt; if the butter had been salted, we'd have omitted it from the dry ingredients, but it wasn't so we didn't.

"I have no bleeping idea," said Bella, but she didn't say "bleeping." "That man has me completely blinking flummoxed."

Only she didn't say . . . well. I hadn't even meant to bring her along with me this morning. But when I'd crept downstairs in the dark, praying that the coffeemaker had gone on the way I'd set it to and the baby wouldn't wake up, she'd already been drifting around the silent kitchen like some unhappy domestic ghost.

Angry, frightened . . . While Ellie and I were out at the lake the night before, my dad had at last agreed to visit the ER and had been pronounced A-OK. But she still couldn't let it go; even in the best of times, she disliked not being in control of a situation.

And in this case, "Bella, I don't blame you a bit," I said. He was being a jerk, and he wasn't even the worst of my problems; still, those chocolate treats weren't going to bake themselves, were they?

"And stopping him would be all well and good," I said as I creamed the sugar into the butter. Next, I beat in two eggs and dosed them with vanilla extract while Ellie carefully eyeballed the amount of cocoa powder in her measuring cup.

Cocoa powder is key, and by that I mean *good-quality* cocoa powder, not chocolate chips or please-God-not-carob, or heaven forbid anything called "chocolate syrup," either; we made our own. Also, don't get me going on anything whose label promises "real chocolate flavoring."

It won't be. You have my word on this. "But stopping him's not the point," I said. "Him *wanting* to quit his antics . . . that's the only real solution."

I beat the eggs into the butter and sugar with a wooden spoon. "So until *that* happens . . ."

Ellie's daughter, Leonora, appeared in the kitchen doorway still in her flannel pajamas. With huge dark brown eyes and her curly dark hair floofed out around an elfin face, she looked like a wood nymph who was ready to do mischief right after she eats her cereal.

"Take it in the family room, honey," Ellie told the child, who scampered away obediently with her spoon and bowl. Then, "Jake's right," Ellie said, turning the oven on to preheat.

"We got to make him think it's *his* idea not to be racketing around in that truck the way he has been, and opposing everything else that's any good for him the rest of the time," Ellie went on.

Correction, I thought. *It's got to* be *his idea.*

And good luck on that one; the smack on the head that he'd gotten by crashing the truck last night had knocked a bit of sense into him, and he'd agreed to hanging around home for a day or so to recover. But once cabin fever redeveloped, what would I say to him, that he was an old guy now so he had to stop having fun?

Sure, that would work. Naturally, it would. I finished beating the butter and eggs.

"Anyway," Bella grumped, changing the subject. Wiping the cookie sheets with an oiled paper towel, she laid them out in a row. The few hours left before the shop opened meant we were in assembly-line mode.

"Anyway, what happened last night?" Between him getting into an accident and us being AWOL for so long, she'd been in high dudgeon when we finally got home. But by then I'd been in no mood to explain.

Now I folded the dry ingredients into the moist, mixed them all very thoroughly, and began placing walnut-sized dollops of the result onto the cookie sheets.

"Well," I replied, "first the ambulance came and the EMTs got Miss Blaine loaded into it and took her to the hospital."

Ellie slid the cookie sheets into the oven. "Bob Arnold showed up, too," she said, "and stayed until the sheriff's deputies arrived."

"Andy Devine told Bob Arnold that he was

just out riding his motorcycle, clearing his head, and that he wouldn't be answering any questions about it," I continued the story.

I hadn't known what to think. The motorcycle speeding past us from Miss Blaine's place when we first arrived might very well have been the same bike that Devine was riding when *he* showed up.

Or it might not have. Honestly, it had been too dark and the bike had been too surprising, not to mention moving too fast, for me to be sure. Ditto for Devine wanting the gun I'd produced from my bag; maybe it was a sign of guilt, him trying to disarm me.

Or maybe he just hadn't wanted to get shot. Bella started washing out the batter bowls so we could get more cookies going; the chocolate snickerdoodles, this time around.

"What were you doing out there, anyway?" she wanted to know.

Ellie got in ahead of me, meanwhile scooping out a serving-spoon full of Crisco. "Okay," she began, "so do you remember how Wade said that cyanide was used for vermin control?"

Bella allowed as how she did. "I don't know why such things have to be discussed in my nice, clean kitchen," she groused.

From the window over the sink I could see past Ellie's chicken coop to where her apple trees' black silhouettes marched across the bluff overlooking the bay. To the east, dawn filled the sky with red and then the sun peeped up, pouring bright gold onto the water.

"When Jake told me about that, it reminded me of when Miss Blaine used to live on the poor farm," Ellie continued. "A sort of supervisor there, she was."

Bella's face smoothed. "Oh, I remember that. A lot of land, some barns, a big bunkhouse, and so on, that the city owned. Out where the public campgrounds is now."

Such public charitable institutions are fast passing out of human memory, but back in the old days in Eastport, Maine, if you were poor and had no other way to manage, you could trade work for your room and board.

"Growing vegetables and raising animals, hammering and sawing or getting firewood, or if you were a woman you could take in laundry or do sewing for people," Bella said.

In addition to all your other women's-work chores, she meant; those animals and vegetables and so on, and, of course, your children. I thumped the final dough ball down onto the cookie sheet.

"Yes, and Miss Blaine was a sort of an on-site manager there when she was young," said Ellie, "watched over all the animal care and took the kids and the new widows under her wing and whatnot."

Widowhood being a reliable way to get

impoverished, and not just in the old days, either. But I digress . . .

"Later, as the school gym teacher she ran girls' sports." Ellie watched the kitchen clock, oven mitts at the ready; she timed baking as if that clock was the countdown timer for a space shuttle ignition.

"And I remember it very clearly, I was on the track team at the time," she said, "and she told all the cross-country runners to watch out for those baited spring traps with the cyanide capsules in them, that there might still be some and not to step on one accidentally."

Of course, maybe they were illegal now, as Wade had said, but in the good old days, if predators got your animals, you didn't eat.

"She'd used them herself on the poor farm," Ellie went on. "So I couldn't help wondering if she still had any now."

"But, Ellie, why would Andy Devine have had any way to know that?" I asked. "About her, or the poor farm, either?"

The oven timer went off with a shrill *brringg!* "And, anyway, we're getting way ahead of ourselves," I added.

We slid the baked cookies out and the unbaked ones in, as Ellie shook her head.

"Maybe we are. And I'm not sure how he would know, or if it even matters," she said. "But I do know that she gave a presentation at the library last winter and it was about that poor farm she lived on."

She set the oven timer again. "And since Sharon's a volunteer there at the library, I imagine if he wasn't on duty he probably went to that presentation. Wouldn't you think?"

I would, indeed. The engaged pair were practically joined at the hip, social-occasion-wise. But whether the beloved retired educator had mentioned any deadly poisons at the library event . . .

"That I don't know," Ellie replied. "I didn't go, myself. I just thought it might be worth checking. It's why I wanted to go out there last night and ask."

She'd already cut the croissant triangles—zip, zop—and placed them in the warming oven to rise. Now she began working on the éclair filling, a recipe she'd followed so often that she had it memorized: whipping cream, sugar, a chocolate syrup that she'd made earlier from scratch, and vanilla.

You whip it into soft peaks and refrigerate it: *finis.* "But when I went upstairs in her cottage I didn't find anything, and then Jake found Miss Blaine," said Ellie.

She began assembling the ingredients for the outsides of the éclairs: flour, salt, butter, eggs, and a measuring cup with water measured into it, plus a large sauce pan.

"So just then she yelled for me to come, and in all the awful excitement afterward I forgot to finish my search."

"Forgot?" Bella looked up impatiently. "How could you—"

"You know," I pointed out, "we were a little busy right then."

And speaking of pointing out things, may I just say right here that if your éclair recipe mentions pudding mix, and especially if it says *instant* mix, throw it out.

The recipe *and* the mix. Also, just because we used whipped cream in our éclairs, that doesn't mean you can't use chocolate custard.

Or vanilla, for that matter, or pistachio.

Root beer, even.

Just not from a mix.

Five

Half an hour later after working along in silence for a while, we'd made good progress in the baking department.

Just not in the murder department. "You've got a point," Ellie admitted, taking up again the conversation we'd been having.

"There's no really good reason to think Andy Devine knew about those cyanide-trap thingies, even assuming Miss Blaine did still have any of them."

"Or that Moran was killed with cyanide at all," I agreed. That whole idea had just gathered steam of its own accord, it seemed to me now.

The croissants were in the oven, filling the kitchen with the kind of intoxicating perfume that can only be produced by butter-pastry. Meanwhile, we were slicing the already baked biscotti logs, readying them for their own last heat treatment.

"And we *won't* know, either, not until the autopsy results come out," I went on.

I nabbed a biscotti-log end and bit into it. Ellie had sliced a quarter cup of candied ginger up and put it into the batter with the chocolate chips, and the result didn't quite blow the top

175

of my head off with its indescribable delicious-ness.

But it was close. "We just couldn't think of a way to get a milkshake that reeks of insecticide into Toby Moran, that's all." I added to Bella, "Not without hogtying him and forcing it down his throat, anyway."

And there'd been no sign of anything like that; if there had been, the guys who'd found him dead would've talked about it and word would most definitely have gotten around.

Ellie nodded agreement. "Sure, but remember that burglary report Bob Arnold got called away on earlier yesterday?"

I used a thin spatula to get another batch of cookies off the trays, sliding them onto a wire rack to cool and putting the trays under hot water immediately. They were the one thing Ellie's cozy old kitchen was short of, because she'd lent a lot of her cookie sheets to the Moose and hadn't replaced them.

"The burglary call earlier in the day was from Miss Blaine, was it?" Bella inquired astutely.

The one Bob Arnold got while he was talking to me on Water Street, she meant; wanting to distract from anything having to do with my dad, I'd filled her in on all this as we drove over here to Ellie's this morning.

"Yes," said Ellie. We'd both heard Bob saying so to the sheriff's deputies who'd shown up out at the lake last night, that there'd been a burglary at Miss Blaine's, earlier. But how that crime fit into any of this, we still hadn't had much chance to discuss.

"I see," Bella replied thoughtfully while she scrubbed the cookie sheets with soapsuds and rinsed them. "But there's more to it, though, isn't there?" she asked Ellie.

Once she finished at the sink and was ready for her next assignment, I handed Bella all the éclair-pastry ingredients that Ellie had gotten together, and she took it from there. If she worked as fast and efficiently as she usually did, the last of the cookies would come out of the oven just as the éclair shells were ready to go in: perfect.

If by perfect you mean phew. By now it was already 7 a.m., and we'd have to stop soon so Ellie could get Lee ready for school.

"Yes," said Ellie to Bella's question. "There must be more to it. Because the way Andy showed up out there last night, just at the right moment . . . and really, two motorcycles? How likely is that?"

The one that had raced past us on its way out the dirt road, she meant, and the other on the paved road later, with Andy Devine on it.

Assuming there'd been two, that is, that it hadn't been Andy both times. I still couldn't be sure, nor could I stop puzzling over it.

Ellie put her batter bowl and spoon in the sink.

"But there's something else, too, that I've been thinking about."

If it had been Andy both times, he'd have raced out toward the main road, passing us on our way in, then returned not much later to . . . what? Find out what we were up to, whether we'd recognized him?

Or to learn whether or not Miss Blaine had survived? Which as it turned out, she had.

"I called, by the way," Ellie said. "This morning just before you got here, and the hospital says Miss Blaine's hanging in there."

Bella listened quietly. She knew what Ellie and I were up against: no money and not much prospect of having any until tourist season got under way, plus enough unpaid bills to wallpaper a room.

She also knew that we were counting on the wedding cake job to tide us over. What she hadn't known was that we now feared Andy Devine might really have killed Toby Moran, but she was quick on the uptake.

"So," she mused aloud. "Let's say he got cyanide from Miss Blaine somehow and used it, then thought about it and realized that the real cause of Moran's death would surely be identified sooner or later—"

"If it *was* the cause," Ellie reminded her. "We don't know yet."

Bella shot us an *oh, please* look. I guess she wasn't a big fan of coinky-dinks, either.

"So he went out there to get rid of evidence, or muddy it up somehow," she said. "And Miss Blaine interrupted him, tried to stop him, and got hurt that way. Then maybe he heard you two coming, so he had to get away fast?"

"Nice theory," I said. Also, my plan to distract her from her other problems was working, I thought. And then to Ellie, "Where do you guess she was yesterday morning, maybe here in town at the Senior Center lunch?"

When the earlier break-in happened, I meant. The lunches were a well-established social activity for the elderly here in Eastport, and Bella had been trying to get my dad to go to one since forever.

But he said that if he wanted to spend his noon hour hearing about a lot of other people's aches and pains, he'd go to the doctor's office and maybe get a flu shot while he was at it.

"If she was in town, though, all Devine would've had to do was catch sight of her here in Eastport . . ."

Which would've been likely; it's a very small place.

"And he'd know that was his chance. To get out to her cottage yesterday morning, I mean, and do . . . whatever."

I stopped, thinking about it. Then, "Maybe not to take something away or even destroy something, but . . . to leave something there?"

Ellie glanced over at me; I went on a little defensively. "Well, we need a new angle on all this, don't we?"

But I had to admit I didn't know what might've been left at the cottage. "Maybe something that should've been there all along," I added, "and sooner or later somebody would notice if it was gone?"

"Hm. Maybe," said Ellie, not sounding convinced.

Bella dumped the dry ingredients for the éclair pastry into the water and butter, by now simmering together, then removed the pan from the heat and began beating the mixture to cool it.

And yes, I do know that this couldn't possibly work. Beating the dry ingredients into hot water and melted butter . . . how could it?

The whole thing always sounded to me like an unnecessarily complex recipe for flour paste. But somehow it did work; soon Bella had a dozen éclair shapes made of pastry dough on the cookie sheet.

"Right, into the oven with them," said Ellie briskly, whisking the cookie sheet away from her and setting the timer once more.

Then Bella spoke. "All right, so maybe he'd asked her for the poison and she'd given it to him. Why, we don't know."

That's for sure. Or anything else, basically, but that didn't deter Bella.

"Then yesterday morning he went out there and put it back. Or most of it. To make it look as if it had never been gone."

She began washing her hands, which for Bella is a project that proceeds fingernail by fingernail. "But then he realized . . ."

She stopped, frowning as she worked on her hands, then began wiping down counters and cabinet fronts. Next would come the refrigerator door and the little grooves in the gas stove's knobs.

"Well, I don't know what he might've realized," she finished at last.

At least she wasn't obsessing over my father; I scraped out the last cookie batter bowl and Ellie went back to making the éclair frosting: butter, powdered sugar, and melted semisweet.

That was when Bob Arnold walked in. "I thought you ladies would want to know that Miss Blaine went into surgery a few minutes ago," he said unhappily.

"Oh," I said, taken aback. "But the nurse told me . . ."

"Yeah, she took a turn for the worse. That head bump . . . they think they can fix it, but you know. Dicey until they do."

"And she never said anything?" According to the nurse I'd talked to, Miss Blaine had regained consciousness but wasn't yet fully awake.

Bob shook his head. "No, I'd been hoping she would. But things went the other way instead."

And then it hit me, his expression. "Oh," I said again, and Bob nodded, his pink plump face grim.

"Someone didn't just get surprised by her, did they?" I asked. "I mean, she didn't just happen upon someone breaking in."

To take something. Or put something back. Or maybe just to rob the place; maybe we had this all wrong from the get-go.

"Nope." Bob brushed a strand of his thinning blond hair straight back from his high pink forehead.

"Docs at the hospital say somebody hit her hard from behind with something heavy."

He took a deep breath, his eyes lighting appreciatively on our wire racks full of cookies. But then his look turned serious again.

"Someone snuck up on her, it looks like," he said. "Door was jimmied."

Of course; that's why it had swung open at Ellie's touch.

"I'd told her to lock it when I was out there earlier for the burglary, and I think she did. She was shaken up by the break-in."

Ellie handed him a snickerdoodle and he bit into it. "No sign of a struggle," he went on. "Nothing missing that I could tell. Someone surprised her, knocked her out, dragged her down to the water."

He swallowed. Then, "There's drag marks on

that path to the dock. Someone tried kicking 'em away, but you look close and they're there."

"You were out there already this morning?" Ellie asked.

He nodded. "Waiting for it to get light. The shoulder wound was from a sharp nail in the dock. I think it was meant to look as if she fell in, hit her head on a rock, and drowned."

"So is everybody else done out there now, too?" Bella inquired. She was scrubbing the already-spotless kitchen sink so hard with Ajax, it was a wonder the porcelain didn't peel off.

"Because," she went on with a glance at me, "Jake and I were thinking of going to get her a few things. Her hair and tooth brushes, her own hand cream, maybe her robe and a pair of slippers—"

I glanced back. "Yes, to take up to the hospital for Miss Blaine. For when she wakes up," I agreed.

Bob nodded. "County boys were there late last night, going over the inside of the house. Now that it's getting to be daylight it won't take them long to finish up outside."

He thought a moment. "So, yeah, those guys'll probably be gone," he added to Bella, "and if they're not, you just wait for them to go and afterward you won't be stepping on their toes any."

"Great," I said, keeping my tone light. "We'll go as soon as we're done here."

Meanwhile, Bob didn't seem to know anything about the cyanide Miss Blaine might have had, and I saw no reason to enlighten him. Or at any rate not yet.

Outside Ellie's house I slung my arm around Bella's shoulder and squeezed, and she leaned against me for a moment.

"Good thinking on the toiletry items," I said.

She nodded minutely. But now that we weren't busy with baking, her mind was on something else.

"Why can't he just talk about it?" she wondered plaintively. "About what's going on with him, I mean?"

She'd been married once before, to a guy who was approximately as communicative as a fence post. My father, on the other hand, had never had any problem letting people know how he felt, whether they liked it or not.

Until now. "I don't know," I said when we'd gotten into my car.

The pale early light made the dew in the grass sparkle, and the air smelled like the fountain of youth as we left Ellie's driveway.

"But I think maybe it's got something to do with being old, and feeling like he dodged a bullet with that heart attack," I said.

Downtown on Water Street the shopkeepers were sweeping sidewalks, setting out sale tables, and hanging banners, while in the boat basin a dozen new Coasties were hustling onto their training vessel.

I spotted Andy Devine with them, shepherding them to their assigned places on the boat. I gathered his superiors weren't taking his legal troubles very seriously.

Yet. "I'll make him dodge something, all right," Bella grumbled, "if he keeps on behaving like such a . . . a *butthead*."

"Mmm," I replied, trying not to burst out laughing. Bella's idea of profanity was about as scandalous as a glass of warm milk. But her problem remained serious, and I still had no idea what to do about it.

Driving out Route 190 from Eastport, we were silent, me with my eyes on my driving and her with her henna-frizzed head leaning back on the head rest.

"Pretty," she murmured, gazing out the side window, and it was, too.

The sun was well up now, shedding its champagne-colored light on the rocky shores of Carrying Place Cove. Then came old apple orchards bursting with pink-white blossoms, and salt marshes where deep-purple water lily blooms lay thickly on the water.

"I suppose you want to know why I'm not home with your father right this minute," Bella said conversationally.

Long-legged shore birds skittered across the

sand alongside the causeway. "Because he's driving you nuts?" I replied.

In Pleasant Point, Native American kids whose ancestors had been living in this spot when Leif Eriksson was only a bud jogged to school, lugging Power Rangers lunch boxes and Batman backpacks.

Bella glared balefully at the dashboard, ignoring them. "Because he's going to get himself killed, and I refuse to watch," she said.

"You don't think," I pressed her gently as we rolled up to the Route 1 intersection, "that maybe he can take care of himself?"

He'd done all right until now, after all, even reuniting with me here in Eastport after a long mutual misunderstanding. And he'd had sense enough to marry Bella. But she was convinced that he was heading for trouble.

"He will get his neck broken in another accident or drive off the end of a pier at night," she predicted darkly. "That dratted truck's on the road to ruin and him with it."

She turned exasperatedly to me. "And you of all people, I thought you had better sense. But all you do is encourage him more."

I turned left onto the lake road. In bright daylight the old farm fields rolled away uphill, newly sprouted with pale-green hay and bordered by rock walls that were slowly falling into lichen-encrusted heaps.

"You think he listens to me?" We passed the old railroad trestle that once had brought everyone and everything to Eastport. Now it hung lonesomely in the air, its connection to the remaining railbed lopped off at both ends so that it resembled a chunk of ancient Roman ruins.

"*They* had the right idea," stated Bella, pointing to this piece of unceremoniously amputated infrastructure. "If you don't want people doing something, you just take away the ability to do it."

Trespassing on the trestle, she meant, by daredevils leaping the gaps at either end on their ATVs and dirt bikes. Which made me wonder . . .

"What happened here, anyway?" We drove down a winding lane between a double row of willow trees, their new spring leaves silvery in the sunlight. "To make them cut off the trestle ends, I mean?"

Because there must've been an incident of some kind. In downeast Maine, where we can barely keep the schools open and the roads paved even in good times, the money wouldn't have been available otherwise.

"Kid flew off it, broke his neck," Bella said flatly.

Which didn't do much for my argument about Bella maybe taking it easier on my dad, or for her mood, either. But only a few minutes later we turned in at the road to Miss Blaine's cottage, and there her attitude softened.

"We used to come out here to swim," she said softly as the blue lake water appeared glittering between the leaves.

I slowed the car, partly on account of the road's rough surface, but more for her sake.

"My cousins had a cottage; we'd come out here in the summer and stay," she said. "But I haven't been back here in, oh, years."

We passed the place where the mystery cyclist had roared past us in the dark the night before; moments later, we were in the turnaround where I'd left the car, and where somebody had disabled it.

Wade had come out with a compressor and re-inflated the tires, and put the wires back so I could drive home. Now I parked and we got out; no county officers were around, and no squad cars, either.

So we were alone. "Oh," breathed Bella, her big grape-green eyes widened wonderingly as she gazed around.

Light slanting through the leaves fell on lady's slippers and trilliums, hyacinth and vermillion bloodroot growing from the rich black leaf mold at the bases of the big old trees.

"Oh, I remember the way it *smells,*" she said, breathing in the cool, damp aroma of lake water mingled with pine sap.

"Come on," I said, not liking that I had to rush her.

But neither of us would enjoy getting discovered here by anyone but Bob Arnold; his tacit permission notwithstanding, I thought the county cops whose jurisdiction this was might not share his casual approval of our visit, especially if they knew the whole story.

And if I found what I was beginning to suspect I might inside Miss Blaine's lakeside cottage, they'd like it even less. But first we had to *get* inside, which was a project.

Bob had nailed the jimmied door shut to stop vandals getting in, and I'd neglected to ask him about a key to the other one. The windows were all too high to try climbing in through, and the cellar bulkhead door was secured by a sturdy, gleaming padlock.

So I was stymied until Bella spoke up. "Ladder," she said.

"Huh?" I'd been gazing around dumbly, trying to figure out what to do.

"Ladder," Bella uttered again. "On the shed."

I looked where she pointed, found the aging but solid-appearing wooden ladder hung on the tool shed's shingled side, and hauled it down from its cast-iron angle brackets it was mounted on.

Then Bella and I hauled the ladder to the house and propped it, and I clambered up. Soon I had a window open, and after that it was simply a matter of shoving myself through it head-first, losing my precarious grip on the frame at a most inopportune moment, and landing on the floor at an awkward angle that didn't quite break my neck.

"Are you all right?" Bella called from outside.

The cottage was cold, the fire in the woodstove having gone out and the still air smelling of ashes.

"I'm just ducky," I called back to her grumpily, and once I had gotten myself up off the floor I let her in.

"Good," she said, brushing past me and stopping. "Oh, this is lovely, nothing like the old camp house that we used to—"

"Yeah, never mind that." From the windows overlooking the deck I could see straight out onto the lake.

Across the water, one of the cottages that had been dark the night before was now abuzz with activity: kids swimming around a dock, dogs romping and barking happily at them, a woman spreading a yellow tablecloth out onto a picnic table.

Also, there was a boat leaving the dock. A small boat, with a little outboard engine on it . . . two guys in the boat, it looked like.

Coming toward us. As they got nearer I could see them looking up at the cottage. "Go," I told Bella, and she didn't hesitate.

"I'll take the upstairs," she said, "and you

stay down here." Her quick step hurried up the staircase to the second floor, where Ellie had gone the night before.

I yanked open drawers and cabinets: in the kitchen, where a hand pump over the sink provided water, and in the living area, where the cottage's solar power was augmented by glass-globed gas lamps mounted at intervals on the ceiling beams.

From down on the lake, the distant mutter of an outboard engine grew to a nearby snarl, then shut down entirely.

I pulled the lids of the window seats open: board games, extra pillows and blankets, gas lantern parts—globes, mantles, the little metal inside mechanisms that regulate the gas—and in the final bin, a plastic tackle box with a lot of rubber bands wrapped around it.

I rolled the rubber bands off. Down on the water, a boat's metal side thunked the dock; then footsteps thumped the dock planks.

The box had compartments for lures, hooks, and the other doodads needed for freshwater fishing. No doodads, however, were in the box. Instead there was another, smaller box made of clear hard plastic.

The box had a printed label on it: POISON! CAUTION! NOT FOR USE NEAR PETS, CHILDREN, OR DOMESTIC ANIMALS!

And other warnings along those lines. You

were not, I gathered, meant to eat any of this stuff. Or feed it to anyone, which, of course, was the question for today: had someone?

Or administered it some other way, perhaps. I opened the box. Inside were four shiny white plastic cartridges along with a leaflet of instructions. The trap itself came packaged separately, maybe.

"Bella," I called, but she didn't answer. Outside, the men from across the lake climbed toward the cottage, their shoes crunching on the graveled path. I could hear them talking to one another, just not what they were saying.

But they didn't sound happy. And the little gun I'd had was at home in my dresser drawer, now. I'd meant to turn it over to Bob last night after Miss Blaine got loaded into the ambulance, but then Wade had arrived and I got distracted again.

Now the two guys climbed the deck steps. Probably they weren't bad guys, but I didn't feel like taking chances. Urgently, I scanned the cottage's open living area, hoping to spot a weapon.

An iron poker leaned against the woodstove, but no way was I a fighter. Me trying to use that thing as a weapon might be hilarious to watch, but forget about it being dangerous to anyone but me.

Because, unfortunately, if I can bonk myself

with an object, I will. Talking, though, I can do, sort of.

"Hey, guys!" I greeted the two men who appeared on the deck. "Something I can help you with?"

Brightly, cheerfully . . . because when people who are up to no good sense that you know something is wrong, they move faster. And I didn't want that, even though I didn't know quite yet who these guys were.

Up to, I mean, if anything. "I'm here getting a few things for Miss Blaine," I said, keeping my tone genial. "I don't know if you heard, but she's in the hospital. She took a bad fall last night."

The men were in their thirties, shaggy-haired, stubble-chinned, in jeans and sweatshirts with battered sneakers; one had on a gimme cap with a local trucking outfit's name embroidered on it.

"Oh," said the one wearing the cap. TWO GUYS MOVING & HAULING, it said. "She gonna be all right?"

They seemed very . . . normal. "Yes," I said, feeling my suspicions fade somewhat. Looking down at the plastic box I was still holding, I closed the top and gently put the box back in the window seat.

If either of them thought there was anything strange about that, they didn't say so. I still didn't like the way their eyes darted around, though.

"Okay. Uh, yeah." They backed toward the

door. "We, uh, we just wanted to make sure you weren't, like, burglars or something."

I smiled hard at them. "That's nice of you. I'll let her know you were watching out for her, she'll appreciate it."

I closed the top of the window seat and put the cushion on it. And then, because I just couldn't help myself: "Pretty isolated spot for an elderly lady. You guys live out here year-round?"

Their faces hardened simultaneously, not much to my surprise, and then the silent one spoke. "No, we just brought the kids swimming."

He angled his head back toward the cottage they'd come from. "Us and his wife. Soon to be ex-wife. Whatever."

He turned to his friend. "We gotta go."

"Take care," I called after them as they hustled back down the path to the dock. Their little outboard whined and their boat snake-waked its way back across the lake to their own place.

Then, "Hmph," came a voice from behind me, and Bella came down the stairs. "There's a likely-looking pair."

She sniffed. "Checking for burglars, my great-aunt Fanny. Those two were casing the joint."

When my dad was an invalid, she'd read a lot of old detective fiction while she sat keeping him company. And while I wasn't sure the lingo was still current, she had a point.

It was what they'd looked like. I opened the

window seat bin again and lifted the poison out. "I wonder what they wanted."

Because while the cottage was comfortably furnished, it wasn't by any means luxurious; so far, I'd seen nothing worth stealing.

"No jewelry or such upstairs," Bella agreed. "Or fancy-looking furniture, paintings and what-not. Nothing like that."

All of which was consistent with what Ellie had said about her old teacher: a solid person, someone who took seriously the idea of treading lightly upon the earth.

So why *did* she still have enough cyanide to kill a . . . well, I didn't know what it would kill, did I? But it sure seemed like a lot of poison. And she wasn't a farmer or rancher or a government land manager, so I was curious about her keeping what amounted to a mass-murder weapon in her window seat.

But I could ask her about that later, after she'd recovered. For now, "Okay," I sighed, getting the plastic box back out and carrying it to a window where the sunlight streamed through.

It was a four-cartridge set, you could tell by the way they were packed in the box, and by the look of it none of the cartridges had been used.

Or . . . had they? Bella leaned in to peer at what I was doing. "Keep back a little," I warned.

Because I'd looked it up late the night before. "You don't have to eat or drink this stuff to die from it," I said. "You could just inhale it, or get it on your skin, and whammo."

She blinked respectfully. "Let's not have any accidents," I said, leaning in cautiously to inspect the plastic cartridges more closely.

And at first they all looked perfect: smooth, white, and shiny, about the size of a wine cork but rounded at both ends. Some kind of a spring-loaded piercing device was supposed to hit it and shoot cyanide out its front, I gathered from the diagram on the instructions.

But . . . "Look," breathed Bella, and then I saw it, too, a tiny pinhole on the barrel of one of the cartridges.

Bella's green eyes narrowed. "I'll bet someone took some of the poison out of that thing. With a hypodermic needle or something."

I glanced sideways at her, pleased; half an hour earlier I'd have done just about anything to get her thinking—even for a minute or two— about something besides my dad and all his many recent misdeeds.

And now here she was, looking bright as a new penny. "You know, I think you could be right," I said.

But I thought something else, too, as across the lake the little outboard engine went silent: whoever had invaded Miss Blaine's quiet lake-side cottage hadn't been here to take something from it.

I'd been right. Unless I missed my guess, they'd been here to return something.

The walls of Eastport's newly refurbished downtown municipal building were decorated with photographs of the old trains that had once served Eastport. Passing the photographs on my way into Bob Arnold's office, I'd wished very heartily that I was on one of those trains . . . and for good reason, as it turned out.

"A firearm," Bob Arnold said, eyeing the ugly little .22 pistol I'd deposited on his desk.

I'd dropped Bella off at home, then come straight over here to tell him what we'd found at the cottage and to give him Moran's weapon finally, too.

But now I almost wished I hadn't. "Yes, Bob, I know it was out of line to keep the gun. But at the time I was a little distracted by—"

"A firearm that you found while rooting through the belongings of a murder victim. You should never have been there in the first place."

Oh, but he was hot. "I told the state guys I found those photos of Sharon Sweetwater," he said—I *had* given him those—"so as not to get you and Ellie involved. I said I'd had an idea where they might be based on something Moran said to me once."

He sucked in a furious breath. "I lied, in other

words, to cover your foolish tails," he added angrily, "and look what it's got me."

I didn't blame him. Still . . . "Bob, I really am sorry. But they were done with the place; they'd even told the landlady she could—"

Clean the room, I was about to finish, so there was nothing wrong or illegal about us being there. But Bob didn't give me a chance.

"You told me about the pictures, you remembered that much, but somehow you forgot the gun you found. Yeah, sure you did. . . ."

He shook his head, tight-lipped. "Once you were in there, you should've left the damned thing where you found it, that's what you should've done."

He got up from behind his desk to pace a green indoor-outdoor carpet whose glue smell still tinctured the air years after they'd installed the thing.

"But," he continued, "now that you *have* brought the gun in to me, I suppose . . ." His blue eyes regarded me balefully. ". . . now that you *have,* I suppose I can figure out something to do about it."

"Something that doesn't involve us?" I asked hopefully.

He eyed me. "You don't deserve it. But yeah, I'll tell them I tossed it in the lockbox in my car last night, and in the aftermath of your dad's crash, I'm the one who forgot about it."

"They'll believe that?" Not wise of me, I know, but I couldn't help it.

Bob made a face. "They already think all us small-town cops are fools. More ammunition for their opinion is just what they like."

But then he faced me. "Thing is, though, we're not. Fools, that is, so how about you tell me now the rest of what went on at Moran's place last night?"

And when I hesitated: "Come on, Jake. Moran's room was torn up and tossed to hell . . . you and Ellie didn't do that, I know you both better than that."

He leaned forward, hands pressed flat on his desk. "And Mrs. Starne, she was all upset, nervous and defensive . . . like maybe somebody just scared the wits out of her and she's ticked off about it."

He really was a very good cop. "Yeah, well . . ." I told him the whole story. "But, Bob, she absolutely insisted that we not call anyone or tell anyone, and—"

He sighed resignedly. "Yeah, and she's a real piece of work, too; that sounds just like her. Anyway, I'll take care of this."

Which meant he thought that I could go now.

But: "Um. There's a little more." I held out the clear plastic box with the cyanide cartridges in it: three loaded ones, and—

"That one on the end, there," I told him, "it

looks like somebody stuck a needle in that one."

Bob's pale blond eyebrows went up. "Whoa," he pronounced, setting the box down on his desk and gazing at it.

I gave him an abbreviated version of how Bella and I had gotten it. "All I want," I said, "is not to be in possession of it anymore."

Although, in fact, it wasn't all I wanted. Also, as I'd feared, he was still stuck at the how-we'd-acquired-it portion of the program.

"You weren't there getting anything for Miss Blaine," he said. "That was a cover story, socks and toiletries and so on."

He gestured at the box. "You were out there looking for . . . Jake, why the heck are you and Ellie so wound up in all of this, anyway?"

So then I did have to tell him all of it, starting with Sharon and Andy's wedding, the enormous whoopie-pie cake that Ellie and I were baking for it, and our need to do the job and get paid, or else.

Plus, of course, what Ellie had said about moving away, somewhere she and George could find work that wasn't (a) uncertain; (b) poorly paid; and, in George's case, also (c) backbreaking.

Bob listened carefully, hands clasped on his desk.

"So if we could just clear Andy of Toby Moran's murder by finding at least one other reasonable suspect," I said.

"Then Ellie could stay right here in Eastport, where she belongs," Bob finished for me.

He shook his head unhappily. "She's serious about this?"

"As serious as a—"

Heart attack, I'd been about to say, but then I remembered just in time about my dad and his truck. I wasn't sure if any laws had been violated last night when he'd crashed, and I didn't want Bob thinking about clarifying the subject—for me, or for himself.

"Anyway," I went on, "if Andy Devine's guilty, and now it seems to me there's some serious doubt about that, then there won't be any wedding at all."

Bob nodded slowly; he still didn't approve of the gun-and-poison show I'd brought to his office this morning. But he didn't want to lose Ellie and George, either; we all loved them, not just me.

"But if he's *not* guilty," I said, "then seriously, Bob, we need to know it. Because those bills of ours—"

"I get it," he interrupted as I stopped, suddenly overcome. The whole idea of Ellie leaving Eastport was just impossible.

Except that it wasn't. He handed me a tissue from the box of them that he kept on his desk and looked away as I blew. "Sorry," I said.

He busied himself moving papers around.

"Hey, some days you just gotta run the water-works," he replied understandingly.

Then he filled a foam cup from the coffee urn in his utility closet and brought it to me. The thick black liquid smelled like battery acid, but I drank it gratefully anyway.

"Okay, listen," he went on, changing the subject. "The other thing about last night . . . in case you're wondering, I'm not going to try to get your dad's driver's license suspended."

I hadn't even known that possibility was on the table; if I had, I'd have been working on Bob about it already.

"Yeah, I know that's what you and Bella would like," Bob went on. "But, Jake, there's no legal cause. Just being old doesn't cut it, you know, if he's safe to operate a motor vehicle."

It was what my dad had said, too. Bob looked out his window at the boats puttering on the water. "His eyesight's okay, his mental status is good—"

Turning back to me, he frowned suddenly. "It is, isn't it? I mean, he doesn't think he's Napoleon or anything?"

"He's sane," I confirmed, recalling our conversation outside the Moose the day before. "As for his eyesight, since he had his cataracts removed he can practically see through walls."

It was another thing we'd nursed him through over the winter. Now I sat up straight in Bob's office chair. The coffee was repulsive to drink, but the result was excellent, especially if you like the feeling of having caffeine shot straight into your brain.

"It's his *attitude,*" I went on, "that's making me crazy. Like a kid who can't help keep testing the adults. It's infuriating."

The phone console on Bob's desk began blinking; he ignored it. "He hasn't left the island today, though, has he? In the new truck?"

Wiping my eyes with a clean tissue, I confirmed that he hadn't. "Truck's still at the garage getting possible damage from last night checked out, so he can't."

Bob went to the other window, overlooking the parking lot. By the rumbly-thud sound of it, some boys were riding skateboards out there, an activity that was strictly against town ordinance.

He turned his back on them. "Good, because I want to keep an eye on him for a while, just to be sure. But no one's complained about speeding or driving recklessly," he went on. "There've been no reports of open containers, loud mufflers, or any other kind of misbehavior."

He sat again behind his desk. "In fact, as far as I can tell he's been a model citizen, rules-of-the-road-wise. The kind of accident he had last night could've happened to anyone."

It was another thing my dad had said, and it

was true that deer were a constant menace to motorists all over Eastport.

"So, let me ask you, Jake, are you absolutely sure it's your dad's attitude that's the problem?"

I stared, unable to believe what I'd just heard. And when I could finally speak: "I'm sorry? After all we've done, his illness, his convalescence, now we're struggling to get him as near back to normal as we can. . . ."

It was too much. I got up. "You're telling me now you think *we're* doing something wrong?"

Bob took all this patiently, his plump pink face serene and his hands resting loosely on the desk in front of him.

"I'm saying that maybe he's behaving like a teenager 'cause that's how you're treating him. You and Bella both, but he's a grown man, so he's pushing back. That's all."

"Right, we've all got opinions about things, I guess." I tossed the Styrofoam cup into the trash. "Thanks for the coffee."

"I understand. But think about it," he said, not backing down.

Of course, he wouldn't; over the years he'd faced guys swinging boat hooks, fire axes, and 12-gauge shotguns, to name but a few; he wouldn't fall into a funk just 'cause I'd gotten annoyed.

Especially when he was right. . . .

Outside, I stomped across the parking lot amidst

the skateboard boys zooming and swooping. Slamming my car door, I frightened a bunch of seagulls away from a crust of bread they'd been squabbling over.

But behind the wheel, I cooled off; maybe I'd heard some things I didn't want to. And maybe, based on what I'd heard, I'd even have to consider changing my own behavior somewhat.

Or maybe not; I could think about it all some more later. For now, though, the important thing was what Bob had heard, so that he at last had the whole picture.

The wedding and why we so badly needed it to happen on schedule, the cut-and-paste lingerie photos of Sharon Sweetwater, and the poison from Miss Blaine's.

Oh, and the gun. We'd already told him the night before about the motorcyclist speeding out from Miss Blaine's cottage, whereupon he'd eyed Andy Devine with enough skepticism that I thought I didn't have to say any more about that.

And on top of it all, I'd gotten the cyanide cartridges out of Miss Blaine's cottage so no one else could take them, and out of my own possession, as well.

What Bob did with it all was his business; I just hoped he'd manage to keep our names out of it, as he'd . . .

Well, not promised, exactly. But close; thinking this, I backed out around the skateboarders, turned the corner onto Water Street to head home, and instead spotted Ellie out in front of the Moose.

And then it hit me, what Bob Arnold *hadn't* said. "Get in," I told Ellie. Because . . .

"He didn't say we should quit," I told her after reporting the whole conversation with Bob.

Well, not the part about my father; I was still digesting that. But: "He didn't say mind our own business, or anything like it."

"You think he knows something we don't?" Ellie handed me one of those newly baked biscotti loaded with candied ginger and semi-sweet morsels.

"I think he *doesn't* know something," I said around a mouthful of chocolate bliss, "but he *wants* to."

The chocolate was no direct help for any of the situations I was facing, but it made me feel much better and it got the taste of Bob's terrible coffee off my tongue, too.

"I could be wrong, but you know Bob. He's not shy about telling you what he wants and doesn't want."

Or what he thinks, I added silently, still smarting from Bob's assessment of my dad-handling technique.

"And I think what he *wants* is for us to snoop around some more in Toby Moran's murder, and possibly find out what he thinks the state cops *won't,*" I added, pulling away from the curb.

Downtown, it was all just as busy and cheerful as if no murder-by-poison had happened here at all, much less just thirty-six hours earlier.

Across from the hardware store, trucks backed onto the fish pier to load lobster traps. In the boat basin, men called to one another across the decks of fishing vessels rafted together three abreast.

"Something local, then," Ellie mused aloud. "For the motive, I mean. Or someone local, for the killer. That's what Bob thinks."

On Key Street, my big old white clapboard house stood with its windows all glittering and the gauzy white curtain panels behind them fluttering pristinely in a little breeze off the water.

"And he thinks if someone else besides Andy *is* guilty," I agreed, "the state cops won't know enough about local people to figure out—"

In my driveway, the red truck was back from the garage, showing not even a scratch after its mishap of the night before.

Those garage guys were fast. "Who," I finished, slowing to turn into the driveway, myself. "But he doesn't want to dig around in it. It'd be stepping on toes, as he puts it."

"And *that's* why he hasn't told us not to. Dig around in it, that is," Ellie added thoughtfully.

Next to my dad's truck sat Sam and Mika's

little Honda sedan, and behind them Wade's pickup, parked at a hasty angle; it was the way he did it when he was only here to grab lunch.

Bella was home, too, of course; that's how those windows had gotten so glittery, and the curtains washed white as snow. All of them were here except for Mika, who was at the Moose; I drove on past the driveway entrance.

Ellie looked questioningly at me; she'd have liked lunch, too, probably, and despite the biscotti I was also famished. But: "There's not a single person in there who won't start yammering at me about something the minute I walk in," I said.

So I kept on driving, out Key Street between neat, small houses with their yards all freshly mowed and picket-fenced, to County Road, past the ball field, the youth center, and the fire station, then around the long curve between the gas station and the big new Baptist church, headed out of town.

"Lately it seems like anything I do with, for, or about any of them only ends up making things worse," I said.

We shot past the airport, the old gas-fired power plant, and the garage where the town plow trucks and roadwork equipment were kept.

"Well, not including Wade, of course," I amended, "but still." On the causeway, we slowed for the speed limit sign in Pleasant Point.

"So," I said, "first we're going to get some food. Real food, I mean, not just cookies and cake."

Because right then what I needed was the solid nutrition of a battered fish sandwich on a soft white sandwich roll with plenty of tartar sauce, fries dipped in a little bowl of blue cheese dressing, and a paper cup full of cole slaw so well dosed with celery seed that a single bite could change your whole idea of cabbage.

Plus a Coke, cherry if they had it. Which was why, five minutes later, we pulled into the parking lot of the New Friendly Restaurant on Route 1 overlooking a tidal marsh, where green-headed mallards paddled and dove. Just five miles from Eastport, it was nevertheless a world away in the not-dealing-with-my-family-right-now department.

And that, too, was precisely what I needed.

"And *after* lunch," I began as we got out of the car.

Mika had told me she could stay in the shop all day. She was trying out a new babysitter, a young teenaged girl from across the street, and from her tone I got the sense that a little break from her daily home-and-baby routine might be right up her alley, as well.

"After lunch," I said, "do you remember what Marienbad said about Toby Moran's last girlfriend? Who it was, I mean, before Sharon?"

Ellie nodded. "Yes, Carrie Allen. I went to school

with her and she's a veterinary technician now; I saw her at our reunion. Before you ask, though, I don't think she even knows Norm McHale."

The disgraced veterinarian . . . a short laugh escaped me. "Yeah, that would've been too much to hope for, wouldn't it?"

We crossed the gravel parking lot toward the low-roofed, red-painted eatery with the big plate-glass front door.

"But I know her, too, actually," I said, pulling the door open. "We've taken Max to the clinic she works at."

The big old German shepherd had needed a thorn removed from one of his paws. "Right up the road from here, on Route 1, and I think she lives near here somewhere, too," I said.

The smell of French-frying hit me as we entered the restaurant. "Sam bought some old washing machine parts from her, once, and had to come out here to pick them up," I added.

What he'd been doing with the washing machine parts was another story, but he could fix anything, that kid.

"And after we eat we're going to find her and talk to her," I said.

Inside, we found seats at the counter while behind us the busy waitresses zipped between tables and booths.

"Okay," said Ellie, "but I want to get home before Lee does, so no goose chases."

Turning, I scanned the room where flannel-shirted men, ladies lunching with friends, and tables full of mothers and children munched happily on noontime feasts. But that wasn't all I saw.

"What?" said Ellie distractedly. She sipped some of her water while checking out the specials on the whiteboard by the kitchen door.

I didn't; check them, I mean. "Hey, Ellie? Looks like we're not going to need a goose chase," I said.

At the other end of the counter, a woman stood waiting for a refill on her fountain drink.

"Why?" Ellie wanted to know. "Have you changed your—?"

Thirty or so years old with a slim build and short, curly brown hair, the woman wore a pair of baggy green uniform pants, a beige smock top, and sneakers. There was a small plastic name tag pinned to her smock-top's breast pocket.

On her lunch break, obviously. I couldn't read the name tag. But I didn't need to, because when she turned her head and I saw her whole face, I knew for sure who she must be.

At some time in the not-too-terribly-distant past, she'd had her nose broken, and now that the swelling had mostly gone down you could tell that it was never going to straighten out quite right.

And I was pretty sure I knew who'd broken it. Ellie looked up questioningly at me again.

"We won't need any chase at all," I told her as the woman with the nose Toby Moran had given her took her drink back to her table.

On the table in front of me, the day's menu informed me that the fish sandwich I wanted was not only available, it was also on special.

"Because the woman sitting over there with the tossed green salad in front of her is Carrie Allen," I said.

Six

"So how was Andy Devine supposed to have gotten the poison into Toby Moran's milkshake, anyway?" Carrie Allen wanted to know.

The fish was wonderful, the cole slaw divine. I'd washed it all down with another Cherry Coke and a slice of the New Friendly's famous chocolate-raspberry pie, which if the restaurant hadn't already been making it, The Chocolate Moose would have done so, it was that good.

Then Carrie had walked over to our table and sat down without any invitation. I'd glanced over at her once or twice while we were eating—Ellie had a tuna melt plus half my French fries, and that worked out well since otherwise I wouldn't have had room for pie—but not *that* often.

Still, I guessed she was touchy about being watched, and when she sat with us and ordered her own cup of coffee, we found out why.

"No idea," I said in answer to her question. "We don't know how the killer got the milkshake and cup from our shop at all, much less got the poison into it and got Toby Moran to drink it."

"If someone did," Ellie put in. "The autopsy report's not out yet. So the truth is that we still don't know what really happened."

"Seems like Moran knew how to make trouble

for a lot of people, though," I said. "Was he like that with you?"

I knew he had been. At close range, her nose deformity was worse than I'd thought. But I wanted her to say it, and she did.

"Yeah, he stalked me." Her voice hardened with rancor. "He called me, he followed me, he harassed me on social media. I basically had to give up being online completely, which was hard because until then I did the Facebook page for the veterinarian's office I work at."

She took a breath. "But that wasn't all. He showed up wherever I was and told lies about me, hung around my place late at night and scared the crap out of me, and generally made my life hell."

Another breath. "And that was all *after* he hauled off and slugged me, on account of he'd lost his temper and wanted to punish me for the crime of breaking up with him in the first place," she said.

She touched the crumpled place in the bridge of her nose with a careful fingertip.

"So I guess that's the end of my modeling career. I still feel really self-conscious about it, in case you hadn't noticed. Thanks a lot, Toby."

"Oh, now," Ellie jumped in consolingly. "You've always been gorgeous. Now you're unusual looking *and* gorgeous," she declared, "and that's even better."

Carrie looked pleased but unfooled. "That's nice of you," she allowed. "But even if it was true, it's not what you wanted to talk about, is it? The fallout from my poor choice of romantic partners?"

Pretty *and* smart . . . I still didn't understand how Moran reeled these excellent young women into his clutches. But I had a feeling Carrie was about to explain, or at least maybe give us enough more dots so that we could connect them ourselves.

Meanwhile, the lunch crowd was thinning out around us, only a few old codgers in buffalo-check caps left gabbing over their coffees at the counter, and a tableful of young women with toddlers still trying to get a bite to eat into their own mouths after satisfying the kids.

Carrie got up. "Anyway, what happened between me and Moran is no secret. So if you want to hear about it . . ."

Slinging her jacket over her shoulder, she headed for the door. "Why don't you follow me to my place?" she called back to us.

"I've got a new batch coming out of the cooler and you can help me test it."

"Batch of what?" Ellie wondered as we followed Carrie Allen's old Econoline van uphill away from Route 1 onto the Shore Road.

Past the abandoned redbrick schoolhouse

with its twin front doors, both now barred and padlocked, and its windows boarded over, we took a left and soon emerged from the dense green thickets lining the pavement, out onto an open ridge overlooking the bay.

"I don't know what," I replied, frowning; somehow the van had disappeared. "Where the heck did she . . . ?"

Spring-green fields bounded away from us downhill toward the water, with here and there an old barn or metal Quonset building set up to store the baled hay after it was cut.

But no Econoline . . . until a mailbox with ALLEN stenciled onto it beckoned from the end of a dirt driveway. Around it the forest closed in again even more thickly than before.

"Hmm," Ellie said doubtfully, digging in her bag to make sure her phone was there, and that it worked. Because this driveway . . .

"Yeah, kind of . . ." Creepy-looking, I'd have finished if my voice hadn't trailed off; suddenly I felt uncertain.

"Haunted," Ellie finished for me, and she was right; hemmed in by old trees, the unpaved driveway stretched ahead, then vanished around a curve out of sight.

The undergrowth on both sides seemed to watch silently as we drove on, somewhat against my better judgment. *Deeper and deeper into the woods* hadn't been my plan for this afternoon.

But here we were. "What's she want us to help test, anyway?" I asked. Through the trees, the remains of an old cellar hole formed a depression that resembled a half-filled grave.

"I don't know," said Ellie, staring at something dangling from a tree branch; white and fabric-wrapped, surely it was not an old doll turning in the breeze.

Surely it wasn't. "But I guess we're about to find out," she said; then we pulled up alongside the house.

Carrie Allen's place didn't look haunted, at any rate, I saw with relief. Just the opposite; it was a modern tan-shingled structure with a dog run on one side and a perennial garden, its dark-mulched, stone-bordered beds just now beginning to show a little green, on the other.

As I turned off the car, one of the dogs danced out from behind the house, sniffing and yipping; two more followed, one with a stubby flap where one ear used to be and the other galloping on three legs.

They all looked good, clean and happy and energetic. Then Carrie appeared, calling them all back with a shout, after which she guided us inside, too, past a clutter of leashes, collars, and fuzzy toys with their cotton guts ripped out.

The first dog, I saw now, was blind, with one eye heavily clouded and the other entirely closed. But it didn't seem to bother him.

"Please do *not* tell anyone you saw them," Carrie said hastily. "If anyone finds out I'm rescuing animals at all, much less any sick or crippled ones, I'll be swamped with the tragically unwanted."

She put enough of a twist on that last bit to let me know she'd been taking in dogs for a while, and dog-saving, I knew from sad experience, was not a job for the soft-hearted.

"Yup." She caught my assessing look. "You work at saving strays, you get realistic real quick. Not," she added, "that it helps me much with human beings, apparently."

With Moran, she meant. I glanced around; from the driveway, all I'd been able to see was the garden and the dog run. But inside, the house was a serene marvel.

The downstairs was one open room with a kitchen, dining area, and the living space arranged on the kind of expensive faux hardwood that doesn't scratch easily and needs no upkeep besides regular mopping.

Which it obviously got; it even smelled clean in here. "Nice place," I remarked.

The windows, all uncurtained, looked out onto an unspoiled view: beach, waves, islands, sky. Ellie gazed out to where a bald eagle had nested in a dead treetop about fifty yards distant.

"I like it," Carrie acknowledged my compliment. "Although it can get a little lonely."

The nest, made of dead branches as thick as my arm, was about the size of a Volkswagen, with three little heads sticking up out of it.

Maws gaping, wickedly hooked beak tips already visible . . . the long driveway's bleak, haunted feeling washed over me again, reminding me that I would not want to be alone and in trouble out here.

"Over here," she called, waving us to the dining area, where a row of miniature beer mugs had already been arranged.

When we got there, Carrie popped the stopper from a brown pottery jug and poured, and we spent the next few minutes tasting the kind of beer I'd only read about in gourmet publications, previously.

"Fruity," Ellie pronounced of one, smacking her lips.

"Nutty," I said of the next glass I tasted. And, "Like honey," I remarked of the next. But then came the pièce de résistance.

"Oh!" Ellie looked up, beaming. "It's chocolate! It's—"

"Not beer," Carrie said, clearly pleased. "It's a kind of ale. I wondered if you guys would be able to tell."

I took a sip. The cocoa bean flavor, dark and luxurious, filled my head. "You make this stuff? It's like a chocolate brain infusion."

She looked pleased. "It's a hobby of mine. I

have the brewing equipment in the basement. It had sat down there for a while unused, but I spent a lot of time alone out here after my . . ."

She stopped, touching her crooked nose self-consciously again. "Anyway, I needed something to do," she finished. "You really like it? Because honestly, I thought I'd enter some competitions with it if . . ."

"It's lovely," I assured her, setting my glass aside. "But much more of it and I won't remember why we came here," I added warningly.

Ellie had put her glass down already, as well. "Right," she said, blinking. "What we came for."

She gathered her thoughts while I searched for a way to phrase what we needed to ask; that beer was *potent*. Then: "What we want to know," she said simply, "is what a person like you was doing with that terrible little blot on humanity, Toby Moran?"

I let a breath out. She'd said it perfectly; she generally did.

"Yeah," I echoed. It wasn't *all* we wanted to know, especially now that I'd found out what a capable person Carrie was.

But it would do for a start. She seated herself on the beige-upholstered couch in the living area. On the blond maple end table beside her, a small gold clock chimed the quarter hour.

"Interesting question," Carrie allowed, smiling ruefully.

It was a quarter past one. Ellie would need to leave, soon, to be home when her daughter got there. Carrie frowned faintly, perhaps thinking of what she was about to say.

That was when I noticed what the room was missing: there were no mirrors anywhere. Not that people always had mirrors hanging, but when I excused myself—the Coke, the beer—I found none in the bathroom, either.

Not even on the medicine cabinet. Which was when I really began to wonder about it. "What I ever saw in Toby Moran," Carrie was saying when I returned. "Good question."

I'd left her alone with Ellie deliberately. People like talking to her; they confide in her, and she can spot a lie a mile away.

But Carrie had taken a while formulating her reply, as if maybe she hadn't yet quite come to terms with the answer, herself.

"Okay, so here's the thing," she said at last. "Toby was fun."

Her sigh was reminiscent. "I mean," she added, "you know how when you were younger, you maybe wanted to be . . . oh, I don't know. Cool, I guess? And with a cool boyfriend, somebody a little dangerous, maybe."

Ellie's eyes softened. "Yes," she smiled. "Ninth grade, Jeffrey Bingham. He played bass guitar, but, of course, I got over all of that when . . . oh," she stopped suddenly, spying Carrie's expression.

221

"Right," said Carrie. "I didn't. Get over it, I mean. I had to work, go to school, and then at home . . . well, I never had time for a boyfriend."

Another sigh. "And Toby was adorable at first. I mean, really. Romantic, attentive . . ."

I guessed I could imagine it, if it was all just an act on his part. "But later?"

By now we were getting ready to go, Ellie glancing at her watch and the dogs jostling excitedly around us.

"Later he was a son of a bitch," said Carrie. "So bad, I nearly even lost my job over it."

We were at the door; she waved out past us. Who knew how many wooded acres lay between her and the next neighbor, or the road.

"And, of course, way out here it was nerve-wracking at night," she added. "Which is the thing I really want to tell somebody about."

Okay, now we were getting to it. I gestured to her to walk us to the car; the dogs followed along, too.

"These guys," she said, gesturing at them, "got so anxious about Toby, they'd go nuts barking whenever he came around."

"They didn't bark at us," I pointed out as we got into the car.

Carrie nodded as I backed the vehicle around. Afternoon light filtered greenly down through the trees into the clearing.

"Right," she said. "Only at him, no one else.

And he hated it, I know because he sent me e-mails about it, threatening to poison them."

I hit the brakes. She was just outside my car window. "Poison them," I repeated.

She nodded again, her brown curls bobbing. "And what I heard is that that's what he ended up dying of, himself. Is it true?"

Beside me, Ellie glanced at her wristwatch again. "True," I said. "But . . . look, Carrie, if there's something you have to tell us—"

She nodded, tight-lipped. "I do. About the dogs, about him saying he'd poison the dogs. Because the thing is, he tried."

The words came out in a rush. "It was late, I heard them barking, they ran out the dog door. I got to the hamburger he threw down before they did, luckily. I couldn't believe it, that he would . . ."

She stopped, overcome for a moment by the memory of what must have been a terrifying event. But then she gathered herself.

"Anyway, right about then he seemed to lose interest, and pretty soon I found out he was dating that pretty teacher, Sharon—"

She snapped her fingers, searching for the name. "Sweetwater," I supplied, and she nodded.

"Yes, it's why I never told anyone about what nearly happened with the dogs. I didn't want to attract his attention again. But if that information is of any help to anyone, now . . ."

That wasn't why she was telling us this. "So you don't mind us informing the police about him trying to poison pets, but I'm guessing you want to stay out of it," I said, "is that it?"

She touched her bent nose again unthinkingly. "Yes, if you can. Because—"

I understood, or hoped I did. He'd ruined her face, nearly ruined her life, and she wanted no part of the investigation into his murder.

Especially since from what I could tell, she had a great motive of her own and the cops wouldn't miss that; if they hadn't had Andy Devine already in their sights, they'd be interested in her. I put the car in gear while she was still talking.

"Because maybe what he died of wasn't something somebody else got to use on him," she was saying.

Above, an enormous bald eagle sailed toward the big nest. I let the car creep forward some more.

"Maybe it was something he already had, that he'd gotten hold of so he could do bad deeds with it, himself," Carrie Allen finished.

"Yeah, maybe," I told Ellie as we went back down the driveway. Ominous-looking thickets of small trees still lined it and the cellar hole still gaped, but the doll I'd thought I'd seen dangling was gone.

"Deeds like trying to poison people's animals,

for instance," I said, and Ellie's reply was exactly what I'd been thinking.

"Sure," she said. I turned back onto the main road, heading toward Eastport. "That's possible."

"But," she added, "on the other hand, what if Toby gave Carrie the idea by trying it on her dogs, and she did the last one of those poisoning deeds, herself?"

"So it seems Toby Moran liked his revenge served hot," I told Bob Arnold soon after our visit with Carrie Allen.

I'd dropped Ellie off, and now I was working the final two hours at the Moose so my daughter-in-law could go home. A whole day of peace and quiet had been too much for her, as it turned out, and anyway, the babysitter brought the baby home early on account of family problems.

The babysitter's problems, that is; her parents' separation and imminent divorce was screwing the kid's life up terribly, according to Mika.

"Yeah," Bob said sourly. "Guy had no patience. You hit him, Moran would punch you back harder, and right away, too."

The way he'd done to Carrie. . . . I relayed the rest of what she'd said. "She doesn't want to be involved, and I don't even really know if what she said is true, but I thought you should know—"

The sweet, spice-sharpened aroma of a mocha

pound cake baking in our big oven mingled with the strains of a Mozart violin concerto on the sound system in the shop.

"She says he tried to kill her dogs. With poison," I said.

Bob crunched into a chocolate biscotti and chewed. "Interesting. So maybe she wanted revenge, too, you mean, for her broken face?"

He swallowed. "Nice theory, but I'm afraid it doesn't get Devine off the hook. Plenty of people hated Moran, sure. But only one was in a fistfight with him just before he got croaked."

It was lovely in the shop: fresh coffee, good things to munch on, a cool, salt-smelling breeze coming in the front door . . .

Too bad it was all going to end, soon; that is, unless I managed to do something about it.

"Let's face it," Bob went on, "Devine was the last person known to have seen Toby Moran alive, and I don't care what he says about how he walked into a door, or some such nonsense. Ask me, their meeting was violent enough that he came out of it with a gashed forehead."

He eyed me sharply. "And he still won't say who stitched it up. You and Ellie don't happen to know, do you?"

I ignored the question, hoping he might not notice. Luckily, just then Bob changed the subject, himself.

"So, anybody could take one of these?" He

pointed at the paper milkshake cups stacked atop the display case, then picked one up.

"Cute," he remarked of the cartoonlike moose grinning toothily from the cup. Then he eyed me sharply.

"Seriously, Jake, when the state cops get around to asking you ask if Devine could've gotten one of these cups without your noticing, what'll you say?"

He waved at the glass shaker full of antler-shaped chocolate sprinkles on the counter.

"Or those? I mean, who else has access to them is what the state guys'll want to know. Assuming," he added with the hint of a sly grin, "they don't decide you killed the little bastard."

"Bob," I replied tiredly. By then I'd had another conversation with Bella, and it hadn't gone well. "If I were of a mind to commit murder, Toby Moran wouldn't be very high on my list."

The guy who'd sold my dad that red pickup truck, though . . .

"But to answer your question," I went on, "like I've said before, just about anybody could waltz in here, take one of those cups and shake some sprinkles into it, and walk right out again with them."

One of us might notice. Or not. Mika hadn't been able to say. "And the milkshake ingredients?" Bob asked. "Anyone could get them?"

He made it sound as if milkshake-making was rocket science. But: "Absolutely. All the fixings, right there at the IGA," I replied.

Well, except for Ellie's secret ingredient. The pre-measured bags containing malt powder were stored in a breadbox behind the counter, and I doubted anyone could've filched any of them, or found the can in the kitchen cabinet, either.

On the other hand, I doubted Toby Moran had been a milkshake connoisseur, so he probably hadn't missed it. Heck, probably he hadn't had time to miss it . . . Bob's pale blue eyes narrowed.

"So," he said, raising an index finger. "Access to the cups, the ingredients, and the sprinkles."

Another finger. "Possible access to the poison, if like you're thinking cyanide does turn out to be the real method."

I turned to him: so he *was* taking my idea seriously.

"Miss Blaine did discuss cyanide at her library talk, by the way," he added. "*And* she revealed that she still had some."

I'd included the possibility when I'd spilled my guts to Bob earlier in the day, and just as obviously, he'd checked it out.

"So Devine at least knew about it," he went on. Another finger went up. "Then there's the motive. The pictures of Sharon Sweetwater, plus a couple of beers and some spur-of-the-moment anger: bingo."

He took a breath. "And last but not least, good old-fashioned opportunity, which Devine also had." His ring finger went up.

"Right." I snapped the cash register drawer open and began to count the money in it. "But there's the rub."

He sighed, crunching another biscotti. "Yeah, I know. It's not just a chance to shoot or stab Moran that the killer needed, was it?"

He took a napkin and wiped his fingers on it. "Somehow, someone either forced or persuaded Moran to drink a poison-laced milkshake."

Which might not've been so hard if that's all it had in it. But it didn't. It stank of bug killer. The smell would've been obvious.

"Right." Bob's lips tightened. "That's what I don't understand."

Me, neither; not for sure, anyway. So far, we only had a theory.

"Also, how's Andy supposed to have known he'd run into Moran? This murder wasn't spur-of-the-moment, remember."

Bob shook his head impatiently. "Nah, he could've planned it, got all his materials together in advance, then gone home and whipped that shake together in the Coast Guard station's kitchen, run back to the Duck with it."

He thought a moment. "Behind the Duck, I mean. Where he'd have known Moran was probably still hanging around, half in the bag."

That's what a prosecutor would argue, at any rate, he meant, and I had to agree; it could have been done that way.

I just didn't think it had. And my big question still wasn't answered. "Look, Bob, even with the nasty bug killer smell rising off of it, are you sure we should assume Moran understood that the shake was poisoned?"

Because that was the part I really couldn't come up with a theory for; not unless our cyanide idea panned out.

"What if instead of forcing it on him, some-body presented him with the drink as a sort of peace offering?" I said. "Remember, he was intoxicated. Not thinking clearly."

"Huh," said Bob. "So the killer just handed it to him, maybe he was too drunk to notice the stink, and . . . down the hatch."

"Maybe, but . . ."

"That's right," Sharon Sweetwater inter-rupted, the little silver bell over the door tinkling as she came in.

"Down the hatch," she repeated. "He took it, he drank it right down, and presto, one less lousy bastard in the world."

She looked at both of us. "Toby was a greedy little creep with a mean streak a mile wide," she went on, "and he got what he deserved."

We stared back. Sharon's short dark hair was disheveled, her face splotchy and without makeup, and instead of her usual impeccable outfit she wore grubby jeans, an old gray sweatshirt, and sneakers so raggedy they looked as though they might actually fall off.

"Have you heard?" she demanded. "Well, have you?"

I tried gently ushering her to a chair, but she resisted. "I mean, have you heard that Andy just got arrested?" she clarified.

Oh, Lord. "No, I haven't," I replied while Bob just shook his head in annoyance. Not being told things in advance by the state cops was par for the course.

But that didn't mean he liked it. "What happened?" He took out his cell phone, punched numbers into it.

"This morning," Sharon reported, her voice full of misery. "He met with them, they'd asked him to come in. Just to talk, they said."

A little sob escaped her. "But," she added, "he never came out again until they led him out, into one of their squad cars."

She wiped her eyes with a napkin. "I was waiting outside, but they didn't let me talk to him. They took him away."

"Does he have a lawyer yet?" I'd figured this must be coming, but I hadn't expected it so soon.

Sniffling, Sharon shook her head. "Not his own. He'd talked to his C.O., but he was just so confident that this was all a mistake."

Bob turned his back to us, still talking on his phone.

"And I believed him," Sharon said bitterly. "But now I've got to straighten this mess out, before Andy takes the consequences for—"

"Stop," I said sharply as Bob Arnold turned to us.

Because I knew what else was coming now, or thought I did, and I don't care how good a friend Bob Arnold was to all of us; you don't admit to having committed a murder in front of a police officer.

You just don't.

But then Sharon Sweetwater did.

"Bob," I said when he was getting ready to leave the shop. He'd sent Sharon up to his office, telling her he'd meet her there.

"Bob, about something else." I mentioned the babysitter Mika had hired and told him about what had happened with her earlier.

"Mika says the girl had to bring the baby back to our house, and that she seemed upset. Do you know anything about the family?"

Was there some situation in the girl's home besides the ongoing divorce, I meant, that would make her unreliable or unsafe around the baby. He understood.

"Well, the mom and dad are separated, you know that, I guess, and the dad's a twerp. Thinks the mom is turning the girl against him."

"Is she?" My ex-husband had tried tricks like that. He told Sam once that I was planning to send him to military school.

Sam was five at the time. Bob sighed heavily.

"She doesn't have to turn anyone against him. He does it, he's like a two-year-old, has a tantrum if the kid doesn't want to spend time with him even if she's got a good reason."

Because she's babysitting, for instance . . . "Okay," I said, "I appreciate the information."

I handed him a croissant and he went out with it in a napkin so he could munch it without getting crumbs all over his squad car, and twenty minutes later I locked the shop and departed, myself.

Driving home past the fish pier, I watched a barge unloading wooden barrels full of lobster bait, plus bales of the brightly colored nylon netting bags that the bait went into before being fastened into the lobster traps.

At the corner of Water and Key streets, the library's benefit garden sale was in full swing, fresh green seedlings and perennials on display all around the log-stuffed cannon mounted on the library lawn.

Along Key Street the tiny white-picket-fenced front lawns, all neatly trimmed as if with manicure scissors, gleamed in the afternoon sunshine like rows of square-cut emeralds.

Everything was in good order in Eastport today,

in other words, and then I got to my house. There, a red pickup truck sat alongside Wade's big work pickup, the Honda sedan that Sam and Mika drove, and an open-backed REO farm truck with a railed wooden platform instead of a standard truck bed mounted behind the cab.

Oh, goody, I thought uncharitably; I'd never seen the farm truck before, or the items crammed into it, either. Striding past it, I counted a lawn tractor, a push mower with a wheel missing, a rototiller, and a wooden barrel with a lot of yardwork tools stuck into it—rakes, hoes, shovels, and so on, plus a coil of garden hose hanging around the tool handles—crowded together on the truck's platform.

I mounted the porch steps and pulled open the screen door; inside, the baby cried lustily while Mika walked haggardly back and forth, trying to calm him. She adored little Ephraim—we all did—but just then she was wishing hard that she'd stayed in the shop, I could tell, and I didn't blame her.

I already felt that way, myself. At the stove, Bella scrubbed burner tops with one hand while stirring a cream sauce destined for her famous shrimp-and-spaghetti casserole with the other.

That is, if the baby's yells didn't curdle the sauce. "Smells delicious," I shouted to Bella over the din, and she glowered at me in reply, from which I gathered that the Pickup Truck

Wars had not yet reached a satisfactory conclusion.

"Your father," she snapped furiously at me, "is the most *annoying* man I ever met!"

Her voice, harsh as a raven's croak, cut through even the baby's eardrum-lacerating cries. "He's got his keys upstairs with him, and he won't give them up!" she grated out.

Suspicions confirmed; leaving the kitchen, I went on into the dining room, where I found my son, Sam, disassembling a small gasoline-powered engine on the dining room table.

Like I say, Mister Fix-it. He'd put newspaper on the table, but still.

"Hey," he said, looking up as I came in. "Look, I got a perfectly good gas weed-whacker engine for nothing. All it needs is some . . ." His voice trailed off as he noticed my expression. "Oh, don't worry, there's no gasoline in it," he assured me.

He waved around at the small engine parts spread out all over the papers. "No solvents, nothing that might hurt anyone to breathe."

"Sam." The square, 1830s-era dining room with the tiled hearth, tall draperied windows, and elaborate cranberry-glass chandelier was like a little jewel box, most of the time.

But now it looked as if one of the repair bays from the Mobil station had been moved into it. "Sam," I said calmly again.

Very calmly. No wonder Bella had looked at me like she might explode. On top of her annoyance with my father, she must've found Sam with his project in progress and not dared open her mouth about it, for fear of what might come out.

Sam's look turned to one of caution as he caught on. "You know," he said not-quite-casually as he got up, "maybe I'll just clear all this stuff away right now and find some other place to work on it."

"Uh-huh," I said evenly. "That'd probably be a good idea." Then: "So I guess that awful farm truck outside is yours, too?"

"Uh, yeah. Summer people'll be here soon, thought I'd go into the yard-work business," he offered nervously.

He already had a job. Or I'd thought he did, at the marine store where he'd worked summers in the past. Now, though . . .

"Ma, I don't want to work for someone else my whole—"

I found my voice, and the only thing that kept me from using it on him was the pair of hands that clapped themselves to my shoulders.

"Hey," Wade said pleasantly, squeezing meaningfully. "How about you come on with me?"

I half-turned just as a look passed between the two men. "Oh, I get it, you two are in cahoots," I said.

Wade wrapped his arms around me. "Yes, but let's not get too involved in that idea. Let me"— he bent to murmur warmly into my ear—"take you away from all this, over there to all that."

Which was when the oily engine parts slipped out of the newspaper Sam was clutching and clattered down onto the gleaming-clean hardwood floor all around his feet.

"Fine," I said to Wade, letting him lead me out of the dining room. Because wherever *that* was, suddenly I was all for it.

"So she confessed? Sharon Sweetwater did, I mean. In front of Bob Arnold?" Wade speared a stuffed mushroom with a frilly toothpick and ate it.

"Oh, she sure did," I replied, sipping a dry martini.

Two hours had passed since I'd left Sam moving the engine-repair operation out of the dining room. Now, thanks to Wade's swift, accurate assessment of what I needed, we were at Fernando's, an old-fashioned supper club twenty miles from Eastport, way out on Route 9.

Candlelight flickered in the diamond-paned windows in the cozy dining room, music tinkled from a piano in the bar area, and no one was complaining or worrying at me about anything.

"In front of Bob," I added. It was my second martini, which if Wade hadn't been driving I wouldn't have had the first one.

He was drinking Sprite. "So now what happens?"

We'd ordered: chicken picante for him, veal medallions for me. A basket of breadsticks was on the table, along with some butter pats.

I crunched into a breadstick. "Now the state cops will question her. But I doubt her word alone will get Andy Devine off the hook."

Wade nodded. "Yeah, they wouldn't have charged him if they didn't think their case was pretty solid, I suppose."

"Nope, they wouldn't. And Sharon's story isn't exactly dense with detail," I added.

I had no idea whether it would even make sense, only that she was desperate to clear her fiancé.

"All she's really done, besides causing a lot of trouble for herself, is make it even less likely that the wedding will go on as planned."

Our food came; the veal was so tender, it hardly even needed a knife.

"What I still don't get is why," I said between bites. "Why would Andy risk everything—his upcoming marriage, his whole career—just for payback about some stupid faked lingerie pictures?"

Wade ate more chicken, then some scalloped potatoes.

"Because for one thing they were so obviously not Sharon," I went on. "I doubt her students' parents were fooled. And for another, I'm pretty sure that girls in underwear aren't exactly X-rated, nowadays."

I put my fork down. "You can see the same thing in the Lands' End catalog, for heaven's sake."

Well, maybe not those black lacy numbers, but still. The piano in the bar room finished "Autumn Leaves" and started in on "I'm in the Mood for Love"; it was a romantic little roadside supper club.

"Why commit murder," Wade mused aloud, "with all the possible ruination that could cause, when a punch in the nose would've done the trick?"

"Precisely. But what still really gets me is that bug killer in the milkshake."

Before Wade and I had left the house, I'd squirted some Raid into a paper towel. Now I described the experiment to him.

"No way I could even get the towel anywhere near my face, much less into my mouth," I reported. "I just don't believe Moran guzzled that stuff down. I don't care if he was drunk."

I took a breath. "Something else happened, and it's something that involves that cyanide, somehow. I don't *know* it yet, but I'm still sure of it."

"Okay. And meanwhile . . ."

Wade was a good listener; also, he hadn't had two martinis.

"Meanwhile, mean as he was, you're also absolutely right. Moran wasn't worth it," I finished.

Around here, there was a phrase for guys like him: all trap and no lobster. So it wasn't "why kill him?" that I should be wondering about, or even exactly how.

In Andy Devine's case, at least, it was more like "why bother?" Which meant . . . I sat up straight.

"Wade, I've been thinking about this all wrong."

I began devouring my dinner, talking between bites. "Andy might have gotten the poison, the milkshake, even the cups and the antler-shaped sprinkles," I said.

We didn't know precisely how yet, but nothing we knew so far said any of that was *not* possible.

"And we know already that he had the opportunity," I went on. "But so did Sharon, or, anyway, she hasn't got an alibi for the time. And she knew Miss Blaine had the poison cartridges as well as he did; she was at the library lecture, too."

She'd also said she'd handed the poisoned milkshake to Moran and he drank it without hesitation, not mentioning any cyanide at all. But I'd already tested the insecticide-only idea and come up with a big *nope*.

"So . . ." Neither of us wanted coffee. Wade laid some money on the tablecloth and we got up, waving our thanks to the waiter.

240

"So the bottom line here is that Andy's got a motive," he went on when we got outside, "plus at least as much method and opportunity as she does."

"Right." Under an indigo sky pricked with stars, the breeze had an edge of ice in it. "But not a *good* motive."

Not good enough to commit murder. Something else entirely had happened, so why was he lying about any of it?

Wade dropped his jacket over my shoulders and got the truck door open; I hoisted myself onto the bench seat. On Route 9, highballing eighteen-wheelers roared by, as massive as locomotives with their big headlights glaring. "And Sharon had a worse one," I said.

Motive, I meant. Wade nodded, keeping his eyes on the road. "Let me guess. Something about how she snapped, or some such foolishness?"

"Got it in one," I agreed. Warm air blew from the truck's heater; I rubbed my hands in front of it.

"And never mind that to do all that had to get done before Toby Moran could even *get* murdered that way, she'd have had to *stay* snapped for . . . oh, I don't know how long."

Long enough, anyway, to get the poison, the cup, the sprinkles, the shake ingredients . . .

"Even Bob Arnold rolled his eyes at her story," I added.

But he'd still had to call the state cops. Wade took the Route 214 shortcut past a highway maintenance yard, a liquor store whose sign glowed dingy yellow, and a farm-machinery graveyard, where the jagged outlines of ancient plows and hay-baling contraptions bulked darkly.

And then it got *really* dark. No moon, no streetlights . . . only our own high beams broke the velvety blackness crowded in all around us on the shortcut.

Wrapping Wade's jacket more closely around myself, I rolled the window down. Through it came a chorus of peeping and croaking and chirruping, as the inhabitants of a nearby frog pond made their early-summer happiness known to anything that would listen.

Basically, I thought, frogs lived in a puddle, ate flies, and never got warm; still they yelled out their happiness in doing it and I found that encouraging.

Or maybe it was the martinis. "On top of which," I said, "Moran really knew how to make enemies. Ellie and I have already met one of them."

I summarized our talk with Carrie Allen earlier. "And I'm sure there are more, but like Bob Arnold says, it was Andy who was either there or very nearby when it happened," I finished.

As we passed Round Pond, the starry sky shed a thin, pale gleam onto the flat water. "And if he doesn't work out for them, there's still Sharon for them to go after," Wade said.

"Right. And she's already confessed, for Pete's sake."

Something else, though, something we *didn't* know, kept nagging at me. Past the sawmill at the end of the Route 214 cutoff, we came out of the woods at Route 1 and turned north, back toward Eastport.

"So has Sam mentioned his new business idea to you yet?" Wade said, accelerating past a tiny post office building and a mom-and-pop restaurant not yet open for the summer season.

"Yes," I said, my tone conveying my opinion. "And I really don't see why he has to—"

My phone trilled an interruption; anxiety pierced me as I dug the thing from the bottom of my bag.

"Hello?" I said into it. A familiar voice came from the device.

"Jake?" It was Ellie's voice, but garbled. "Jake, she's gone."

"What?" I pressed the phone to my ear. Reception wasn't great on this stretch of Route 1. "Who is, what do you—?"

We passed the fish wholesaler's Quonset barn near the old Shore Road intersection and the connection cleared up.

"Miss Blaine. Jake, she's dead."

I heard Ellie suppress a sob for her beloved old

teacher, and at the news I felt like letting loose a few tears, too.

Of frustration, that is. We'd been waiting for Miss Blaine to wake up and tell us who'd attacked her. Only now . . .

"Oh, Jake," said Ellie sorrowfully. "She took a turn for the worse this evening, Bob Arnold said, and about ten minutes ago—" . . . Now we were on our own. "Also, the toxicology report on Toby Moran just came back," Ellie went on.

She summarized what was in it: just as I'd thought.

I heard her suck in a shaky breath. "Bob knows already because the homicide team called to tell him to go tape off Andy's locker at the Coast Guard station, and Sharon's place, too, so they can come back and search them for—"

Yeah. "Cyanide," I told Wade when Ellie and I had hung up. "A lot of it."

And that settled that, at least. Wade turned off Route 1 onto a curving lane leading down to the Pennamaquan River. In the darkness I felt rather than saw the massive bulk of the big stone dam, whose flow in the old days had powered sawmills, a grist mill, shingle mills, and a lathe.

All gone, now. Water tumbled down the dam's venerable old sluice channel with a sound like heavy rain, while Wade looked thoughtful. Finally, "So, can I ask you a question?"

244

"Go for it," I said as we rolled down a long hill between old farmsteads, their outbuildings dark except for the warming lamps in the henhouses.

A mother fox led a bunch of kits into the road and he slowed.

The babies were cute, sweetly tumbling and roughhousing. The mother wasn't, all ratty red fur and feral expression. When they'd crossed: "What would be the point of putting that stinky bug killer in the milkshake at all?" he asked.

"Well, because . . ." I explained about covering up the cyanide method for long enough to silence Miss Blaine.

"I see," said Wade, and we drove along in comfortable silence for a while, until we reached the end of the side road and Wade pulled the truck back onto deserted Route 1 again, aimed toward Eastport. I sat there in the darkened cab with him, leaning against his shoulder, listening to the whine of the tires on the pavement . . . and then I had it, the answer to the question I *hadn't* been asking.

"The method," I said. "That's what I haven't been able to make sense of. I'd been puzzling over it without realizing it. But now . . .

"Wade, what if the cyanide wasn't in the milkshake at all? What if it wasn't only the smelly bug killer that covered the method, but the whole milkshake that covered it?"

He glanced at me. "To cover some other way of

. . . like, what, put the cyanide in a squirt gun or something?"

It wasn't specifically what I'd been thinking, but . . .

"Yeah, something like that. Probably we could come up with a lot of ways to—"

I stopped, hearing again the heartbreak in Ellie's voice and feeling a burst of anger rising in me at the memory. She didn't deserve this, and neither had Miss Blaine.

None of us did. "Yeah," I said again as we sailed across the dark causeway toward the lights of Eastport.

"A lot of ways," I repeated, thinking about Miss Blaine's cottage by the lake and her retirement in it: peaceful and well-earned.

Until someone ended it for her, selfishly and savagely.

"And you know what?" I went on, feeling those martinis fall away suddenly. "I'm going to figure out what method it was, and whoever used it, I'm going to deliver them to the cops on a platter."

Because revenge may be a dish best served cold for some people.

But in this case, I wanted mine hot and sweet.

Seven

The next morning, Ellie and I met at daybreak on the fish pier, on Water Street in downtown Eastport.

"Oh, I can't believe this," she said miserably as the gray dawn grew pink-tinged, then blazed up fiery red.

On the bay, the dark shapes of fishing boats already well into their day's work showed as silhouettes, then took on detail: men's shapes, stacked traps, the sharp, thin lines of chains and winches.

"Miss Blaine would be encouraging us now, though, wouldn't she?" I said. "To go on, I mean, not get bogged down in . . ."

"She certainly would." Ellie turned to me. "And the two different poisons aren't even the whole problem, are they?"

"Nope." We sat on the pier's end, looking out over the waves. "It's *all* of it that we need to reconsider," I said.

She'd brought milky coffee and fresh croissants: plain ones, warm and generously buttered. Legs dangling, we began eating our breakfast.

"How's everyone at home?" she asked.

I shrugged. "Bella's upset, my dad's dug his

heels in, the baby's fussy, and Sam's got a new brainstorm."

I told her about the yard-care business, how I thought it was risky for him to go out on his own with it. "And if he buys any more junky lawn-care machinery, we'll have to build a shed for it all."

I finished my croissant. "So things are a little hectic." Which was putting it mildly, but she didn't need to hear that.

"Listen, those two guys who showed up at Miss Blaine's cottage," I said instead.

Gulls swooped in for the croissant crumbs and rose with them, flapping and screaming. Ellie dropped our napkins into the bag she'd brought the pastries in and crumpled it.

"I mean, if they *weren't* just checking to make sure *we* weren't up to something bad, what would *they* be doing at Miss Blaine's place?"

"I don't know. But even if we did find out . . ."

I'd had plenty of time to think about this because the baby had cried every half hour the night before.

"There are still so *many* questions," she finished.

In the brightening dawn I saw the tear slipping down her cheek, and it fueled my resolve.

"Look," I said, dropping an arm around her shoulders. "We could have one more crack at all this."

She swallowed hard. "I don't know. . . ."

"We could just try ruling those two guys out of any involvement," I went on. "It might not do any good. But I'm stumped, otherwise, and it might be our only chance to clear Andy Devine."

I took a breath. "And Sharon. And get justice for Miss Blaine's murder, too," I added.

"Well," Ellie said slowly, brightening as she began to catch my drift, "it is pretty early still."

That was more like it. We got up, as out on the water a barge glided by, loaded with bales of fish food and headed for the salmon farms in Sipp Bay.

"Yes, it is early," I agreed. "So if Lee's going to be okay—"

"George came home last night," Ellie said, answering my question. "He'll be up to get her off to school and so on, he loves to do it."

Because, of course, as things stood now he rarely got the chance. "We could go out there once more," she went on, "and . . ."

We had four hours still before The Chocolate Moose had to be opened. Ellie turned tentatively to me.

". . . to Miss Blaine's cottage again, maybe, but also to the one those guys came from?"

Pleased at the way her mood was recovering, I watched the idea of further snooping take hold in her. "Yep, we surely could," I agreed.

"They might not even *be* there," she speculated. "Then it'll be easy."

Which was what I was hoping for. Even though they'd been there during the day, the nights were still chilly this time of the year. They might've been out fishing, then gone home to hot dinners, flat-screen TVs, and their own warm beds.

Meanwhile, if we sat around doing nothing there'd be no wedding, no more Chocolate Moose—and no more Ellie here in Eastport, either.

"George is already looking at rental houses in Bangor," she said, reading my thought. "So . . . yes," she finished determinedly, "let's go."

We tossed the empty croissant bag in the trash can at the end of the fish pier, and moments later we were in my car: out over the causeway, across Route 1, and onto the Lake Road, still murky with night mist that drifted between the trees like pale ghosts.

On Miss Blaine's lane, the first real sunlight began sparkling in the cobwebs between the tree trunks. The air was clear and still very cold out here by the lake.

At the house all was quiet, and although the phone didn't work here, we were going over *there,* weren't we? So I muted my phone in case it betrayed us at some inopportune moment, and Ellie did the same with hers.

Across the water, the guys' little camp was

equally still, the lake as smooth as glass. "Let's have another quick look around here first," I said.

There'd been two kayaks by the dock, I recalled. "That way we can scout out their territory from a distance, and if they are there we can pretend we're just out for an early paddle."

The cottage doors were still locked, of course. But this time I knew where to place the ladder. Inside, the air still carried a whiff of wood smoke, and the clock on the kitchen shelf ticked hollowly.

Ellie took the downstairs this time, and I went up. The pine-paneled bathroom was tiny but functional and clean; I felt a little pang of envy at the neatly folded towel, the spotless wash basin without even a drop of water marring it.

Bella rode herd on the bathrooms at my house, but even she couldn't stay ahead of six adults and an infant for very long. I went on poking around, feeling a pang of guilt at invading the dead woman's privacy: a guest room, a spare room . . . but nothing interesting in them.

"Jake!" Ellie called, and I hurried down to follow her excited gesture out the window facing the lake.

"They're over there," she said, "they've got a fire going. You can see the smoke from their chimney."

A wisp of smoke twirled up lazily. Then two

men appeared, and moments later a small boat moved away from the dock.

"They're going out fishing," Ellie said, pleased.

Perfect, I thought. We wouldn't need much time. My only worry was, what if they came back while we were there?

She read my thought. "We could go back out to the road and try calling Bob Arnold. Ask him to—"

"What," I interrupted, still watching the small boat puttering on the calm water, "ask him to perform an impromptu and probably illegal dwelling search, based on our cockamamie suspicions?"

It wasn't the way I thought of it, but he would. "I don't think so," I went on. "Besides, just because Andy's phone worked out on the road doesn't mean ours will. And, anyway, you already know what we need to do."

At my words I watched her resolve return. "You're right. Let's do this thing."

Two blue life jackets hung by the door; grabbing them, she ushered me out ahead of her.

"But we'd better get a move on," she added as we trotted down the dock path together, "before they catch a fish and decide to come back to clean it."

In theory, it is perfectly possible to get into a kayak without soaking more than your feet.

Kayak-entering has never been a talent of mine, however. It goes one way, I go the other, and before you know it the spot I was aiming for with my rear has been cleverly replaced with lake water.

Cold lake water; so much for dry pants. "Yeesh," I grated out, repositioning myself, whereupon the floating kayak tipped crazily once more. It didn't capsize, however, since from the kayak's point of view why even bother at that point, right?

Or so I thought while, reveling in the charming sensation of wet clothing clinging cozily to my backside, I settled at last into the kayak's cockpit and grabbed the paddle off the dock.

By now the guys in the boat were halfway across the small lake, idling along with a mutter of outboard engine that barely broke the pristine silence.

"This way," said Ellie, paddling her own kayak between me and the lake's thickly treed shoreline.

"If we stick to the shallows they're less likely to see us," she advised.

Luckily, the kayaks were camouflage green, not highway orange or, God forbid, pink. In the cool, fresh-smelling mists of an early summer morning in Maine, we eased among the lily pads and the marsh reeds.

"Hey," I heard one of the guys cry out, and

froze; had they spotted us? But it was only that one of them had indeed caught a fish and was leaning over to net it.

Their boat didn't turn back, though; I let my breath out.

Ellie paddled beside me, her cheeks pink and her eyes intent. "I'm glad we came," she said, her momentary hesitation forgotten.

"I am, too." A green frog eyed us unblinkingly, then sprang splay-legged from his rock and swam. A hawk circled overhead.

"The shoreline by their own cottage is the one they're most familiar with," she said. "The look of it, I mean, from a distance."

So we should be most careful there, she meant. We slid forward silently some more, until a shallow, rocky place stopped us.

"Drat," I uttered quietly, pushing with my paddle.

But I was stuck. The kayak's narrow nose had poked forward hard into a crevice between two boulders. And now it wouldn't come out.

"Push," Ellie whispered urgently, maneuvering herself around to the other side of the obstruction.

I was already pushing with the paddle's blade, and when that didn't work I rolled out of the damned kayak and yanked on it, bracing my bare feet on another big rock.

Which turned out to be slimy. No warning,

just splash, feet up and head down like I was going off a diving raft backward, only with less pleasure and a lot more swear words.

Gosh, that water was cold. I came up spluttering. Ellie hovered above me with her eyes wide, her index finger pressed to her lips.

"Ssh. Jake, they heard that."

She waved out across the water. A thickish stand of last year's cattails shielded us, their spiky chocolate-brown heads unravelling to wads of soggy-looking wooly stuff.

But the sound of an outboard was getting louder. Voices, too: not alarmed, but they were interested and they were coming this way, now.

"Ellie, what're we going to—"

Do, I was about to finish, and then it happened.

"Bow-whonnnk!" The sound nearly startled me out of the water, as yet another frog, this one an enormous green bullfrog with big, googly eyes, leapt muscularly from its hiding place among the cattails right out into the lake, and landed with a huge splash.

The boat's engine sound revved, then faded. "They're going away," said Ellie in a whisper. "They're . . . yes!"

I poked my head up, brushing a mess of wet hair back off my face. In the distance across the water the little boat was indeed heading for the other end of the lake.

As I watched, it swerved around a small island,

then passed a low, barren peninsula with a single pine tree jutting up from the tip of it . . . and then the little boat was gone.

"Phew," breathed Ellie.

Or words to that effect. I, however, was still wet and cold, and by the feel of it something hungry was nibbling one of my toes. Also, I'd lost my kayak paddle, which was probably lucky; if I'd had it I'd have gone after the nibbler with it and likely amputated my foot.

So instead I just grabbed my pant leg, yanked my foot up, and removed the drowned piece of tree branch stuck to the bottom of it.

No nibbler. Still seated in her kayak, Ellie observed my antics, very carefully not laughing.

"Oh, Jake," she managed. Well, sort of not laughing. I grimaced at the merriment in her eyes.

"Yeah, yeah," I groused, maneuvering myself back into the kayak with all the grace of a bunch of drenched cats being herded into a burlap sack.

A *wet* burlap sack, and have I mentioned how much I enjoy having soaked clothing clinging to me? Clammy, skin-crawlingly . . .

Oh, never mind, it was repulsive, was what it was; nevertheless, we made it at last to the cottage's dock area, got out, and shoved the kayaks in among the pilings under the dock, out of sight.

Two more kayaks lay pulled up onto the beach.

"All right, now," said Ellie, peering up at the cottage's empty windows.

Or at least we hoped they were empty. Glancing nervously back over my shoulder in case the fishermen decided they needed more bait, I followed Ellie up to the house.

Although house might be too fancy a word for it. Unlike Miss Blaine's pretty lakeside home, this was more at the hunting-camp end of the spectrum: in the rock-encircled fire pit on the beach, someone had been burning milk cartons and Little Debbie cake boxes.

Inside—they'd left the door unlocked—the smell was of burnt bacon, damp boots, and beer cans. A couple of sleeping bags hung over a clothesline strung near the woodstove.

On the wooden card table near the stove lay a deck of cards, an empty bottle of Allen's, and a loaded .38 revolver with the safety off, a situation I recognized from observing Wade's gun-repair work.

Junky little .22 pistols aren't his style, but this gun was. "Huh," I said, plucking up the weapon and disarming it, replacing it on the table, and dropping the bullets into my pocket.

At Ellie's look, I shrugged. "They could come back, you know."

"Right." Her expression was businesslike. "Let's just do what we came for and get out of here, and we won't have to worry about that."

"Agreed." I glanced once more out the window at the lake; no motorboats. Then I turned to the task at hand: finding . . .

"Ellie? Any ideas about *what* we're looking for?"

She looked up from where she was already rummaging through an old canvas trunk. Inside were some fishing lures, a boat cushion, boxes of stick matches, and a dog's well-chewed Nylabone.

"I don't know. Just . . . something. Right? Something that might tell us something new or aim us in some new direction."

Wherever that might be. I hoped it was warm, though, because I was still wet and cold, and beginning to shiver.

Luckily the woodstove still had some fire burning in it; grasping the pot holder tied to the stove's doorhandle, I opened the firebox to get closer to the warmth, then found a last slim stick of kindling in the firewood basket and stuck it in there, too.

Meanwhile, Ellie began opening and closing drawers and cabinets in the cabin's open kitchen area. "Nothing so far," she reported.

The cabin was plainly equipped, and not decorated at all: two pans, a skillet, and a percolator were the cooking implements, while the plates, cups, and implements were all plastic or paper.

On the counter between the kitchen area and

the rest of the room lay a letter with some official-looking paperwork clipped to it. The letter was about an upcoming court hearing related to a divorce, to decide the custody arrangements for two minor children.

The ones we'd seen swimming here, maybe, I thought. "Nothing here, either," called Ellie from the closet under the stairs.

I put the letter down, wondering if I dared put another stick of wood in the stove. A little more heat and I thought I might be able to get warm, if not particularly dry. But there was no kindling left, and a big log would be a giveaway that someone had been here.

"Darn," Ellie said, rummaging through the jumbled canned goods on a shelf over the sink's hand pump.

"Maybe there really is nothing here. Maybe we're wrong and those guys really were just checking us out."

"Could be." I rummaged the wood basket again, hoping for just one slender branch that might burn up in a few minutes.

That's how much longer I figured we might still be here, snooping around. But what Ellie said next as she glanced out the window again changed my opinion, fast.

"Uh-oh. Jake, we'd better—"

Not what I wanted to hear. "They're coming back?"

But, of course they were, what else could it be? She hurried back to the kitchen area and began slamming drawers and cabinets shut.

"Look around, try to put back anything we've moved."

Starting with all the firewood I'd pulled out of the basket and set alongside it while I was searching for a small piece . . . I stuck the first chunk of wood into the basket again, then looked down to see where to position the next.

I wanted it to look as if no one had been rummaging in it. But what I saw then at the basket's bottom made me dump the whole thing out onto the floor.

"Ellie?" I whispered. A few sheets of old newspaper were there amidst the splinters and bits of bark. For fire-starting: twist up some newspaper, build a teepee from lengths of kindling positioned over the newspaper spills you've made, touch a match to it all, and voilà!

Or *viola,* as Sam always pronounced it. But newspapers weren't all I'd found, and now I could hear the engine on the guys' fishing boat, getting closer.

"Ellie? What's *this* doing here?" I said, holding up a plastic hypodermic syringe with a needle on it. A *capped* needle, I was glad to see, not one just lying uncovered there, waiting to stick me.

But still. A shiver that had nothing to do with the lake water went through me. "Ellie?"

She was staring. "Bring it. But come on, we've got to go *now*."

Voices drifted up from where the guys were already tying up their boat. Crossing the room in a few strides, she seized my arm and kept going, dragging me to the cottage's rear door.

It opened onto a sun-dappled clearing. A thick carpet of pine needles from the trees around the cottage made our escape soundless. But we still had to get back down to the kayaks, where we'd hidden them under the dock; that or fight our way through the underbrush, two or three miles around the shore back to Miss Blaine's place.

Cutting across the lake had been the short way to get here, like going across the middle of a circle instead of around the outside. And with the sun now high in the sky, the mosquitoes were out.

Also blackflies, tiny caraway-seed-sized monsters whose painful bite produced red, itchy welts, a headache and swollen glands, and a fever in people who were badly allergic to them.

As I was, and don't even get me started on deerflies, ounce for ounce the world's most ferocious flesh-eaters. At this hour of the morning the lakeside forest was like a diner for biting insects, and I was the main course.

"Come on," breathed Ellie, peering anxiously through the trees, and by then I needed little urging; swatting, slapping, and trying not to inhale tiny airborne bodies with stingers, I hunkered beside her.

The guys mounted the deck; then the porch door slammed. Inside, footsteps stomped the floor.

"Now," said Ellie, and we flew downhill to the water's edge. Cringing, I strode behind her into the chilly water and ducked under the dock to hide.

The slimy green wooden dock pilings glistened around me; minnows, disturbed by our plunge into their habitat, darted away flashing as Ellie grabbed a kayak and shoved it at me, and swung smoothly into her own while I hesitated.

"Lean back onto it, drop your butt in, swing your legs up," she recited just as the guys came running back out of their cottage again.

That's when I realized that I'd left the woodstove door ajar. And, of course, they'd noticed; why wouldn't they? We may as well have left a note: *Hi, we invaded your house!*

Thinking this, I leaned back until my body was crosswise over the kayak, dropped my backside firmly into the seat, and swung my legs up over the bow. My feet dropped down into the cockpit, and I was in.

"Wow," I said to Ellie, stupidly pleased.

But she was already gone, pushing from between the pilings and out from under the dock and into a thicket of reeds. Then, just as I was about to follow, a pair of boots strode out onto the dock and stopped right over my head.

Boots with feet in them, that is, and at the same time I noticed that my paddle wasn't down here under the dock with me. Instead it was out there on the water's surface, floating in plain sight.

But for the moment, whoever was up there had his back to it; I could tell from the way the boots were pointing. I stretched my hand out for the paddle, fingers straining.

He turned. I yanked my hand down, catching the skin inside my arm hard and painfully against one of the dock pilings. Instantly blood streamed down my arm; also, there was a splinter jutting from it.

Grimacing, I gave the splinter an experimental tug and it slid easily out. This might not have been my best move, however, since once the splinter was gone the stream of blood from the newly unobstructed puncture wound became a steady spurt-spurt.

Darn, I thought with a flicker of panic. Meanwhile, Ellie was nowhere to be seen and I didn't dare call out to her.

And I still didn't have the paddle. Holding my breath, I braced myself with my hands against two of the cold, wet, slimy dock pilings, trying not to think about the kinds of things that probably lived down there in the water around them.

Like leeches, for instance, and just then I suddenly zigged when I should've zagged; the kayak capsized, tumbling me out.

Swiftly and as if summoned by my worst imaginings, through the water a squadron of inky-black, thumb-sized shadows began separating themselves from the pilings they'd been clinging to, then propelling themselves toward me.

The guy on the dock was walking back up toward the cottage now. The paddle was nowhere in sight, while the kayak itself had somehow gotten shoved up underneath the dock again. To reach it I would have to wade back there, too, through a swarm of leeches.

"Gah," I breathed, pushing myself cringingly along with my toes. At least it wasn't mucky, but this seemed small comfort. A whimper escaped me as I spotted something dark clinging to my left leg: like a streak of mud, but it was *long,* and it was *moving.*

And it was attached. Squeaking with disgust, I grabbed the end of it wincingly between my thumb and forefinger, but instead of coming off it merely . . . *lengthened.*

Trying not to imagine the thing's round, toothy mouth fastened into my flesh—trying, but not succeeding—I gave up on the horrid creature, hustling instead through waist-deep water to the kayak.

Grabbing it, I gave it a shove and it slipped

away from me, and popped out from under the dock. *Oh, great . . .*

If those guys were watching, I was completely screwed. "Psst!" Ellie gestured frantically to me from the reed clump she'd been crouched in. "The kayak! Push it over here out of sight, quick!"

So I did, and then I did something else, too, something I hope I never have to do again.

I *put my face* down into that leech-infested lake and I *swam underwater* to where Ellie and my kayak waited, and never mind the fact that those bloodsucking little monsters might slither into my ears.

Or *up my nose . . .*

"Eeyaghh," I said when I came up, or something like it.

The feeling of leeches attaching themselves to me was hideous; by the time I hauled myself into the kayak again it was a wonder my whole skin wasn't just shuddering itself right off my body.

"Pick them off me," I whispered, not wanting to look.

Ellie was busy doing something to the front end of my kayak. "Please," I said, feeling that at any moment a maniacal shriek might come out of my mouth. "Please, they're all over me."

"What?" My eyes were squinched shut, but her voice came nearer. "Jake, what in the world are you even talking about? There's nothing all over your . . ."

Then she stopped, and I could feel her staring. "Oh, my—"

I opened my eyes. The spot on my leg where the leech had been attached was a small, inflamed circle, courtesy of the creature's raspy teeth; apparently I had dislodged it, after all.

And there were no other leeches anywhere else. My arm, though . . .

Ellie looked scared. "Oh, Jake, we've got to do something about this."

The arm where the dock splinter had been stuck streamed with red. The hole, small and purple, pumped fluid steadily, each crimson *bloop!* looking to be about a tablespoonful.

And being a morbid little twit, I happened to know that there are approximately ten pints— or only about 320 of those tablespoonsful—of blood in a person my size.

Luckily, Ellie was already stripping one of the straps out of her life jacket and wrapping it around my forearm. Scanning around, she snatched a floating stick up out of the water and twisted it through the strap.

"There," she said. Turning the stick, she tightened the strap on my arm until the blood spurting from the hole lessened and stopped.

"Hold that," she instructed me. I was too scared to talk, still trying to wrap my head around the fact that I was injured at all.

Gradually, though, it dawned on me that this

thing wouldn't heal by itself. From the way the wound bled, it was obvious that I'd poked a hole in an artery.

Not a big artery, but still. "Jake, you're going to be fine," she said. "You just sit there and don't lean over at all, okay?"

Oh, you betcha. By now if I leaned over, I might fall over.

"And I'm going to get us home," she went on, looping the line on the front of my kayak through a cleat on the rear of her own. Then she paddled, sticking close to the shore but otherwise moving right along.

And for a wonder, no one spotted us doing it. We'd been lucky not to get caught and it just didn't occur to the guys, I guessed, that their home invaders had been water-borne.

Even the paddle I'd left behind might've come from one of their own kayaks. So five minutes later we were at Miss Blaine's dock, and on our way to the hospital not long after that.

And whether it was because I was in shock or just anxious in the extreme by then, time seemed to pass swiftly; moments after I walked into the emergency room I was waking up from IV anesthesia.

"Ptthhh," I said, reaching for the glass of water someone held out. But the arm wouldn't work right, and when I looked down I saw the white gauze wrapping my arm from elbow to wrist.

"So much for keeping all this just between us," I joked to Ellie, letting my arm fall back down onto the bed. The anesthesia I'd had was wearing off swiftly and I already felt clearheaded again.

Unfortunately, its painkilling properties were fading fast, too, and from what the wound felt like now I gathered they'd had to dig around in there quite a bit.

Like with a steam shovel, maybe. "Ouch," I said calmly. Then: "Ellie, do you know where my clothes are?" I kept my voice mild. Right now, I was in a hospital gown and socks. "I left some things in them," I enunciated meaningfully.

Like, for instance, the hypodermic syringe that I'd swiped from the guys' cottage. Luckily, Ellie caught right on.

"Anything that was there, I've already taken," she said. "Don't trouble yourself about that."

You've got worse things to worry about, her tone implied, and I couldn't disagree. My coming home from the hospital with a ripped-to-bits forearm, for example, would interest Wade very considerably, and Bella hadn't heard from either of us for hours; she'd be amused, too.

At last when my vital signs suggested I could be discharged, the nurse took my IV out and I started pulling clothes on again, stopping when

I got to the part about my wrapped arm fitting through a sleeve.

Luckily, the bandage kit on the bedside table contained scissors. Ellie slit the shirt sleeve, then fastened it again with adhesive tape from the same kit. Finally, with instructions and prescriptions, I was let go, and from the car I did call Bella, to give her a much-edited version of what had occurred.

"But I'm fine now," I added when I'd finished, figuring that the survival portion of the program was the angle that I should pursue.

"Oh," Bella replied distractedly, not sounding as if she'd really heard me, or if she had, she wasn't impressed.

"Good," she added, and then to someone else there with her, "No! Don't do that! No, I said I'll take care of it when—"

Sitting in the driver's seat of my car, Ellie heard the sounds coming out of my phone and looked quizzically at me.

"It sounds like something's wrong," I said, "but I can't—"

Then Sam came on. "Mom?" He sounded bad. "Mom, they took him."

A shot of fear went through me. "Who, Sam? What's going on?"

"Mom, we can't find Ephraim. He was here asleep in his playpen, only alone for a couple of minutes. But when I came back just now . . ."

His voice broke. Ellie started the car and pulled hurriedly out of the hospital's parking lot.

"When I came back to the kitchen the back door was open and the baby was gone," he said, then sucked in a ragged breath.

"Mom, I think someone must've taken him!"

Eight

All the way home, I kept beating myself over the head with it. "If I hadn't just taken off without telling anyone, and if I hadn't turned off my phone . . ."

"What?" Ellie countered, speeding us skillfully up, down, and around the hilly curves on Route 1.

"You think even if the phone worked, some kidnapper was going to call you, give you a fast heads-up on what was about to get done?"

We slowed for the turns in Red Beach, then shot up out of the shoreline hamlet and along the straightaway to Mill Cove.

"So you could rush right home and prevent it?" Ellie went on.

At low tide, on the wide, sandy beach, small black-and-white birds skittered between tide pools.

"No." We sped past the Red Sleigh gift shop, and after that the convenience store with the gas pumps out front.

"But I should've been there," I repeated stubbornly. "Besides, you know darned well this is probably because of us."

She glanced at me, frowning. But I noticed she didn't deny it. We drove between stands of white pine, balsam fir, and the remnants of ancient apple orchards, their gnarled branches exuberantly in bloom.

"Okay, though, so what if you're right?" she said eventually. "Someone took Ephraim to do what, divert our attention?"

The painkillers I'd gotten at the hospital had worn off all the way by now; my arm felt like somebody was simultaneously blowtorching it and chopping it to bits. Through gritted teeth I replied, "Something like that." We sped past the airport, then on into town between the bank building and the hair salon.

"If the guys at the lake figured out what happened in their cabin," I went on, "maybe they called someone. Whoever they're in on this with. Whatever *this* is," I added miserably.

"I guess it could be possible," Ellie gave in reluctantly. "If they also figured out somehow that we were the intruders. And who we are, even. Our names and so on."

She swung us onto Key Street. "But it's a lot to accept. How would they know who we are? And they'd have to have done it fast."

We pulled up in front of my house. Bob Arnold's squad car was in the driveway, and when we crossed to the front porch we found my daughter-in-law, Mika, sitting on the front steps with her face in her hands, her glossy black hair shielding her sobs like a curtain.

In the doorway, Bob stood waiting for us. "If it's true, though, and someone's got the baby on account of it," I went on quietly.

"Then I guess we can probably figure out what they want for him in return," Ellie finished for me.

"Yeah, for us to quit snooping and shut up," I said, mounting the steps. "I hope that's all they want, anyway."

Oh, this was all my fault. . . . A wave of pain rolled through my arm and up my neck, so intense that I stopped, gripping the porch railing.

"Ellie, I've got to take something for this." With my good hand I dug in my pants pocket for the small orange bottles we'd gotten at the hospital. But shoved down there with them I also found something else.

"What is that?" said Ellie, just as Bob Arnold turned from the door, looking as if steam was about to start boiling from his ears.

Meanwhile, Mika just went on weeping, and I wasn't sure which hurt worse: my arm with the fire exploding in it or seeing her so wretched.

"This," I said, pulling from my pocket the syringe and needle I'd taken from the guys' cottage.

Ellie had given it back to me. "I'll bet this is what they want."

"Because it's proof of something?" Ellie

wondered aloud. "But of what? And even if all they want is to get it back, how would we—"

Get it to them, I knew she'd been about to say, but just then I looked past her, across the street.

In the big front yard there, another old apple tree shed creamy pink petals onto the green grass. But something else was on the soft grass, too, amid the apple blossoms. . . .

Someone, rather. "We won't have to," I said as across the street, the small shape on the lawn rolled over and kicked its feet happily.

"All we've had is a warning," I added, rushing toward the figure.

By now Bob Arnold had seen it, too, and was hustling down off the porch. "All units," he began into his radio.

I raced across the street. The house belonged to the family of the young teenaged girl who'd been babysitting for Mika. In the yard a fenced area made of picket sections enclosed a square of the lawn.

Little Ephraim lay inside the fence, on a blanket with pink and blue moons and stars embroidered on it. "Gah!" he greeted me.

Bob followed me. ". . . has been located," he was saying into the radio, and when he was done: "That arm," he said furiously when he reached me, "had better be broken. I mean, you'd better have a no-kidding compound fracture there, Jake, or—"

On the carpet of fallen blossoms beneath it, the baby looked puzzled to be alone in the great outdoors but otherwise unharmed.

"Glrp!" he said brightly when I picked him up. Gazing around, he spotted Bob Arnold and grinned toothlessly, waving a tiny fist.

"Glrp, yourself," Bob retorted as his radio sputtered. "Yeah," he pronounced into it, "the searchers can stand down."

As he spoke, his index finger moved as if drawn toward the baby's grasping hand, then was seized by it.

"Yeah, he's fine," Bob said into his radio.

By then Mika had seen us and come scrambling across the street at us. She took the baby from my arms and cradled him, sobbing.

"What happened?" she managed through her tears. "How did he get there, who—"

Bob Arnold was pounding on the door of the babysitter's house now, but no one answered and it seemed clear that no one was at home. I put my good arm around Mika and guided her back across the street to our place, where Sam and Bella had come out, too, with my dad and Wade hurrying behind them onto the porch.

Ellie's daughter was there as well, her dark hair pulled back into an elastic and an apron tied on over her school clothes.

"I called her from the ER while you were still out cold," Ellie explained as we all went inside, "and told her to come here if George had to leave before I got back."

Which made sense; George rarely got more than one night at home, and the little girl was familiar with Bella, and with my kitchen. Now while Mika took the baby upstairs, the others began peppering Ellie and me with questions.

But I had no good answers. It was all I could do, even with my arm now pulsating with anguish, not to rush out and find whoever had dared even to *touch* my infant grandson.

But those feelings would have to wait, along with the guilt that I still felt like a dagger in my heart. Because this was my fault, I was certain.

Going out to the lake at all, then across it to a place we had absolutely no business being, and taking the syringe and needle . . .

All my idea, I berated myself, every foolish bit of it. And now, of course, here was my comeuppance, wasn't it, since, after all, what in the world else could have provoked an awful incident like this?

"Any word from Sharon or Andy?" I asked Bob Arnold before he could start in on me. I'd explained by then the basic details of what had happened to my arm, and he'd calmed down a little.

"Murder cops've got 'em in separate rooms at City Hall," he said. "They both turned down having an attorney. Nice kids, but neither one of them's exactly a Rhodes scholar," he added in exasperation.

The rest of my family were in other parts of the house. Ellie shot me a look that said *talk to you later,* then took off as well, to get Lee back to their place in time to do her homework before supper.

Grabbing the chance to speak with him in private, I told Bob the truth about where we'd been and what we'd been doing, then went on.

"So I'm responsible for this, Bob. Whoever feels threatened by what Ellie and I have been doing, this was a message from them."

"Oh, yeah?" He eyed me skeptically. "Well, I'm not so sure about that. But if it is true, it just makes it plain that whatever you've been doing, you need to stop doing it."

Like that wasn't obvious, right? "Oh, I know. Believe me, I . . ."

"I'm responsible, too, though," he added. "I should've laid down the law in the first place, that you two should—"

"Right," I agreed humbly. "Mind our own business."

Because for one thing it was all over, our chance of clearing Andy Devine or his fiancé, Sharon Sweetwater.

And once I'd admitted this and promised to keep my nose out of Toby Moran's murder from now on, Bob departed the house, too. His look on his way out wasn't comforting; there was, he obviously knew, more going on than we'd told him even now.

Then when everyone else was gone: "Here." My dad's voice startled me. I looked up; he held out a whiskey glass.

With whiskey in it. "Down the hatch," he commanded.

Warmth spread through my chest, loosening up a bunch of tears that had been stuck there. Struggling against them, I bit my lip hard enough to draw blood.

He put his arm around me comfortingly. "Hey. Everything's okay. The baby's back."

He poured me another shot. This time I only sipped at it, still thinking I might get a chance at another one of those pain pills.

"No harm," said my dad, "no foul."

But that was the thing I was least sure of right now, wasn't it? The *no harm* part . . . And even without knowing any details he saw that much, his bushy eyebrows rising in comprehension.

"Feeling rotten, huh?" he asked sympathetically.

In his younger days, if you got on my dad's bad side he'd build a small explosive device and set it to go off in one of your trash bins. Or if you were very unpleasant (and he was going to be around to make absolutely sure that nobody got hurt), he'd put it under your porch.

And there were other things; bigger ones. I'm

not excusing any of it, you understand; I'm just saying that it was a different time, back in the radical 60s.

Also, he'd paid for it all, legally and in other ways. Now as he poured a drink for himself and pulled a chair out, waving me into it, his gaze fell on my bandaged arm once more and I saw his mind working on the idea of finding out who'd hurt me.

"It's okay, Dad," I told him, "I did this to myself."

"Oh, you did, hey?" he replied skeptically. He sat across from me at the kitchen table, clasping his gnarled hands on it.

Someone turned the heat up on the blowtorch they were holding to my arm. I pulled the pills out, shook a tablet from the bottle, and swallowed it while he watched calmly.

"Well, then, maybe you'd better tell your old dad all about it," he said, whereupon I finally did just burst into angry tears.

A couple of hours later, after another one of those damned pills and a good dinner, I felt better.

Wade had inquired kindly about my injury and had accepted my explanation; that I'd been retrieving one of Miss Blaine's kayaks and snagged my arm on the edge of the dock.

Hey, so it wasn't a *detailed* explanation; so sue me. Meanwhile, nobody blamed me for getting little Ephraim kidnapped; they couldn't, because they didn't know.

Only Bob Arnold and Ellie did. But no one had to blame me because I still felt bad enough about it all by myself.

And about something else, too; so bad, in fact, that by eleven o'clock that night with everybody else in bed and asleep, I slipped fully dressed downstairs carrying my shoes and a flashlight.

Past the dark living room and dining room with their massive old cast-iron radiators looming like strange zoo animals, I tiptoed like a cartoon burglar toward the back door. I had no excuse— or at least not one that I wanted to tell anyone about—for going out.

Still, I had to. So it was crucial that I not wake anyone. But as I passed the kitchen, where a night-light glowed over the old soapstone sink: "Going somewhere?"

My dad sat at the kitchen table, dressed in a dark sweatshirt and navy pants with a black knit watch cap that his stringy gray ponytail snaked out the back of.

He got up, pushing his chair in soundlessly; black high-tops on his feet, I noticed. Like the rest of his garb, they'd be less visible in the dark; he hadn't known what I might be planning, I supposed.

But he must have suspected I'd be going out, and wanted to be dressed for it.

"Hey," he said, crossing the room toward me. Not as limberly as he used to, maybe, but he looked plenty spry.

"Why'd the harbor seal cross the bay?" he asked, hoisting a dark cloth satchel over his shoulder.

I shrugged helplessly, glancing at the back door: *close, but no cigar*.

"Because he had a sense of porpoise," he answered himself with a dry chuckle.

It got a small smile out of me, as he'd always been able to even when I was little. "Now," he said, "let's get this show on the road."

"Okay," I gave in, not bothering to argue. I was glad that he was coming with me, suddenly.

"Oh, I thought I'd find you here," said a voice from the kitchen doorway.

I spun around to find Bella standing there, wrapped in a pink chenille robe and fuzzy slippers and looking dubious. But she didn't argue with my dad or with me, either, or ask any questions.

In fact, from the look passing between them now—he adored her, and she thought he walked on water when she wasn't so angry with him she could've spit nails—

Now it seemed as if maybe they'd been talking over a few things.

Bella's green eyes were narrow slits in the glow of the kitchen night-light, her henna-red hair frazzling out from beneath a hairnet.

"You just be careful, the two of you," was all she said. Then we got out of there, hurrying across the porch and down the steps to the dark driveway before she could change her mind.

"Just out of curiosity," said my dad from behind the wheel of my car, "how were you planning to drive?"

My arm now felt more like a dead log than a burning one, but I had let him take charge, anyway.

"I'd have figured something out."

I would have, too, but I was glad not to be required to. Through the car windows the chilly night smelled like cut grass and chamomile, and from somewhere nearby in one of the small, seasonal ponds that were common here on the island, a lot of spring peepers were yelling their heads off.

We backed out of the driveway. "Where to?" he asked with a little nod of mock courtliness in my direction.

I laughed despite myself, but then pain slammed my arm suddenly; I bit the inside of my cheek. If he knew how bad it was, we wouldn't be doing this.

But I had to do this. "The police station," I commanded, and in response he started down Key Street under a canopy of just-fledged maple leaves.

As we made the turn onto Water Street, past

Peavey Library, with its windows full of moon-light, and the Happy Crab restaurant, where a few last-call lingerers waited to be thrown out—

"Huh," he said quietly, glancing up into the rear-view mirror.

But the car behind us turned the other way, and moments later we were outside Bob Arnold's office.

"And you waited so long to tell me this because why, again?" Bob wanted to know when I'd finished with my story.

I'd called him from home before even bothering to get dressed and go downstairs, and when my dad and I arrived we'd found the police chief waiting in his squad car in the otherwise empty parking lot.

Moonlight lay on the water. The boat basin, now still and silent, gave off the smells of mud and seaweed, gasoline fumes, and cold brine tinctured with a little fresh boat paint.

"Once we had Ephraim back I just wanted everyone to settle down," I said. "If I'd had to describe in front of everyone how reckless I'd been . . ."

"Yeah, yeah, I get it," he said when I finished explaining. I'd put the needle and syringe into a plastic freezer bag; now I handed them to him.

The movement made me wince. "How's it

doing?" he inquired of my arm, meanwhile peering down at the bag.

The answer was *awful,* but he wouldn't have liked that, so I just changed the subject.

"They're doing a complete postmortem examination on Moran, are they? Blood work, what he'd eaten and drunk, the whole shebang?"

Not just quit when they found out what killed him, I meant; I didn't know the exact routine at a murder victim's autopsy.

Bob grimaced in reply. "Oh, yeah. Right down to the hair and fingernails, they'll be all over the actual physical evidence in case the defense throws a curveball they need to answer. Why?"

Then he got a better look inside the bag I'd given him, and his face creased unhappily. "What the heck is this?" he demanded.

So I told him, and I explained where we'd gotten the syringe and needle, as well. "But here's the thing, Bob," I said, and went on. "We'd been trying to figure out how somebody got Moran to drink that milkshake, when the awful poison smell should've stopped him."

"Yeah," Bob replied. "I wonder about it, too. So what, though? It doesn't matter how they got him to do it, only that they—oh."

He looked down at the needle and syringe again, and I could see him thinking about those poison cartridges from Miss Blaine's: one opened, the others still full of a killing mixture so potent, it would take only a few drops to finish a person off.

"Right," I said, watching enlightenment spread across his face. "What if he drank it because no bad taste *did* stop him, because there *wasn't* any poison in it? Not until afterward. And then—"

I waved at the injection apparatus, still in the bag in Bob's lap. "Sure," he said slowly to himself. "Why not?" And then to me: "You know, the guys who found him told me there was blood on his shirt. Just a smear, but—"

He let out a low whistle. "So if you're right, there ought to be poison in the needle track, wouldn't you figure? In the soft tissue, I mean, where the stab went in and out."

Which was a little more clinically detailed than I felt like getting, but I agreed.

"In which case," I added, "the milkshake itself and The Chocolate Moose cup it was put into, *and* the insecticide, were all merely window dressing, meant to turn our attention away from the real method."

I took a breath. "The real poison, drawn out from the cartridge at Miss Blaine's with a needle, and put into the victim the same way."

"So there'd be poison in Moran's stomach, all right," Bob mused, "but he'd never have had to taste the stuff to get it there, or even have it in his mouth at all."

"Correct. Somebody poisoned the milkshake

after Moran drank it." I floated the rest of my theory. "It was the needle part of it that they wanted to cover up."

The more I thought of it, the more he *couldn't* have drunk it; based on the whiff I'd had, it might not even be physically possible.

Bob nodded; he'd been thinking harder about all this than he'd let on, I was willing to bet. He just hadn't been in a position to do much about it, since it had already been made very clear to him that the state guys didn't want his help.

Him with his small-town police department, his ten-year-old cruisers, and his community college degree . . . He bore it all with his usual quiet dignity. But . . .

"You know what?" he said. "I bet you're right."

He shoved the bag with the needle and syringe in it over onto the squad car's passenger seat and put the car in gear.

"I think I'll put a call in to the medical examiner, myself," he said, sounding pleased.

The car crept forward. "I might be someone's idea of a throwback, too far out of the loop to know how modern police work gets done," he went on.

"But I know a few people, probably they're still willing to give me a couple of minutes," he finished.

But then he sobered again. "Baby all right, is he?"

"Ephraim's fine." I outlined again why I thought the baby's faked kidnapping—because clearly it was faked, we'd obviously been meant to find him right away—might've been meant as a warning. When I was done, Bob looked almost as troubled as I felt.

"Jake." Right hand on the steering wheel, left elbow out the window, Bob peered up at me.

"Two things. Like I said earlier, I know I didn't shut you guys down very hard at the start of all this. But now I'd appreciate it if you and Ellie would cut it out. It's time, okay?"

The snooping, he meant. "Things are getting dicey, we don't know yet what's going on, and I just don't want any of you getting hurt."

Of course he didn't. I understood. But: "Yeah, Bob. Okay, we'll do that," I assured him, carefully keeping a straight face.

Thinking, *Right. Sure we would.* Because I'd thought about things some more, too, and now my opinion was that, of course, we'd just lay back and let the whole unhappy business, including our own personal and professional futures, get handled by a bunch of people who hadn't been smart enough to keep Bob Arnold involved in the first place.

"What else?" I said. Through the darkness I could hear the radio in my car booming so loudly that the vehicle should've been rocking on its wheels; my dad liked Creedence.

At the sound of the lyrics having to do with moonlit things that were bound to take your life, another shiver went through me, one that had nothing to do with the chilly night.

"Sharon Sweetwater and Andy Devine," Bob answered me. "They both got taken into custody a little earlier this evening, after the homicide investigators from the state completed their questioning."

He sighed heavily. "So there's really no reason for you and Ellie to do more about them anyway. Because it's over, Jake; even if they do get exonerated eventually, there's not going to be a wedding."

"Whoa." I blinked, considering this. "Both of them? But that doesn't make sense, wouldn't it have to be one or the other?"

But then it hit me, why it did make sense. Bob nodded, seeing me getting it.

"The homicide cops have decided they're both guilty," he said. "That the two of them killed Toby Moran together."

When I got back to my car, my dad was staring across the street at something, squinting intently.

"What?" I asked, but he only shrugged as he pulled out of the parking lot and drove slowly past the fish pier.

All around us, late-night Eastport shimmered in moonlit silence. On the breakwater, the haloes around the dock lamps' sodium-yellow bulbs teemed with flying insects massed so thickly, they were visible from here onshore.

Other than us, they were the only things moving. Even the Rubber Ducky's neon sign was turned off, the darkness in the windows like a discouraging cherry on an already gloomy cake.

"Quiet," my dad observed.

He went on peering out the windshield as we drove slowly past the Duck, the pet supply store, a fabric shop, and, of course, The Chocolate Moose itself. But if he saw anything interesting, he didn't say so.

"Tomorrow morning, Ellie and I will get together and decide what to do about the shop," I said, although I guessed I probably knew.

If we weren't doing a wedding cake, plus all the other little goodies and mini-desserts an affair like this also included, there was no point pretending anymore that we'd be doing anything else.

Or that she'd be staying in Eastport, either; my heart thumped miserably at the thought, but there was no getting around it.

"It's too bad," my dad said sympathetically as we went by. "But listen, have the state cops even talked to you and Ellie yet?"

I shook my head, then gave him the news about Sharon and Andy. "So the investigators have been busy," I finished, "but don't worry, they'll get around to us. They have plenty of time."

"Hmm. I suppose so. But *when* they talk to you . . ."

"It'll change their minds about their suspects? Or they'll figure out that Moran wasn't a one-off and Miss Blaine's death was connected to this whole thing, too?"

I shrugged. "I do think they'll get it right sooner or later. Just not soon enough for us. The poison's not what they thought, Andy is still lying about something, and they can't very well just ignore Sharon's confession, so everything's all screwed up."

"And straightening it all out will take time," my dad agreed, glancing up at the rear-view mirror.

"Right. Which we don't have, at least as far as The Chocolate Moose is concerned." A sigh rushed out of me.

"And yeah, it's too bad, all right," I said. "All of it."

He turned left, up Washington Street past the big old granite-block post office building and Spinney's Garage, where the geraniums blooming in the office window glowed a radioactive-looking crimson in the glare of Spinney's yard lights.

"At least I've told Bob everything, now," I said. "So, you know, I've got that going for me."

Although . . . not *absolutely* everything,

actually. Later I wondered if I would ever forgive myself for that. But at the time, of course, I didn't know; I didn't even think it was important.

At High Street the yellow caution lamp over the intersection blinked steadily. "Anyway, now you know why I couldn't sleep."

We passed through the silent crosswalk. "I just couldn't stand Bob not knowing about that needle and syringe," I went on.

My dad drove in silence as we rounded the curve past the bank and the Mobil station. He didn't tell me where we were going, and I didn't care; I just knew I didn't want to go home yet.

Also, he didn't say anything stupid like, "It'll be all right," or "You'll get over it," two statements that I personally despise.

Or "cheer up," which is arguably the worst of all. "So now he knows all about them and where we got them," I said. "He's got the photos we found out at Moran's place, too," I added. The cobbled-together, supposedly racy pictures Moran had, meant to show Sharon Sweetwater in skimpy lingerie.

He turned from Route 190 onto Clark Street and back toward town, between towering fir trees growing close to the road in thickets. As I rode, I felt a tear leak down my cheek; after she left I'd see Ellie every week at first, probably, then every month.

Thinking this, I swiped furiously at my face

just as a motorcycle flew up over the oncoming hill straight at us, headlight glaring, and roared by in the opposite direction.

"That was him," said my dad at once. Craning his skinny neck, he watched the motorcycle's brake light flare at the intersection, then speed away on Route 190 out of town.

"Downtown, just now," my dad said. "I wasn't sure if it was someone in a doorway or not. There was a big, round thing hanging from his hand, and it made me think my eyes were deceiving me, somehow."

The bike had gone by way too fast for me to know for sure whether it was the same one Ellie and I had seen out at Miss Blaine's.

"Like he was holding a severed head or something," my dad said.

One thing was for sure, though, it wasn't Andy Devine on this one. Because according to Bob, Andy was in custody and so was Sharon, and now it occurred to me that maybe that was a good thing.

For now, anyway. "Motorcycle helmet?" I speculated. The big, round thing, I meant. My dad didn't reply, instead pulling a U-turn.

"Hang on," he said mildly. And then . . .

And then holy heck did he ever hit the gas.

"I don't care," he replied to my every objection as the moonlit scenery flew by: that he was exceeding the speed limit, that the tires on this car were old, that—

"Dad, there's a deer in the road ahead, oh, we're going to—"

But we didn't hit it, or anything else, either, and considering how late it was and how far out at the back edge of beyond Eastport was located, it was unlikely that anyone was enforcing the speed limit out here at the moment.

Also, it occurred to me that some of the deeds of my dad's youth had probably involved fast cars; that, or a secret career behind the wheel at the Indy 500. Soon we caught sight again of the motorcycle's red taillight zipping along ahead of us in the dark.

But zipping along to *where?* My dad tromped the gas pedal even harder.

"You know the worst part of getting old?" he asked as we zoomed onto the causeway into Pleasant Point.

"No, wh-what?" I replied as the guardrail posts flew by whap-whap-whap.

"The humiliation of it." His gnarly fists gripped the wheel. "I mean to say, Jacobia, it just never ends."

Leaning toward the windshield, he looked eager and excited; in the dim light of the passenger compartment, he looked *young*.

"Don't do this, can't do that, oh, are you sure you're really up to such a thing."

He glanced at me. "It's infuriating. Like they think you might lose the rest of your marbles at any moment, go running around naked or stick beans in your ears."

"That," I managed, gulping with fright, "must be very annoying."

Meanwhile, I wouldn't have believed my old sedan could even go this fast. As we sped along the last part of the causeway, the vehicle took on a floaty feeling as if the tires had given up even bothering to pretend that they were touching the pavement.

"Anyway," said my dad, "that's the deal. What I've been putting up with." Old age, he meant, and its attendant humiliations.

"I've told Bella how it is, so now I figured I might as well let you in on it, too," he added.

Ahead, the motorcycle had slowed for the speed limit sign just where the causeway ended. My dad let up on the gas, too, staying back a dozen car lengths or so from the motorcycle.

Its rider gave no sign of having noticed us. "Meanwhile, I wonder where the heck this guy's going," my dad remarked conversationally.

Then the blue rotating beacon of a squad car flared suddenly in our rear windshield. A short *whoop-whoop!* came from the car's siren.

My dad pulled over. "Hello, Officer. What's the trouble?"

Hands visible on the steering wheel, body deliberately relaxed, he looked up mildly at the Pleasant Point police officer.

The cop already had his ticket book out and open. But we hadn't *been* speeding, we'd slowed down even lower than the limit, so . . . ?

"Do you know you've got a taillight out?" The cop frowned, his glance quickly assessing us both along with the car's interior.

My dad handed over his newly reissued driver's license and the car's registration and insurance cards, while I thanked my stars that I kept the latter two documents together in the glove compartment and not just knocking around loose in the vehicle somewhere.

The cop handed the documents back, along with what turned out not to be a ticket, after all; it was a warning to get the taillight fixed promptly or pay a big fine next time.

"Thank you, Officer," my father said politely; then we were free to go.

Only by that time there was nowhere to go to. The road stretched emptily away into the darkness; while we'd been getting our warning, the motorcycle had gone ahead, out of sight.

Silently, we turned around, passing the patrol car again; back in Eastport, we rolled slowly through the darkened streets. At the Coast Guard station, Andy Devine's motorcycle stood parked in the lot beyond the heavy black iron gates.

"So the guy on the bike had been following us?" I said. "Earlier, that is."

First the car that had been behind us, then the figure that had either been in the downtown doorway or hadn't . . .

"At least now we know there's definitely another bike around here besides Andy's," I added.

Had to be; there was only one way onto the island, and no one had passed us on it. So the bike we had been chasing couldn't have gotten back here ahead of us.

"And whoever's on that other one was out at Miss Blaine's place the night she was attacked," I finished. I was sure of it now.

Because I supposed I could accept that just by chance two very similar motorcycles might be owned by different people in one small geographical area of downeast Maine: Andy's and someone else's.

But not three of them. For one thing, those bikes were *expensive*. And as I may have mentioned, downeast Maine isn't exactly boiling over with spare money, especially in early summer.

So as far as I was concerned, the biker we'd been chasing just now was the one who'd zoomed by us going *out* the long dirt lane from Miss Blaine's place when Ellie and I had been going *in*.

And that meant it hadn't been Andy out there, after all, when Miss Blaine was being attacked. He probably really had shown up by chance out on the Lake Road afterward, not because he was a culprit.

In short, he'd been telling the truth. But there wasn't much I could do about it, because for one thing just try telling a homicide detective that kind of story; go ahead, I'll wait.

Besides, other than the two similar motorcycles part of it all, I still had not the slightest idea what the heck was going on.

"Hey, we gave it a shot," said my dad as we drove once more up silent Key Street. The moon sank toward the west, a blurry disk in a sky gauzy with incoming fog.

"Yeah, thanks." We pulled into the driveway. "Sorry about that taillight."

The porch lamp was on, a lot of shiny brown June bugs bopping themselves silly against it. The rest of the house was dark.

"Don't worry about it. I can fix it tomorrow." We got out. Mist drifted like pale ghosts across the dark back lawn.

"Been quite a while since I've come face-to-face with one of 'em, though," he added with a small chuckle.

A police officer, he meant. Back in the old days there was a time he'd had so many warrants out for his arrest that he'd—

Well, I didn't know what he'd done about it, actually. I hadn't had any connection with him for that part of his life, or mine.

But I had one now. "Nice driving," I said as we climbed the porch steps together.

A reminiscent smile creased his face. "Used to do a lot of that, back in the day."

"Yeah, I can tell." He'd enjoyed it, too, and even as nuts as it had felt while it was happening, I had to admit so had I.

In the house, Max, the big old German shepherd, got up from his dog bed and padded out to greet us, his tail wagging slowly.

"Listen, Dad, about the truck . . ."

But before I could finish, he held up a hand. "Back in the day was a long time ago, though, Jake. How about if right now we just let an old man go on up to bed?"

There was plenty more that I could have said, and that I wanted to ask him, too, now that we were getting along so easily together. But he was right; we were both tired, and tomorrow would be a difficult day.

Because tomorrow, I'd decided sometime during the course of the long evening I'd just been through, was when Ellie White and I would be accepting the inevitable, and shutting down our beloved Chocolate Moose for good.

Nine

"What we need," said Ellie the next morning, "is a frosting that's substantial enough to decorate with, *and* sticky enough to keep the whoopie-pie cake sections from sliding all over the place, but—"

"But doesn't taste like lard," I finished for her, lard being the secret ingredient to a frosting so stiff, you could cut yourself on the edge of it while still raving about its flavor.

But that wasn't what I wanted to talk to her about. "Ellie," I began after I'd told her that Andy and Sharon were in police custody.

It was 7 a.m., and when I'd arrived she was already set up in the kitchen of The Chocolate Moose, cranking out cookies, cupcakes, and another four dozen ginger-chocolate biscotti for a special order plus an extra dozen for me to take home.

These, by the way, are in my opinion the perfect food, with enough fresh grated ginger as well as slivers of the crystalized kind to spark inspiration, plus enough good chocolate to fuel action.

Too bad that Ellie wasn't giving me the third thing I needed: opportunity. But since she didn't want to do the only thing that was currently on my list of what we needed to take action about, I guessed that was understandable.

"Ellie, we're going to have to get it over with sooner or later," I tried. But it was no good; she'd come to a decision, too, and she was sticking with it.

"When the sheriff comes and throws us out into the street," she declared stubbornly, "that's when I'll leave the Moose."

"Oh, Ellie, you know that's not going to happen," I sighed.

Or at least not soon; in Maine it is so difficult to evict people from rental property that we'd be driven out by our own embarrassment long before anything official could happen.

But in my heart it was how I felt also. "I am going to miss this place," I admitted.

Out front in the shop area, the old paddle-bladed ceiling fans turned slowly, moving the air heavily laden with spices and chocolate and with the aroma of the fresh coffee now brewing on the counter.

In the glass-fronted display case a few dozen cookies, some chocolate éclairs, and a chocolate sheet cake that we were selling by the piece awaited our last few customers. Meanwhile, she was readying our final big catering order for a party in Machiasport, an off-the-beaten-track waterside hamlet thirty miles south of here.

Luckily, the customer was coming to pick up the order herself, since while my arm felt a good deal better this morning, I still had no interest in driving all that way to deliver the stuff.

"Oh, I am so much going to miss it," Ellie agreed, her hands moving mechanically through another attempt at a suitable frosting for that dratted whoopie-pie wedding cake.

She seemed to feel that as long as she worked on the wedding cake—even though with both Sharon and Andy in custody there was not going to be a wedding, obviously—she didn't have to give up on the Moose.

I stirred cocoa powder into the rest of the dry ingredients—flour, baking powder, baking soda, pinch of salt—for the cookies, then beat the eggs and vanilla into the creamed butter-and-sugar mixture. The éclair shells were done and the biscotti were already in the oven; once these cookies were frosted—

And while I am on the subject, may I just say right here that a plain chocolate cookie, made with quality ingredients and with a plain chocolate frosting generously spread onto it, is one of the truly good things in life? Because it is, especially with a cup of coffee.

Anyway, once the cookies were frosted, the Machiasport order would be complete: a sad milestone. "So listen," I began again.

Ellie's expression darkened. "No, no, just hear me out," I said. "Because it's true, one more day isn't going to kill us."

It was what she'd been arguing for. "And we even have milkshake ingredients left," she said, brightening at my remark.

But not at her bowl of frosting. Licking a bit of it off the tip of her finger, she made a face that said this stuff, like the batches before it, tasted like lard. And even though there was a well-known way of getting around this, Ellie would use bottled imitation butter flavoring when pigs flew, so I didn't mention it.

"Also, I suppose there could still be developments," she said. "Ones that we haven't had to dig up by ourselves, that is."

In the murder case against Sharon and/or Andy, she meant, and I supposed she might be right. Someone else could confess, for instance. Or Toby Moran could turn out not to be really dead, which to me seemed about as likely.

Mostly, though, when it came right down to it, I just couldn't stand to be the one to break Ellie's heart. She'd see reason when she was ready; she always did, sooner or later. And I was going to give her all the time in the world, I decided; all the time she needed.

Out past the shop's front window, gulls dove and flapped behind small boats puttering industriously around in the boat basin, while on the bay a flock of sailboats scudded, their sails billowing tautly.

Then as if triggered by our decision to stay open at least for today, a customer appeared at our locked front door. And although we didn't open until ten, we figured what the heck, and let her in.

Marilyn Gibson was a pleasant, energetic local lady with short salt-and-pepper hair, twinkly dark eyes, and harlequin glasses on a chain around her wattled neck.

"I heard you might be closing, that's not true, is it?" she wanted to know as I wrapped up six pieces of sheet cake for her, for a luncheon she was hosting at noon.

"Because we just don't know what we'd do without you," she added.

By "we," she meant the ladies of Eastport; women's club members here tended not to dress elaborately or to display elegant mannerisms; no doormen assisted them nor headwaiter ever ushered them to any chic restaurant tables.

But they still had their many civic projects to talk over and fund-raisers to plan. This year so far they'd paved the tennis courts, reseeded the ball field, and bought new litter baskets for downtown, plus a professional service to empty them regularly.

"You aren't, are you?" she demanded again, accepting her change. "You aren't closing the shop?"

Like I say, word gets around. "I'm so sorry," I murmured as it struck me again how much I had enjoyed all this.

"I'd say we could still cater events just for you ladies," I went on, "but since the most important member of the team won't be here—" I waved toward the kitchen just as Ellie peeped out from it, while Marilyn Gibson pushed her glasses up onto her nose and looked seriously aghast. "No! Ellie? You're leaving us? Oh, that's too bad."

She shook her head comprehendingly. "But I understand, we all do have to make a living. Good luck to you, dear," she finished kindly.

The little bell over the door jingled as she went out. "So you told her?" Ellie said as Marilyn strode past the window outside.

I nodded, not quite able to speak. Ellie felt bad enough already; there was no sense my making it worse by bawling my own fool head off.

"We don't have to really do it," I managed. "Close, I mean. Like we said, if something illuminating comes up today, some . . . some *clue* or something, we can always change our minds."

Bob Arnold drove by in the squad car, heading for his office. Norm McHale passed in the other direction, driving the little dark-green two-seater MG sports car we'd glimpsed in his car barn. He'd put the top down, and the tan leather upholstery shone richly.

"I just thought the club ladies deserved a heads-up, after all the business they've given us," I finished, swallowing hard.

"Poor Jake," Ellie said sympathetically, putting her hand gently on my shoulder. "It's okay. It's all going to turn out fine."

But it wasn't and we both knew it. Our dream of a chocolate-themed bake shop, where everything was made the old-fashioned way and with all the best ingredients, had turned to a heap of rubble.

I was in the shop's little washroom when I heard the phone ring, and when I came out again Ellie was putting all this morning's product onto trays.

"It turns out the lady in Machiasport can't pick up her order," she explained. "So I thought I'd just drive it down there."

"But, Ellie, what about Lee's recital? The violin students' big spring concert?" I reminded her, and she looked vexed, glancing up at the clock on the wall behind the cash register.

"Darn, you're right. It's an hour each way; the concert's right after lunch, and I wanted to be there with her before the—"

Lee was going to play "Greensleeves." I'd heard her practicing it, and she was good; besides, she had to have at least one parent at the recital, didn't she?

"I'll go," I said, and twenty minutes later we had my car loaded.

"You're sure your arm will be all right?" Ellie worried aloud.

I wasn't; the incision felt like acid was being poured onto it. "I'll be fine," I assured her, lying through gritted teeth.

"Just watch out for other drivers, then," she cautioned as I started the car. "I don't want to have to finish shutting this place down all by myself."

So she was coming around to the idea. I wasn't sure if that made me feel better or not. Either way, I figured a couple of hours alone in a car full of chocolate wouldn't hurt me.

Maybe the fumes would even improve my mood, and if worse came to worst I could always bite into one of those biscotti, which at the customer's request had been baked so crisply, you could've hammered nails in with them.

But as I pulled out of the parking space in front of the Moose, Jenna Waldrop came quick-stepping down the sidewalk toward me, waving at me to stop.

When I did, the ringleted and bracelet-bedecked young teacher got into the car beside me and slammed the door.

"I have to talk to you." Her bracelets clinked as she clasped her hands in her lap.

"What is it, Jenna?" I sighed. The last thing I needed was an earful of her bitterness. "I mean, I'm sorry you're so unhappy, but . . ."

"The other night at the Duck," she said, ignoring me. She'd decided to tell me something and now she was going to, no matter what.

"There's something no one's talked about. But I was there."

I drove slowly out Water Street toward Jenna's house. "And?"

"After Toby got thrown out and then Andy left, I did, too. To go home, I mean."

Which was what Marienbad had said. "But I stopped in the ladies' room," Jenna went on. "And . . . well, I'd drunk too much. Mom was on the warpath again, I didn't want to—"

Yeah, yeah. Same old story. "Hey, Jenna, cut to the chase, okay?"

I thought she'd be annoyed, not that I cared. Right now I had my own problems. But she just laughed a little wildly.

"The chase. Right. Well, the chase is that when I came out of the ladies' room, no one in the place knew I was still there. Norm McHale, specifically."

Jenna and her mom lived in a tiny wood-frame cottage backed up to a granite ledge, on a side street so steep it was a wonder anything but birdhouses was built on it.

I pulled up in front and set the parking brake. A curtain in the front window twitched; dear old Mom, I supposed.

Jenna sucked in a breath, seeing it, too. "So

307

I was just getting myself together to go out the door when I looked back. And there was Norm, just then going out the emergency exit."

The curtain twitched minutely again. I may or may not have made a rude gesture in its general direction. "Really," I said to Jenna.

She nodded firmly, her auburn ringlets bouncing. "Really. I know he didn't see me, he didn't look back. No one did, I sort of slid out the door quietly. I was," she added shamefacedly, "kind of a mess."

I considered this. "And . . . before or after this happened, did you see anything else unusual?"

Her forehead creased. "Just . . . well, some scuffling sounds. From down there behind the Ducky on the walkway. Not loud, though; I didn't think much of it."

Where Andy and Toby had gotten into their altercation, she meant. Andy said there hadn't been many words spoken, just punches thrown.

"Jenna, have you told anyone else about this?"

The young woman shook her head miserably. "No, and I don't want to. Mother doesn't know I go to the Duck at all, she thinks I—"

The curtain hadn't moved again. *My work here is done,* I thought, feeling a touch of glee.

"Jenna, I want you to go right now and find Bob Arnold, and tell him about this. Do you want a ride?"

Jenna glanced at the house. "No, I've got to

go in for a minute first and settle her down. But I will do it, I promise. Walking back to Bob's office," she added, "will keep me away from here longer."

She put her hand on the car door, but I stopped her. "Jenna. One last thing. Why are you telling me this?"

She paused, considering. "Well, I've been thinking for a while now about what's going to happen when she dies. I mean, nobody lives forever, do they?" she added worriedly.

Yeah, if Mother Waldrop had been my mom, I'd have been concerned about that, too. Looking up at the house again, Jenna went on.

"I mean, she's my mom and I love her, but she's a bitter, unhappy woman."

She turned to me. "And if I'm not careful I'm going to end up just like her, aren't I?"

I didn't know what to say. Another small laugh, then: "Oh, don't worry, you don't have to answer that. I know what you think of me, and I deserve it. Sharon Sweetwater definitely hates me, and I deserve that, too, the way I've behaved to her."

She bit her lip. "I wish I'd tried to be friends with her, back when . . . but that'll never happen, now. Serves me right."

As she reached for the car door again I found my voice. "Jenna."

She turned inquiringly. "Jenna, if you tell

Sharon what you've just told me, that you'd like a fresh chance, I'm certain she will—"

"Right," Jenna replied bleakly. She leaned back into the car.

"Anyway, what I saw in the Ducky the other night. I thought you'd want to know, that's all. And I will tell Bob."

Before I could answer, she strode away toward the house, and I drove off. I'd have gone downtown to talk to Bob Arnold myself, but those baked goods we'd promised to the lady in Machiasport weren't going to deliver themselves, and now I was behind schedule.

So minutes later I was sailing over the causeway with the water wild and whitecapped to my right while to my left, a sandy expanse of clam flats gleamed. I'd put the windows down and the breeze smelled like smoke from a bonfire someone had built of driftwood on the beach.

At the Route 1 intersection I pulled up behind Marienbad Jones, who was waiting to make the turn. Wearing a pair of movie-star shades and with her masses of brunette hair sticking out from beneath a bright pink ball cap, the proprietor of the Rubber Ducky was driving an old Ford sedan that by the sound of it had a hamster wheel under the hood.

Behind her, and just ahead of me, was Norm McHale in his little green MG. Still with the top down, he looked jaunty in a beret, wire-rimmed sunglasses, and a navy windbreaker; tossing me a friendly wave when he spotted me in his rearview, he pulled out heading south, opposite the direction Marienbad was going.

But as he made the turn, he took the glasses off and looked hard at me again, watching—or so it seemed—to see which way I would go.

To see, I mean, if I was following him. The thought wouldn't even have occurred to me if not for Jenna's recent revelation, but now I turned reflexively the other way, then drove another quarter mile to the Farmers Union store and turned in.

Silly, I told myself as, inside, I bought a bottle of water and a package of pretzels. By then I'd had a chance to consider, realizing that Jenna's story about Norm was odd, but that she'd been fairly drunk even by her own admission and might have misconstrued what she saw.

Or the whole thing might've been, as Sam would've put it, a Fig Newton of her imagination; anyway, by the time I got back on the road headed south again, I was well and truly late.

Fields, farms, forests, and the tidal reaches of rivers zipped by; forty-five minutes later with my arm aching miserably, I turned off Route 1 onto a narrow, winding road along a cove's edge.

Soon I was passing between small houses and mobile homes, their driveways piled high with lobster traps. Here and there stood antique center-chimney colonials, their front walks flanked by ancient trunks of trees that were saplings when the houses were built.

Finally, I reached Jasper Beach, a wide, curving expanse of stones all polished smooth by the ocean and heaped by the tides, so you had to climb up to get to the beach, then down again to the water's edge.

Neither of which I did, instead continuing past a small, haunted-looking collection of a dozen or so identical ranch-style houses lining both sides of a gated-shut cul-de-sac: KEEP OUT, said the sign on the chain-link fence.

Unnecessarily, I thought; who'd want to go in there? The ominous-looking dwellings had been homes to families stationed at a nearby, now-decommissioned Air Force base. But now they resembled the set of a horror movie: blank windows, boarded doors. Leaving them behind with a shiver, I drove uphill through a pine grove, then past more vintage homesteads, between ancient stone fences lining the twisty roadway.

And then I was at my destination. The house was a nicely revived old shingle-sided water-front cottage with a slate front walk, massive granite chimney, and an arbor with neatly pruned grape vines spreading by a gravel path that led down to the yard and the rocky shore.

Mulched perennial beds lined the path. When I got out of the car all I heard was the rush of waves on the stony beach and a few gulls crying distantly.

Then a woman came out of the house. "Hello!" She hurried toward me. "Here, do let me help you with those."

She was mousy and pale, with gray-blond curls falling loosely around her face and small, soft-looking hands. But her arms with her cardigan sleeves pushed up were tautly muscular and already tanned; all that gardening, I supposed, but always in gloves.

"Thanks so much for coming, I really appreciate it. I'm afraid I don't drive anymore." The glasses she peered at me through made her eyes look huge, each pale blond eyelash magnified.

"Oh, no trouble at all," I lied as she took two trays of baked goods and I took the other two—with difficulty, but I did it—and followed her in.

"Here we are, then," she called over her shoulder to me. "Home sweet home."

I'll say it was; the cottage's interior smelled clean and sweet, like the inside of a well-maintained cedar chest. Pine-plank floors glowed with polish, a green glass jug of English ivy stood on each windowsill, and a small fire blazed cheerfully on the hearth.

I set my trays down on a cherrywood side-board. Chintz covered the neat but comfortable-appearing furniture. Bright pillows put splashes of color everywhere.

Rich-looking rugs lay on the floors, plush under my feet. "Would you like coffee? Or tea?"

Sally Sanborn was her name, I recalled just in time. "No, thanks. I'm afraid I can't."

The only blot on the interior was the blob in the corner. Wearing a gray sweat suit, a Red Sox ball cap, and a pair of sneakers so horridly disreputable-looking it was a wonder the health department hadn't confiscated them, the blob shifted and spoke. "Umph."

Which I thought probably translated to "hello." With no further remarks the blob left the room, its hunched shoulders and averted gaze telling me that it did not want me to see its face.

The smell of stale tobacco hit me as it—he, rather; a glimpse told me it was a young man of about twenty-five—went by. Then Sally was there again, holding up a coffee carafe inquiringly.

I shook my head regretfully. "I've left my partner alone in the shop, you see."

Yet another thing I'd be losing when the shop closed, I groused inwardly: my best excuse when I wanted to get away from anywhere. But the view was too spectacular to resist when she waved me toward the long row of windows overlooking the water.

"Wow," I breathed, letting my gaze range inland along the curving shoreline, all the way to Jasper Beach on my left and out to the misty shapes of the Spectacle Islands on the right. Then, "Huh," I said, because there was a car in the beach's primitive parking lot. I hadn't seen it on my way in here; you couldn't, from the road. But it was a *small* car. . . .

"In fact," I said, hastening from the window, "now that I think of it, I'd really better get back there to help her as soon as I can."

No more sign of the blob, although a nice, late-model sedan in the driveway said that he at least had a way to get around.

"Oh, that's too bad. I don't get much company out here. Those baked things you brought are for a church supper tonight," she added at my questioning look.

A large supper, I hoped; there was dessert enough for an army. Sally walked me out to my own car, a little dog frisking around her feet.

"So . . . do you get out of here at all, otherwise? Besides to the church suppers, I mean?"

Sally seemed nice enough, and I couldn't help thinking that in Eastport, where she could walk everywhere, she could have a social life if she wanted one.

"Oh, no," she smiled regretfully. "It's my own fault, though, I just get so busy and . . . and *involved,* sort of, what with—"

She stopped, glancing back toward the house as if worried that the blob might be listening.

"My son keeps me company. Anyway, thanks

so much," she finished warmly, but the glance had chilled me and by the time I pulled out of her driveway I was even more relieved not to be staying any longer.

"Come back anytime," she was urging me a little desperately as I got behind the wheel, and I assured her that I would.

"And thanks again!" she went on as I retreated, while behind her the bright blue waves rolled onto the pebbled beach and the pines sighed overhead.

Then, hitting the gas, I started back toward Jasper Beach and the lot where I'd seen the small car parked. The small *green* car . . .

Probably, I told myself firmly, it wasn't who I thought it was, and even if it *was* him, it didn't mean anything.

Or . . . did it?

The parking lot at Jasper Beach was a sandy unpaved track leading in from the narrow, paved road and ending in a weedy turnaround.

I parked and walked the rest of the way in, between scrubby sumac and beach-rose hedges covered in pink blooms, past the beginnings of foot trails that rambled off uphill along granite outcroppings, vanishing into the dense brush.

At the place where the sandy soil ended and beach stones began, I found the car I'd spotted from Sally Sanborn's house. As I'd thought, it was Norm McHale's small green two-seater MG; when I touched it the hood was still warm, so he must've arrived not long ago.

I trudged on past it over the massive mound of beach stones that ringed the cove. The round, smooth stones, polished by eons of rolling over and over one another in the tides, slid and slithered under my shoes as I made my way uphill over them, toward the water.

At the top I could see half a mile to my left and right, around the crescent-shaped beach; straight ahead lay the bay with its foamy breakers rolling in and pulling back again, over and over.

Norm was down there, crouched at the water's edge, where the foam dissipated into the stones. I opened my mouth to call to him, then saw what he was doing.

He was burying something, I couldn't see what. A brisk wind off the water made me shiver as I realized just how visible I was, if he should stand and turn.

No one else was on the beach. And call me paranoid, but I was all at once not eager at all to confront Norm McHale on a deserted stretch of remote Maine shoreline with nobody around.

Possibly there was an innocent reason for what he was doing; probably, even. But I still wanted to know what he thought needed burying in a place that was only accessible at low tide, on a beach made of what must have been millions of identical smooth, round stones, each about the size of a baby's fist.

Once he walked away, even he might have no idea where to look for it again. Surely I'd never find it; no one would. Which was the whole idea, probably; slowly I began backing away down the high stone ridge, sliding and leaning to keep from falling.

Out on the bay, a fishing boat strained at its mooring, pulled stern-first toward deeper water as the last of the tide went out. Small birds skittered along the wet stones, and from behind me came the sounds of a group of hikers, starting up one of the trails.

Relief touched me. Norm still didn't turn; as I retreated, my last sight of him was the same as my first had been: digging. Moving the stones, making a hole, placing something in it. Then covering it again, replacing the stones he'd set aside one by one to cover whatever it was he'd buried.

Darn, I thought, but I still didn't want to confront him alone. In my car I backed out quickly onto the narrow shore road, then drove slowly again toward the old, gated chain-link fence that bounded the abandoned housing compound I'd passed earlier.

There was a stone caught in my hubcap, I noticed distractedly as I scanned the edge of the pavement for a place to pull over. *Tink-tink-tink* . . . I hoped he couldn't hear it.

Eventually, a wide, sandy shoulder spread off the road, ending in a clover patch. I parked and waited, rolling down the car window so I'd be able to hear the growl of the MG's engine when Norm started it up. By now the day had grown warm, the stiff breeze I'd felt earlier dropped to nearly nothing; I opened my water bottle and drank.

A flock of goldfinches cheeped excitedly in a thicket of last year's thistles, a springtime banquet for the tiny yellow seed-eaters. A hawk soared overhead with something silvery flapping in its talons.

Bees droned in the beach roses and my eyelids grew heavy in the perfumed warmth. My arm ached, and I wondered if maybe I had it wrong, if Norm wasn't leaving in his car or if maybe it wouldn't start.

And it was, after all, just a short walk back down to the parking lot. It wouldn't be very much trouble to at least find out if he was already gone—could I have *missed* hearing the MG somehow?—and if he *wasn't* gone, I could decide then what, if anything, to do next.

That was what I told myself as headed back down the road on foot, past a row of cedar trees on one side, then an overgrown berry thicket—blackberries, I realized, wincing at the thorns—on the other.

From there it was only a hop, skip, and a jump,

as Bella would have put it, to the parking lot, where the green sports car still sat parked with its leather seats gleaming richly and its wire wheels glinting.

Slowly, I approached the little vehicle. I didn't know much about vintage cars, but I didn't think leaving the seats to bake in the sun was a recommended care strategy. In the distance, out of sight past the barrier ridge of stones on the beach, waves hissed onto the shore and retreated, louder now that the tide was coming in.

Standing there smelling salt water and feeling the sun beating down on my head, I wondered if maybe I should just *find* Norm McHale and *ask* him what he was doing, burying something at the beach.

Phrasing it, of course, in some other, less confrontational way. And while I was thinking this, I must already have made my decision, because my feet were moving: back out to the beach, up the stone ridge and down the other side of it, finally to the water, lapping a little higher than it had been earlier.

But no Norm—no anyone, in fact—was at the water's edge now. Not a person was in sight, and the only sound was the rush and retreat of the waves rolling on the stones, plus an occasional gull's crying.

Suddenly I felt afraid. Even the sun pouring bright, warm light down onto my head didn't encourage me; all I wanted was to go home, I didn't know why.

Oh, stop, I scolded myself. It was a public beach, more people would be along anytime, and the hikers must still be around here somewhere, too. And anyway, I would only be a minute.

Because if I left and came back later, I'd never re-locate the spot where I'd seen Norm burying something. In fact, I was fairly sure I couldn't even do it now.

Still, I had to try. And I had my phone on me—I'd tried it, just to be sure it worked this time—so if anything bad happened . . .

Which it wouldn't, I instructed myself firmly. Then before I could talk myself out of it, I strode to where I thought I remembered Norm crouching on the stony beach.

The spot was nearly underwater now as the tide rose, but luckily he'd left a bit of a depression where he'd been excavating. I bent and pulled out one smooth, egg-sized stone after another and tossed them aside.

But I found nothing, just more stones, cold seawater, and . . .

Suddenly there it was, a small bundle wrapped in a blue bandana. I plucked the bundle from the hole, rose, and turned.

And ran smack into Norm McHale. "Hello, Jake."

He was standing way too close, as if he'd been

about to pounce and I'd foiled his intention at the last instant.

"Hi, Norm," I managed. He'd made it across the beach while I had my back turned. "What's up?"

My hand moved toward my bag, which was slung casually over my shoulder; *speed dial,* I thought.

Norm reached out suddenly and in a fast, utterly decisive grab, he snatched the bag away from me.

Then he jabbed me with something sharp, a warm sensation flooded through me, and I passed out suddenly and completely. I didn't know anything anymore.

"I'm not going to tell you the name of the drug, but it won't do you any harm."

"So you say."

I'd been walking and talking for some time now, it seemed, but I didn't remember it, courtesy of whatever had been in the needle Norm had jabbed me with back there on the beach.

"It just put you out and made you cooperative when you came to again," he said, "so I could get you in here without trouble. And I took no other advantage of you, by the way," he added.

"Gee, that's so reassuring," I responded sarcastically. "Guess I should be glad it wasn't cyanide. I feel so safe and secure, now."

You son of a bitch, I didn't add, but he heard it anyway, as I intended.

"I'm sorry about this, Jacobia, I really am. I hope when it's all over you and Ellie will forgive me."

"Fat chance. Norm, what's going on? What the heck are you up to, anyhow?" I demanded.

Hey, you never know, he might feel talkative. Meanwhile, I took in as much of my surroundings as I could, trying to make a plan; somehow, I had to get out of this mess that I'd put myself in.

But he didn't answer. "Why did you have to follow me?" he wanted to know instead.

"But, Norm, I wasn't . . ." I began, then stopped as I understood what must have had happened.

Back at the Route 1 intersection he'd seen me, and assumed I was following him. Once he didn't see me behind him anymore, he'd have relaxed. But when he found me on the beach trying to dig up what he'd buried, he must've thought it was all part of a scheme.

Right, I wish. Even after what Jenna told me, I'd just thought maybe Norm heard sounds from the walkway below the Ducky, too, and had gone out the Duck's emergency exit to find out what was going on.

There'd be no convincing him of that, though, and, anyway, it hardly mattered. So instead I went on taking in details of my current location, hoping to make it my previous location as soon as possible.

I was in the living room of a house. Sheetrock, pine trim . . . a decent but not luxurious house. Cheap wall-to-wall carpeting covered the floor. A child's faded, water-stained coloring book lay facedown on the kitchen linoleum. An *empty* house . . .

Then I realized that we must be in one of the abandoned military residences, in the deserted compound past the wire-topped chain-link fence. And it was just as creepy in here as I had imagined.

In the time it had been empty, the house had settled enough to throw the walls and floors slightly out of true. The fun-house result would've been disorienting even without the lingering effects of the drug Norm had administered.

Taking deep breaths in hopes of settling my stomach, I noted the empty kitchen cabinets' doors hanging open and the ceiling tiles beginning to fall. Dust motes drifted in the sunlight slanting in the picture window; it was still bright day outside.

"You've been out about an hour," McHale said, seeming to catch my thought.

So no one would even be looking for me yet. "Come on, Norm," I said, trying again for some helpful info, something I could get out of this with. "What's this all about?"

Meanwhile, I tugged at whatever it was he'd tied around my wrists. When I woke I'd been lying flat, but now I sat upright with my back against the living room wall, near where the stained beige carpeting ended and the tile-floored dining area began.

But it was no go on yanking the wrist bindings apart. "What this is all about," Norm replied, "I'm not at liberty to say, I'm afraid."

Me too; the *afraid* part, I mean. Also, my ankles were tied together. "Oh, I see. But you're at liberty to abduct me, restrain me, and keep me here against my will on account of it?"

More yanking, same negative result. The kitchen island's corner had been fractured by repeated forceful contact with, I was willing to bet, a child's Hot Wheels toy; it was a young-family sort of house, the kind people moved out of once the bassinet and baby gate had been put away. Now the fake-wood plastic laminate had a tear in it, a dagger of woodlike material sticking up dangerously from beneath.

Norm looked unhappy but determined. "Sorry about all that. But it's the lesser of two evils," he said. "Now, if you'll excuse me . . ."

He moved toward the door. "Norm! Darn it, Norm, you just can't leave me here like—"

But then I shut up, as more of whatever he'd given me wore off and two things hit me: (a) this house was plenty straight, it had been the drugs in my system making it look crooked; and (b) sure he could.

He could leave. He could do whatever he wanted. He could set the house on fire on his way out, for heaven's sake, and there wouldn't be a thing I could do about it.

Not one single thing. And he might, too, because—

Panic struck me. "Norm, I don't get it."

Trying to engage him, to keep him involved in a conversation. Trying to keep him from leaving me here, because if he did, then I might never be found.

But he wasn't having any. "I'll be coming back for you," he said, "just as soon as I take care of a few things."

I didn't believe him. Burying something on the beach didn't necessarily make him Toby Moran's killer, or Miss Blaine's, either. But this, what he was doing now—

As I thought this, however, a new possibility suggested itself to me; carefully, I looked away from the closet built into the kitchen cabinetry of the house, near where the absent refrigerator once stood.

The closet's door stood halfway open. Any moment now he would remember what was in it. I didn't look at it again.

"Please, Norm," I said, trying to keep his attention, because I was beginning to recall his first few minutes with me in here, back when he was still trying to figure out exactly what to do next.

The memory of it came in fragments; first, he'd spent a little while walking around nervously, peering around, putting things out of sight. After that he'd promised he wouldn't harm me, that all this—him burying the blue bandana-wrapped bundle, he'd meant, and putting me out of commission once I'd seen him—wasn't the way it looked.

That he wasn't a killer. But oh, of course, he was, I realized as more of the sedative drug he'd given me wore off.

He'd killed Toby Moran and Miss Blaine. And now he was killing me. Not directly, but unless I got free or someone found me—

Both were unlikely; from the absence of graffiti or vandalism it was clear that people didn't come messing around much in here, and the bindings on my wrists and ankles were *tight*—

It would take me about three days. To die, I mean.

He slammed the door on his way out.

Once Norm was gone, I spent some time torturing myself by trying to escape the ties around my ankles and wrists. It would've helped a lot if my hands had been tied in front of me instead of behind my back.

But, of course, they weren't. I'd seen self-defense instructional videos of people who were tied up this way, who'd gotten free by some complicated maneuver that started with them pushing their butts backward through the circle formed by their two arms and then hauling their legs through, like a magician's trick.

I knew better than to try it, though; with my luck, I'd get my whole self tied into a knot and then be unable to untie that. Besides, I still had my eye on that kitchen utility closet.

Scooting painfully across the floor on my rear end, I reached the edge of the carpet, where the tiled kitchen-dining area began. Then, scooching along the tiles—slipperier, but harder on the tailbone, as it turned out—I reached the kitchen island, where the cabinet corner had the jagged edge torn partway out of it.

Finally, I turned my back to the cabinet and shoved my bound wrists blindly against the sharp stuff. If the material wrapped around my ankles was any clue, he'd tied my wrists together with package-strapping tape, the thread-reinforced kind. That meant that sooner or later, a sharp edge rubbing against it should cut it.

Emphasis on the "later," apparently; also, by now my hands were numb all the way to my elbows. For all I knew, I could be slitting my own wrists.

Furthermore, although my injured arm was no

longer particularly painful—that numbness—and the wound itself was higher up toward my elbow, I didn't like thinking about what I might be doing to all those nice, neat surgical stitches that had been put into it.

No blood pool spread out from behind me, however, which I found reassuring. Soon I heard faint poppings and snappings as the thin-but-strong threads embedded in the tape wrapped around my wrists were severed.

At least I hoped that was what I heard, and not the stitches themselves letting go. . . . At last the tape fell away entirely; twin bolts of agony shot through my shoulders, which hadn't moved much for a long time, and I spent a few more minutes just rocking and massaging my bruised wrists and moaning in pain while the circulation returned.

But I was free, and now that I could see what I was doing it was the work of only a few moments to get my ankle ties loosened, as well. Then it was time to make my way to that little broom cupboard built into the kitchen cabinetry. I hauled myself up off the tiled floor and flopped face-first down onto the Formica-covered kitchen island.

Which had not been in the plan; the flopping part, that is. Nor was the sudden sound of a car going by outside; *my* car, I realized from the *tink-tink-tink* sound of the stone still caught in the hubcap.

He was moving it, probably to hide it. Which meant that anyone searching for me wouldn't see it and at least know that they were in the right general area. . . .

I mean, if I didn't get out of this pickle by myself. Breathing slowly and telling myself to be patient, that I could handle this, I waited until the sound of my car faded, then straightened again from my flopped-down position across the top of the kitchen island.

"Oof." Sort of straightened. Something about being twisted into a pretzel shape and tied that way hadn't been good for my sacroiliac.

Or for the rest of me. Black spots swam liquidly in my vision, then merged, while the rest of my body was very annoyingly dissolving and flowing back down onto the floor whether I liked it or not.

"All right, damn it," I said, sitting up again. The black spots returned. But by carefully gauging just how high I could hold my head up without passing out entirely, I slid, rolled, and wiggled the rest of the way into the kitchen.

The long-unswept linoleum was gritty with ancient crumbs and smeared with some unidentifiable stickiness that I didn't much want to think about; Bella would've had a fit. Near the stove, the stickiness mingled with grease in a way that, if I lived, I was going to have to throw out every stitch of the clothing that I was wearing, and maybe even my shoes.

And yes, those *were* insect bodies stuck in the grease patches; a shudder of revulsion went through me as my hand mashed down onto them. Springing up in disgust, I got nearly to a standing position, hooked my arms over the sink, and fumbled at the faucet handles, so thirsty suddenly I thought I might die just from that.

But the faucet produced nothing. Of course, the place was empty and the water had been turned off. Disappointed, I made my unsteady way back nearly to the broom closet before collapsing again.

Good old floor, I thought, hugging it affectionately. Whatever Norm had given me, it was definitely still working.

But now I was at the broom closet door and hauling my way up it, first grabbing it by its handle and then latching on to the mop propped just inside.

"Shall we dance?" I inquired slurringly of the fraying mop head, which didn't reply.

Behind the mop, though, was what I really wanted: my bag. Because when we got in here, McHale had carried it over his shoulder while he used both hands to steady me. Then after he let me drop to the carpet, he'd shoved the bag in here, where it still hung on a utility hook.

Maybe he wasn't thinking clearly, or maybe he wanted it out of sight just on general principles. Not that anyone else was likely to be wandering in here, or looking in the windows, either. Behind its forbidding-looking chain-link fence, the abandoned cul-de-sac these houses were built on was like the set of a low-budget zombie film; all it needed were the undead, themselves.

Any hope of my being rescued, in other words, was so far down on the list of likely events that I'd be better off depending on the kindness of one of those shambling deceased folks.

Still, my bag *was* here; snatching it, I turned from the broom closet and helplessly kept turning, sudden dizziness sitting me down hard on the filthy floor yet another time.

But the bag was here; I yanked the zipper open and rummaged inside. And . . . *yes!* My phone was still there. Only . . .

I pushed buttons and stared vexedly at the thing. It was on, it was charged, I'd checked to be sure it worked. So why wouldn't it—?

And then I realized: that fat black wire sticking out of the kitchen wall wasn't a cable TV connection. It was for a telephone. A land line, to be precise; when these houses were built, cell phone service didn't even exist way out here.

So no one would have realized then that on the beach cell phones worked fine, but in this grim little neighborhood—backed up to a high, impenetrable granite ledge—there could never be a usable signal. Like many places in downeast Maine—at the lake, for example, or out on Route 9—solid geographical features simply prevented it.

So I was stumped. I could, I supposed, just get up off the floor and walk out of here, except that getting up at all seemed impossible, suddenly. I swigged from the water bottle in my bag—*Hallelujah!* I thought when I came upon it—but that only added more nausea to the vertigo that hit me every time I tried rising from a sitting position.

Also, the stitches in my arm had gotten dislodged, after all; I wrapped my sleeve tightly around it as best I could, so in addition to being a truly spectacular visual mess of the blood-drenched variety, it now also hurt like hell.

Finally, even though I was not dead or in any danger of being so very soon, someone else was. If Norm thought I'd been following him, it meant he thought I knew or suspected something that he was willing to kill me in order to hide.

And who else would he reasonably expect to know whatever I knew or suspected? Ellie White, that's who. The notion shot me full of a fear at least as powerful as the drug he'd injected me with.

My friend, my partner in baking and in snooping, the one I would share any information with . . . he'd think I must have confided in her, or at least he wouldn't be willing to take the chance. So unless I missed my guess, he was on his way right now to eliminate that whole "sharing information" business, first on her side of the equation.

And then, once he had her out of the way, on mine. And what *that* meant was that I needed to get out of here pronto, not only to save my own life but, even more immediately and urgently, to save Ellie's.

Too bad that while I was thinking this Norm McHale burst back into the house unexpectedly. I scrambled up, heedless of dizziness, but too late.

Now, catching sight of me standing there unsteadily, clearly ready to vamoose at the very first opportunity, he nodded sharply.

"I knew I should've dosed you again." He advanced on me, pulling a syringe from his jacket pocket and yanking the needle protector from it without taking his eyes off me.

The needle glinted evilly. A crystal-clear droplet hung from it. Backstepping, I tried evading him. But he was faster and steadier on his feet, and in an instant he was upon me, jabbing the needle into my hip and pushing the plunger.

I remember my knees going watery and my vision clouding, the walls speeding past me as if I were in a glass-walled elevator going down fast.

But—*damn,* I thought as I fell, *this makes twice in a single morning*—I don't remember hitting the floor.

Ten

"Wha?" I opened my eyes. Bright daylight stuck daggers of pain through them, into my skull.

I was lying on my back, looking up at the blue sky, which seemed to have two round pink moons hung in it, peering down at me.

My vision cleared. It was the two guys from the lakeside cottage near Miss Blaine's.

I blinked again. This couldn't be happening. How had *they . . . ?*

"Jeeze, lookit 'er arm. That's bad, we better get 'er to a—"

I sat up. The world only spun around a couple of times. As soon as I got my coordination together a little better, I would run.

But they had other ideas. I was lying in the weedy front yard of the abandoned house where Norm McHale had recently attacked me for a second time, dosing me back into a chemical dreamland.

I blinked around painfully some more. The sun was now over on the afternoon side of the sky. *Ellie . . .*

The guys seized me, one under my shoulders and one at my feet, and loaded me into an old gray van through the sliding side door. I was still too wobbly and woozy to do anything useful about it, which I guessed put an end to the whole running away idea for the moment, too.

I had the brief, unrealistic notion that I might scramble up into the van's front seat and drive away very fast—the keys were in the ignition, and the guys hadn't gotten in themselves yet—when a new face appeared in the not-yet-closed side door.

"Hello? Is anybody . . . oh, dear, are you all right?"

It was the woman I'd delivered the trays of baked goods to earlier, Sally Sanborn.

"I was out for a walk, I thought I'd come down to the beach, but as I arrived, your car sped past me and you weren't in it."

Norm, that would've been, leaving the scene of the crime. Or one of his crimes, anyway; she sucked in a breath.

"Well, that didn't seem right. And then Popsy got away from me."

She waved at the little dog frisking around happily on the weedy lawn. "He ran up here, and when I chased him I saw that door was open. Which it never is."

Right. They'd all been boarded but this one. She gestured at the house.

"So I crept up and peeked in and there you were, out cold on the floor, and in the grass by the steps outside I found this card."

It was a business card. TWO GUYS MOVING & HAULING, it said.

Those words were also on the side of the van that had just shown up, I realized muzzily, driven by the same fellows who'd been at the camp opposite Miss Blaine's cottage. And they'd been on their caps . . .

Alarm bells rang in my head: *Oh, come on. A dropped business card? Give me a break.*

It was all too ridiculously coincidental; I knew this even in my muddled state, which by the way was still impressive. Whatever Norm had shot me up with still had me firmly in its grip.

"So I ran home and called them," Sally finished just as the two guys returned.

"I don't get it." I drank from the water bottle she handed me. "Why didn't you just call the cops? Or The Chocolate Moose?"

She knew I'd come from there, after all, and she had the number; she'd used it just this morning, calling us to ask for a delivery.

Now she looked away uncomfortably. "I didn't think you needed an ambulance. And unless it's a real emergency I'd rather not call the police about anything right now. You see, my son is—"

The light dawned as I recalled the young man at her house. "He's a fugitive of some kind? He's wanted for something, is that it?"

She nodded gratefully at me. "Nothing huge, it wasn't anything violent, thank goodness. But he's broken the terms of his probation. And since I'm fairly new around here, no one knows I'm his mother. . . ."

"He's moved in on you," I finished for her. "Sounds like a real prince." I stretched my extremities, all except the wounded one that was bleeding again.

"But why not call The Chocolate Moose, then?" My headache was fading and my fear had also decreased substantially, as it occurred to me that as long as Ellie was at the shop, she was probably safe.

Customers coming in, people passing by on the street . . . in front of witnesses, Norm McHale wouldn't be able to do anything to her. And I'd be back there before closing time . . .

"Why not," I repeated after swigging from the water bottle once more, "just call Ellie?"

Sally straightened from snapping her dog onto his leash. "Oh, I did," she said, gathering the shaggy little creature up into her arms.

"I did call. Twice, in case I'd gotten the wrong number. And I let it ring and ring."

Popsy grinned toothily, panting and gazing up at his mistress with bright, adoring eyes.

"But," said Sally, "there was no answer."

I sat up straighter. My arm was a mess, but that was apparently among the many things I couldn't do anything about.

Urgency seized me; Ellie wasn't in the shop.

338

But once these guys drove away with me, who knew if I'd last long enough to look for her? Because *something* weird was going on with them, that was for sure.

"Listen," I told the woman with the little dog squirming in her arms, "did you hire these guys or . . . I mean, how did you get them to come here at all?"

She brightened as she replied, "I did hire them, yes. I'd found their card by the front steps, which meant they could find their way here since obviously they did it once already. So I hurried home and called them, and said I had a hauling job for them, but only if they came right away."

Apologetically, she added, "As I said, I don't drive, myself, and my son's not allowed to. But they'll take you back to Eastport."

Right, sure they would. That's why their business card had been found by the doorstep of a house I'd been left to die in. . . .

"And after that," Sally called, backing away, "you'd better get some medical attention."

Right, much more of that bleeding business and I wouldn't need a doctor, I'd need an undertaker. But first I had to get out of this van, or the choice would be made for me, and not in my favor, either.

Too bad my body was still even slower than my drugged brain. I lunged for the door just as one of the guys slid it shut. As it closed I got a glimpse of his denim jacket, so raggedy that the pockets were tearing off and various papers stuffed into them nearly spilling out.

"Hey," I objected weakly as another wave of nausea rolled over me. After that I had to concentrate on keeping my stomach contents from decorating my surroundings, while he got behind the wheel and the other one took the up-front passenger seat.

I'd have preferred taking it myself instead of the hard floor here in the cargo area. But nobody asked me; on the other hand, it seemed that no one had *recognized* me yet, either, which I took as a good omen.

It was the only good one I'd experienced recently, but what the heck, it was all I had so I clung to it. Hauling myself up, I peered at the clock on the van's dashboard. The numerals said it was 1:45.

That meant Norm McHale had about an hour's head start on me. It was plenty of time for him to get back to Eastport, visit Ellie at The Chocolate Moose, and spin a story—about me being in terrible trouble somewhere, maybe—plausible enough so that she would go with him.

Maybe even without telling anyone about it, if he convinced her that it was enough of an emergency . . .

The van rolled past the chain-link fence through

the gate whose padlock had been cut off, perhaps with the substantial pair of tin snips lying near me on the van floor. There were a lot of other tools back here, too, and a pile of copper piping that looked as if it might have been liberated out of somebody's cellar.

"Guys?" The one who was driving kept his eyes on the road. The other one looked back at me, but he still didn't seem to know me.

That was fine with me. "Guys, could you maybe drive real fast? I mean, not fast enough to get a ticket, of course," I added hastily as we pulled onto Route 1 headed for Eastport. "Just fast enough to—"

But in the next moment I shut up as the van's sudden acceleration threw me back down onto the hard floor; driver guy didn't seem worried about getting a ticket.

Or anything else. They drove up Route 1 as if their hats were on fire and their backsides were catching, as Bella would have put it. Groggily, I kept trying my phone; it had begun working again as soon as we got away from the dead zone around the abandoned cul-de-sac.

But each time I punched in Ellie's number I got the same result: nothing, not even voice mail. The line at my house was busy, Sam and Mika's cells were also engaged, and Wade was at work somewhere, so I doubted he'd be much help.

By the time the van got to the causeway

and onto it, though, I was realizing, through a diminishing but still very substantial drug-induced haze, these guys hadn't killed me. In fact, they were doing as I'd asked, taking me back to Eastport without delay.

So the next time I woke up enough to punch in another speed dial number, I let the guys drive on instead of trying Bob Arnold. I could explain all this better to him in person, anyway, I decided.

But moments later when the van reached The Chocolate Moose, I could see from outside that the lights were out. The door was locked, too, and when I staggered over and let myself in, I found the credit card reader and ceiling fans turned off, and the register closed out.

So Ellie's departure had been orderly . . . unless someone had set things up neatly to allay any suspicions otherwise.

Thinking this, I finally did call Bob Arnold, but when I did the dispatcher told me that he was tied up at a traffic accident, there were serious injuries involved, and did I have an emergency?

Well, no. Not one that I could explain very well, anyway. So I hung up, and back outside while I thought about what to do next I paid the van guys an amount of cash that seemed to satisfy them.

That they hadn't just murdered me and stashed my body somewhere seemed to deserve a bonus—how *had* their business card gotten on that doorstep, anyway?—but since they still didn't seem to recognize me, I didn't mention it.

Then I thought for a minute more, which considering the way I was still feeling was no small feat all by itself. And what I thought was: Ellie had gone somewhere unexpectedly, but first she'd taken the time to close the shop properly, which to me meant she hadn't been kidnapped by force. More likely, as I'd thought earlier, someone had convinced her to go with them. And when I thought about who that someone almost certainly was—Norm McHale, of course; if he told Ellie that I'd been hurt and that I needed her, he could easily have lured her.

Hastily, I punched redial, discovering from the dispatcher this time that Bob had summoned some county sheriff's deputies to help with the accident, and to cover things here in town temporarily. They would be arriving in half an hour or so, and would I like to speak with one of them when they did? No, I replied, then tried all my other numbers again, which was how I learned that Wade wasn't just busy at work; he was on a boat headed to Nova Scotia to help bring a disabled freighter to Eastport.

Also, Sam was halfway to Bangor for some lawn-mower parts he'd found on Craigslist and gotten for a song, and Mika and the baby were at the health center; the baby had an ear infection.

All of which I gathered from Bella, who added that no, Ellie wasn't there, they hadn't heard from her, and my dad was dozing in the screen house in the backyard. But if she could do anything for me—

"No," I said. Our midnight ride had probably taken a lot out of him, and, anyway, I didn't want either of them to get involved in this.

Besides, if I had to try explaining it all to Bella right now I would lose my mind. I didn't even understand it, myself.

"No, I was looking for a lift, but I've got one and I'll be home soon," I rattled off hastily, and ended the call before she could ask me what was wrong with my own car.

Then, glancing around helplessly, I spotted the gray van still in its parking spot outside the Moose.

"So can I hire you to drive me around a little more?" I asked the guys, peeling off another pair of twenties apiece.

I mean, what the heck, they hadn't killed me the first time, and I was desperate. Also, you never knew, I might get information out of them; that conveniently placed business card of theirs, for instance, was still a serious puzzle.

"How about fifty bucks each?" I upped the ante, and they turned to each other.

"Deal," said the driver, and I was just about to get back—but in the passenger seat this time, for fifty dollars I wasn't going to be bouncing around on that hard floor in the back—when a familiar vehicle came tearing down Water Street toward us.

Big, red, and eye-poppingly shiny, it was my dad's new truck, and behind the wheel—looking old, grouchy, and terrifyingly determined—was my dad.

"Hop in," he called to me from across Water Street.

Leaning over, he swung open the truck's passenger door; he'd heard Bella's end of my conversation with her, I gathered.

I'd pulled my sweatshirt on over my arm, so he couldn't see the damage. Hastily, I shoved the money at the guys in the van, all fifty of it for each of them.

For not murdering me, I thought, back when I was still so doped up that they could've done the deed by pressing a hand over my mouth.

But now, just as I turned away, the driver guy's eyes narrowed. "Hey," he began aggrievedly, "aren't you one of them two nosy women who—"

So he'd finally recognized me. "Yes, I am," I replied briskly, then pushed a couple of extra tens at him.

"For your trouble, okay?" Because whatever the hypodermic rig had been doing at their cottage across the lake from Miss Blaine's place, I was sure now that they weren't behind any of this or responsible for the old teacher's injuries, either.

I mean, and you should forgive me for saying so, but these two were a little dim to be responsible for much of anything.

"Thanks for the ride," I told them, then sprinted back across the street.

Idling by the curb, the pickup truck's engine rumbled powerfully, and I could tell that my dad was already getting good use out of the vehicle by the ratty-looking cardboard boxes he'd loaded into the bed, to take to, so I supposed, the dump.

As I hopped in, he hit the gas and peeled out, an act he very much enjoyed, I could tell.

"So I guess you're looking for Ellie, then," my father said.

He did not comment on my appearance, which by that time must've been ghastly. I did him the same favor; I'd been correct about last night taking it out of him.

"Yeah, and I guess you weren't out in the screen house, after all," I retorted. Because clearly he'd gathered enough from listening in on Bella to know how to find me.

"Where to?" he wanted to know.

"Beats me." I'd been so busy figuring out *how* to chase Norm, I hadn't had a chance to think yet about *where* to chase him.

But wherever Ellie was right this minute, I was

willing to bet he'd put her there; for all I knew, he might still be with her.

"I'm not even sure what car we're looking for," I added.

Norm could be driving mine, or his own little green sports car. Or he might have switched to one of his other vehicles.

Nervously, I pushed up my sleeves, remembering only at the stab of pain what was under one of them.

"That arm looks iffy," my dad remarked in casual understatement.

"Right," I said absently, and then a funny thing happened.

As we made the turn up Washington Street past the big old granite post office building, Marienbad Jones came hurrying out of the Rubber Ducky.

Which was odd. "Slow down," I told my dad, and he did, so I could go on watching Marienbad.

Very odd. She hustled across the street and got into her own car, a big old black Cadillac sedan that she'd gotten in lieu of an unpaid bar bill, sometime in the distant past.

It was the same car I'd seen her in earlier, up on Route 1. Now it jerked backward out of its parking spot, then roared forward.

"Go," I said as it came around the corner, and I don't know what kind of an engine was under that shiny red hood, but it was big.

Also, it was *loud*. Little kids looked up as we roared by, and if I hadn't been so scared for Ellie I might have enjoyed it, too; instead I watched the rear-view, and when Marienbad turned left onto High Street I sent my dad around the block so we could get behind her.

Because the thing was, during business hours Marienbad *never* left the Rubber Ducky; I mean, *never*. But now here she was, swanning around in broad daylight for the second time in one day.

Then I realized from the direction she was headed where she must be going. "Stay back. Don't let her know we're behind her."

My dad slowed obediently again and we rumbled along that way through Eastport side streets, keeping Marienbad's big, boatlike car well out ahead of us.

Then, "Pull over," I said. She'd turned a corner, but the street she'd turned onto was a dead end, so I knew she must've stopped in front of Norm's place.

At my gesture, my dad pulled over near the corner. I got out, leaned back into the truck's cab, and told my dad that I thought Norm McHale had Ellie right now and was holding her against her will.

"I don't know why," I added. "I don't know what's going on. But Bob Arnold's busy, and there's no time to wait for him or anyone."

He nodded slowly. No argument, no objections. Even the town ambulances and the fire department were at the crash Bob Arnold was tied up with; I could tell by the distant wail of the sirens.

"You know this is crazy, right?" I asked my dad. "My just barging on in there like this, you know it's . . . ?"

Nuts was the term I was looking for, actually. Because what I intended was to find Ellie if she was in there and get her out.

"Lots of things worth doing are. Crazy, that is."

A short laugh escaped me; he ought to know. "Don't you follow me," I warned. "If I don't come out of there in a reasonable amount of time, get Bob Arnold and drag him here if you have to."

He nodded gravely. "I will." And then, "Jacobia."

Halfway to the corner, I turned back. Up there behind the wheel of his new truck, my skinny, aging, long-haired father resembled an elderly hippie who had somehow gotten into the wrong vehicle.

What he really belonged in was an old VW van with suns and flowers inexpertly painted onto it. Oh, and with machine-gun turrets, too; as I may have mentioned, he was a complicated guy.

Now as if reading my thought he raised two fingers at me: either a V for victory or a peace sign, I couldn't tell which.

I nodded acknowledgment. Then, trying to look casual, I strolled down the sidewalk to the corner, and around it.

And then . . .

A faint cry came from inside Norm McHale's house, quickening my step.

And then the real fun began.

"Keep still, please." Norm's voice, coming from the same front parlor Ellie and I had visited a day earlier, sounded flustered.

Good, I thought, listening from outside on the flagstone path. My intention was still simply to march in, grab Ellie, and skedaddle with her. And for that plan, the less sure of himself Norm was, the better.

As for Marienbad, I had no idea of her part in all this, if any. I wasn't sure now that she was even here, after all; I didn't hear her, and when I'd come around the corner a few minutes after she did, her black Cadillac was nowhere in sight.

But I'd deal with her somehow if it turned out that I had to, I'd decided. I crossed the granite-slab doorstep between the rosebushes, not bothering to knock before I went in.

Dusty afternoon sunshine slanted in through the smeary windows flanking the door, gilding the vases stuffed full of ostrich feathers and the bamboo-legged tables with porcelain card trays on them.

I heard no more voices. Everything was silent as I crept along the flat, red hallway carpet, past the framed mirrors on the walls and the mahogany hat rack with the dusty hats dangling on it.

Or it was silent until that damned parrot started squawking. "Hello!" it yelled from the big brass cage in the hall window.

The cage's door stood wide open, but the big green bird didn't come out. I stood still, letting my heart rate drop; I'd forgotten that it was even here, so the dratted bird had startled the wits out of me.

"Hello!" it hollered again, and, of course, I didn't tell it how much I would've enjoyed wringing its neck, mostly because suddenly someone had both their hands wrapped tightly around mine.

"Urk," I pronounced as my captor propelled me roughly into the parlor.

"You have a visitor." It was Marienbad behind me. She released my throat, shoving me hard. I tottered forward a few gasping, undignified steps.

"Oh," said Norm, sounding disappointed as he looked up, sweaty and red-faced with frustration. He was holding a syringe like the one he'd used on me a few hours earlier.

Trying to inject Ellie with it, apparently. But she hadn't been cooperating. Instead because he hadn't bothered putting her hands behind her before tying them, she'd been using her two clenched fists as a clubbing tool when I came in.

Now she took his moment of inattention as a chance to put her two bound feet together, draw her knees up sharply and suddenly, and kick out at Norm McHale just as hard as she could, aiming for the middle of his chest.

"Oof," he grunted, backing away just in time so her feet only grazed him. His look changed to one of thwarted fury as he raised the glinting needle once more.

But my pal Ellie only took this as an invitation to more mayhem, and her next kick dropped him to the carpet. I rushed at him, shoving ornate end tables out of the way and tripping over a really darling little embroidered footstool.

I threw it at him, then hurled myself onto him and tried holding him. "Norm, what are you doing? What's all this about?" I demanded.

Then, "Ellie, call Bob Arnold," I said. "Tell him that unless he's out there loading victims into ambulances all by himself . . ."

We need him here, I was about to finish. But before I could—

"Jake!" Ellie cried warningly, but too late. Sharp fingernails dug into my shoulders and strong hands hauled me backward, freeing Norm from my grip.

"Ouch!" I yelled as Marienbad grabbed my

arms, pulling them back behind me and upward toward my shoulder blades.

Glancing down, I saw blood dripping off my elbow, which seemed only right for an extremity that felt suddenly as if nails were being hammered into it. Marienbad tied my wrists together, the restraints biting harshly into my skin, while Norm scrambled across the floor, still trying to grab Ellie's ankles.

But by now she'd gotten the twine wrapped around them undone; evading him nimbly, she raised a large vase that she'd snatched off the fireplace mantel and brought it down hard.

Rolling from beneath it at the last possible instant, he slid across the floor, heaved himself to his feet once more, and turned to advance on her again. She hopped up and scampered away from him.

But when she sprinted for the hall, Marienbad blocked her and knocked her backward into the parlor once more just as Norm, his face wild and his hands grasping convulsively at her, seized her again.

And this time, before I could do anything or shout a warning, he bent to grab up the loaded syringe that he'd lost in the struggle and jammed the needle into her thigh.

Moments later, she sagged with a sigh. Gripping her under her arms, he dragged her out while Marienbad frog-marched me after them.

Down the hall toward the rear of the house, past the parrot, who at the commotion had gone warily silent in his brass cage . . .

At the end of the dark, dreary hall, a swinging door led out to the kitchen, a large, fluorescent-lit room whose white-metal fixtures, scuffed wooden table and chairs, and dull linoleum floor gave the room about as much charm as the inside of your average meat locker.

Fly-specked curtains, torn shades . . . apparently Norm's penchant for decoration didn't extend to the utility areas of the house.

"Sit," Marienbad ordered. "Go on, do what I say."

She yanked out a chair and shoved me into it. Theoretically, of course, that was my big chance to jump up again and overpower her, over-turning the table, maybe, to keep Norm at bay just long enough for Ellie and me to escape.

In that theory, though, my shoulders hadn't just been getting yanked halfway out of their sockets and there wasn't a by-now-really-very-scary amount of blood running down my arm.

Also theoretically, Ellie wasn't completely out cold from whatever Norm had injected her with, but in real life she was. So the two of us were, as my son Sam would've put it, fusterclucked.

"Why'd you do it?" I asked. Hey, this whole thing had gone to hell, pretty much. I'd told my dad not to come in here no matter what, since however bright and bushy-tailed he seemed I did not need him having another heart attack.

Also, despite all that had happened, according to the clock on the kitchen wall I'd only been in here a few minutes. So he wouldn't be rescuing us; not soon enough, anyway.

Which was why I decided to wing it. "Come on, Norm. How'd you go from being a nice, wouldn't-hurt-a-fly type of guy to being a bloody murderer in such a short—"

"Shut up." Marienbad was stuffing things into a paper bag: more syringes, the shiny glass ampules of sedative that I imagined went into them, a plastic envelope of what looked like a lot of money—

Wait a minute, a bag of money? Slumped forward onto the table, Ellie moaned and stirred. "Norm," I began, "where did all that—?"

"I said shut *up!*" Marienbad slammed the bag down onto the kitchen counter and swung around to face Norm.

"We're leaving, okay? We're getting out of here right now, get whatever you want to take with you and—"

But Norm just couldn't resist the chance to excuse himself; I could see now how he must have thought that his embezzlement and tax evasion crimes were really okay, if only he had a good enough reason.

And what he said next proved it. "Look, we really didn't have a choice. Toby found out that Marienbad was paying herself a living wage instead of skimping along on ramen noodles half the year, whenever the tourists weren't around."

The light dawned. "A living wage," I repeated. In winter, the beer drinkers at the Ducky would never support that. Like the rest of us, she'd be lucky to keep the lights on, outside of tourist season.

"You mean she was—"

"Yeah, that's right, I was skimming," she cut in snarlingly. "Whatever came in, I took twenty percent and didn't report it. Paid less in taxes, had a few more bucks so I could at least run the heat."

Ellie lifted her head and looked around blearily. "What's going on?" she slurred, then passed out again.

"I don't understand," I said, forcing myself to sound interested. It seemed Marienbad liked justifying herself, too, once she got going.

Keep her talking. . . . "How would Toby Moran find out about . . . ohh," I finished, getting it, finally.

Marienbad scowled. "Right again. Oh, he was a smooth bastard."

She stalked to the sink, ran some water, and drank it. By then I'd have killed for that water, which did not seem like a good sign, and the sleeve clinging to my injured arm was soggy.

"Sweet-talked me into a boyfriend-girlfriend deal," Marienbad went on. "I gave him a bartending job, later I find out he's pouring drinks but not ringing them up, putting the money in his own pocket."

I could see why she'd have been outraged; skimming cash out of the Rubber Ducky was supposed to be her racket, not his.

As she talked, she kept putting things in the bag: clothesline, duct tape, a roll of electrician's wire, a butcher knife . . . yeeks, I didn't like this even a little bit, all of a sudden.

I mean, not that I'd liked it a whole hell of a lot before. Also, it was getting worse; that woozy, weak feeling I'd begun having . . . that couldn't be from blood loss, could it?

Oh, of course, it could. The thought sent a worm of fear wriggling through me as I went on: "So you killed him?"

But that didn't make sense, and Norm seemed to agree. "No, of course not. Of course, she didn't kill him, that's not a good enough reason to—"

"Yes, it was," Marienbad interrupted flatly. "And I should have done it, too, back then when I had the chance. Alone in the bar, late at night . . ."

"But you didn't," Norm said soothingly. "You aren't the type."

I thought current events were contradicting that notion pretty effectively. "You couldn't let him destroy you, though, could you?" I asked. "If he'd turned you in to the authorities, it would've . . ."

Yeah. Tax fraud was a crime, as Norm well knew, and the IRS didn't make any allowances for people who wanted petty extravagances like being able to turn the heat on in the winter.

"That's right," Marienbad said. "I couldn't. Like he says, I'm not the type." She turned, looking straight at Norm.

"So I didn't," she finished. "You did that for me, Norm, didn't you?"

His look turned to one of despair. "But I thought we agreed we'd never tell anyone that unless—"

"I see," I said, cutting him off. "So really, the whole thing was pretty simple. Except . . ."

It wasn't easy, imagining them together: he a sensitive collector of decorative things, Marienbad a woman who would just as soon smash a vase over your head as put it on a shelf to look at.

But now as she told her story, I watched him and understood: he adored her, but the reverse not so much. He'd begun understanding that fact, too, I saw from the way his face crumpled.

I had no more time to worry about his feelings, however; for one thing, I could practically feel my red blood count dropping.

And for another, Marienbad was about to start hustling us out of here; to where, I didn't know, but I doubted that I would like it.

Or that I would have very long to dislike it, either, since she couldn't very well let Ellie or me survive, could she? Not after what she'd just told us.

I hoped that same notion would occur even more thoroughly to Norm: that she couldn't let any of us live to tell this tale, him included. Like she'd said, you do what you have to do to survive.

And you can call me a cynic, but however handy Norm might've been so far, I had a feeling he wasn't in her long-term plans.

She gestured me sharply to my feet while directing Norm also, urging him to get Ellie stumbling forward somehow. Bending, he slung Ellie's arm over his shoulder and lifted, hauling her along bonelessly with her feet dragging behind; I followed, with Marienbad behind me.

But at the kitchen doorway I halted. "Wait a minute."

I braced myself in the door frame. "Just lay it out straight for me, let me understand."

Ticking off on my fingers, I went on: "First Toby worked for you, then he romanced you, then he stole from you, and then, when you'd fired him and broken off what was left of your romance with him—"

I sucked in a breath. "When the romance ended, he threatened to report your profit skimming to the IRS, which would've been disastrous for you. Have I got all that right?"

"Wrong," Marienbad replied harshly. "You left out the most important thing. First he cheated on me. With that silly girl Jenna Waldrop, of all people," she added. "And *then* he stole from me."

I let my hands drop from the door frame; there it was, the bitter personal-emotions cherry on the money-motive cake.

Also, poor Jenna. Still, I didn't move forward. Instead: "But, Marienbad, why did you have to kill him?"

Anything that kept me from going where she wanted to go was good with me, since I doubted I'd be going anywhere else, ever again.

Or Ellie or Norm, either. "Why didn't you just get a bunch of the regulars from your bar, tell them he was giving you trouble, and let nature take its course?"

It wouldn't have been the first time frontier justice got doled out here in Eastport. But: "Don't you think I tried that? Worked, too, for a while. He even straightened out a little. But it didn't last."

She nudged the small of my back with something that felt enough like the end of a gun barrel to get me moving again.

"He wanted his job back. So he could keep stealing. Wanted *me* back, too. Not that he felt anything for me, just so he could . . ."

The parrot watched silently as we went by. Norm and Ellie were already outside. But so was my dad, in his truck . . . I hoped.

"Just so he could lord it over me," she finished.

A small laugh accompanied this last remark. "Guess I showed him, though. And Norm," she added acidly, "was *so* helpful about it. He even helped with the plan and managed to procure the poison."

Right, and inject Moran with it. . . . "Yeah, he's a real trooper, all right," I said, mimicking her tone. Then I stepped out, squinting in the bright sunlight after the gloom inside the house.

Ellie blinked dazedly, beginning to wake up but still leaning heavily on Norm. Ahead between towering rosebushes lay the flagstone path leading out to the street; to my left, the smaller gravel path that went down to the barn where Norm kept his vintage cars.

I hadn't realized before how private Norm's house was. The big, barnlike garage's new metal roof peeked over the tops of the roses, but otherwise the house was shielded from casual view.

Also, no big red pickup truck was anywhere in sight. So my dad must've realized something had gone wrong; that, however, still left me with a big question: where was he?

Because we needed him, now, we really—

"Stay here," said Norm suddenly.

He shoved Ellie at me. She fell into my arms as he pushed past me, sprinting off down the path toward the barn. Moments later, from beyond the roses I heard the rumble of a garage door being raised.

I peered around again. Still no pickup truck. Pulling up right there at the end of the flagstone walk would've been good. But—

"What's going on?" Ellie wanted to know. Still holding her up, I could feel her trying to get her footing. She was coming around, her balance improving and the strength returning to her body.

Not enough to run, though, and any moment Norm would be back.

"What," Ellie quavered, "are they going to do to us?"

Which gave me a bit of hope, because I'd known her for a long time and my friend Ellie White never quavered.

"How are you going to kill us?" Ellie begged Marienbad pitifully. "Tell me, I have to know."

That was another thing I knew darned well that Ellie wouldn't do, because for one thing she never begged, and for another we were both very aware that for our captors to be planning anything in advance was the last thing we wanted.

Because maybe they were evil—heck, of *course,* they were—but they were also unused to this kind of thing, and what we wanted was for them to go on being as clueless and unprepared as possible.

Which meant that Ellie was trying to tell me something. . . .

And then I had it. "Yes," I chimed in to Marienbad, "how *are* you and Norm planning to get rid of us, anyway?"

From out in the street past the roses and flagstones came the low grumble of an engine, then a gravelly snarl as somebody revved it.

"Never mind," snapped Marienbad, urging me forward, but her voice sounded shaky and her eyes when they met mine were desperate. None of this was going the way she'd wanted.

"Because you know what?" I went on, ignoring Marienbad's reply while hoisting Ellie, who'd just then sagged dramatically in my arms as if the sedative she'd gotten was kicking in again.

Or as if she knew I needed a reason not to be marching obediently down those flagstones toward a waiting car. Norm's car, of course, and where the *hell* was that damned red pickup truck . . . ?

"You're going to have to kill us somehow," I answered myself. "I don't think Norm's going to do it for you this time. Not after you just blabbed about him killing Toby Moran."

Marienbad half-turned, looking as if what I'd just said hadn't occurred to her before. Not looking as if she welcomed the thought, either.

"You could just slit our throats," I suggested cheerily. "That's fast, and I saw you brought along that great big butcher knife."

To her credit, at this Marienbad began looking a little green around the gills. *Good,* I thought meanly.

"Right here," I said, drawing a line on the side of my throat with my index finger. My *bloody* index finger; my arm wasn't pumping it any longer, but it was still oozing steadily.

"Of course, there'll be a lot of this stuff." I held the bloody finger out to her. "And until we do die, you'll have to put up with a lot of gagging and choking. . . ."

"Shut up," she grated out, sounding as if she might weep.

I understood; Marienbad had arranged the murder of a passed-out-drunk Toby Moran, and although I didn't yet quite see how, she was almost surely behind Miss Blaine's death, too.

But doing it in cold blood to a couple of fully conscious people was something else again, as she'd already begun suspecting.

Too bad that Ellie's brief bout of alertness really had passed; she was too helpless to run, the thorny rosebushes massed at both sides of the path walling off it as effectively as bricks.

And at the end of it Norm McHale waited with his trusty hypodermic needle.

Speaking of which, on second thought the cold-blooded murder idea wasn't bumming Marienbad out quite the way I'd hoped it would.

"If you must know, he's going to overdose you both first with that stuff he used before," she told me smugly.

Rats, so they *had* planned ahead. "Come on," Norm's voice called from down the path.

Fear stabbed me hard as the knife appeared from Marienbad's bag looking just the way I remembered it: Big. Sharp. Pointy. She jabbed at me, then jerked it back, her eyes widening at the red spot that appeared on my pants leg. Then . . .

The glitter of dark excitement that sprang up in her gaze scared me badly, more than anything so far. Before now, she'd been desperate, and I could understand that.

But something was changing about her; now the phrase "nothing to lose" didn't even begin to cover the look in her eyes, like she was in a trap and didn't care who she hurt getting out.

"Walk," she said calmly. "Take Ellie with you."

Ellie had other ideas, shaking my hands off her shoulders before balling her fists out in front of her and stomping—unsteadily, but stomping nonetheless—toward Marienbad.

"Oh, yeah?" she spat, swaying. Undrugged, she

might not have been so feisty. But: "You think so, huh?" she demanded. She thrust her fists out, jabbed prize-fighter style with them. "You want some of this? Do you?"

Oh, it was glorious to behold. Just not very helpful.

"Pfft," said Marienbad, not bothering with the knife. She merely reached past Ellie's fists and stuck two fingers out, and pushed.

Whereupon Ellie collapsed. "Catch her," snarled Marienbad as Ellie sagged, the drug she had on board taking firm hold again.

I got between Ellie and the flagstones just before she hit them. In an instant Marienbad stood over me.

"Up." She jerked the knife. "Or we can do it here, the way you suggested."

Ellie moaned, her eyelids fluttering weakly. "Oh," she murmured, catching sight of me, "there's blood all over your . . ."

Then Norm was there, too. "What's the holdup?" he demanded, "the car's sitting right out there, let's—"

"Do it," Marienbad ordered. "They're too hard to handle this way, it's too risky. Just put them both to sleep and we'll—"

But he'd already figured this out and was preparing, whipping out the needle and syringe, and fishing two more of those damned glass ampules out of his pocket.

"Quite the Boy Scout, aren't you?" I snarled, but it came out all mushy.

Apparently some important areas of my brain had begun noticing their blood supply getting skimpy; what with so much of it exiting my body lately, I mean. Heedless of thorns I could barely feel through my fear and wooziness, I leaned back against the massed branches of the rosebushes.

Bees buzzed in them. A plane droned, high overhead. Norm loomed near, his face apologetic but determined.

"This won't hurt," he whispered, raising the needle, from which a clear droplet hung, shivering.

He bent toward me purposefully, just as that parrot yelled from inside. "Hello! Hello!"

Wait a minute. The parrot . . . ?

A needle prick stung my throat, just as some sort of commotion started happening behind Marienbad. Then came the explosion, a dully massive *ka-boom* like the sound you hear in the movies when the bomb goes off. Huge smoke billows began rising from behind the roses.

Norm jumped up, the syringe still gripped in his fist. His face sagged whitely as he must have realized what just happened.

"My cars!" he cried. "My . . . the barn, call the fire department!"

Which with me dying there in the bushes like

that was kind of beside the point, I thought as Norm took off back up the path toward the house, shoving Marienbad thoughtlessly aside in his panic.

She let him go and just stood there, looking . . . well, I don't know what she looked like, actually, only that from behind her Bob Arnold appeared suddenly, grabbing her by the shoulders and shoving her again in his haste to get to me.

"Hey." He crouched by me anxiously. "Jake, you okay?"

But he didn't wait for my answer, instead punching the speed dial on his own phone to summon help. Meanwhile, from somewhere on the other side of the rosebushes came the snap, crackle, and pop of a building burning, very nearby.

Marienbad looked stunned. "Sit," Bob snapped at her.

She sat. Hearing that tone out of him, a stone statue would've obeyed. Then three sharp explosions sounded one after the other in the burning barn, and after that came a familiar roar.

A *motorcycle's* roar . . . "Hey, Hannah," Bob said into the phone.

Hannah Blanchard was the emergency services dispatcher I'd talked to earlier, which I wouldn't mention here except that while it was all going on, I was so proud of myself for remembering it.

368

My own name, though, or where I was or who the president was . . .

Not so much. "Hannah, ask Reggie—"

Reggie was the ambulance's driver; another point in the memory department's plus column for me.

"Ask Reggie if on his way up here he'd do me a favor and knock this little goofball off his two-wheeler if he sees him, will you? Guy's taking off from town right about now, I'm a little busy."

He added the location, Norm's description, and the direction he was heading: off-island, almost certainly. But Reggie didn't have to do anything about it, because the next sound I heard—through the distant, insistent hiss of waves rushing on a beach, which I imagined was the sound of my remaining brain cells shutting down en masse . . .

The next sound I heard was the bum-bada-BUM-bumbumbum of an enormous, God-knows-how-many-horsepower engine, the kind that comes on a brand-new pickup truck.

Next came a shriek of tires, the scream of a different, smaller engine revving itself madly into the red zone, and finally silence.

The perfume of roses washed over me, warmly comforting. "Oh," said Ellie sadly from somewhere. "Oh, help her . . ."

Then it got dark again.

Really dark. And it stayed that way for a while.

Eleven

"That cake was fantastic!" my son, Sam, enthused a week later at Sharon and Andy's wedding reception, held in the Episcopalian church hall across from my big old house on Key Street.

"Glad you liked it," I replied, exhausted but happy. I'd been out of the hospital for three days, and the wedding had gone off without a hitch, every sweet, sappy moment of it.

The bride rode to the church in a horse-drawn carriage fit for a fairy princess, which was what she looked like. Andy Devine was waiting impatiently for her, handsome in his blue dress uniform. The jangling of the church bells had filled the air with a joyous clamor, and the ceremony was lovely, too.

As was the reception afterward, catered with an abundance of energy and style by the Eastport church ladies and featuring homemade creamed chicken on hot-buttered baking powder biscuits, just-picked fresh-steamed peas with herbed butter, and a salad of many greens from the gardens full of early produce all over Eastport.

"Has Mika had cake?" I asked, and Sam assured me that she had. Meanwhile, the Coast

Guard officers, their significant others, teachers from Sharon's school, and friends and relatives of the happy couple mingled in celebration, all dressed in their best for the occasion.

Also, there was champagne, about which enough said; I didn't make a fool of myself, but I wasn't fit to drive, either. Not that I wanted to; instead I sat quietly, watching people enjoy what we'd baked.

"Mika's the real hero," I told Sam, gesturing with my champagne glass. Wearing a green dress, his young wife was across the room socializing with the church ladies, looking gorgeous as usual with her raven-black hair and the baby on her hip.

"While she was covering the shop for us," I said, "all those times we were out trying to chase down who might've killed Toby Moran, she worked up a sheet-cake recipe that tastes just like whoopie pie."

Seriously, my daughter-in-law was a genius. "After that, it was just a matter of . . ."

I stopped. Sam was listening pleasantly, an attentive smile on his face. But I knew for a fact that the only part about baking that he was interested in was the eating part.

"Oh, go on," I shooed him away indulgently, and he drifted off happily to find something else to devour; besides the main courses there were pickles, relishes, slaws, cheeses, fruit, and my favorite, a casserole full of homemade baked beans and tiny hot dogs.

Oh, good heavens, but it was delicious, and I was about to go get more of it just to make sure that it was as fabulous as I'd thought it was the first time, when Bob Arnold sat down beside me.

"So." Purse-lipped, he regarded the hall full of happy people.

"So, who knew Norm had a motorcycle, huh?" Because he had, of course, in that car barn of his with all his other vehicles.

Bob glowered. He was still mad at me. "Bob, I couldn't call you," I said. "By the time it all really started to go south, I was out of cell-phone range."

In Machiasport, I meant; the abandoned houses, and the beach. He eyed the celebration going on around us balefully.

"Yeah, yeah. You couldn't have said something to me about McHale earlier, though? Keep me in the loop?"

The part about Norm stitching up Andy's forehead, he meant.

"Yeah." I felt my shoulders sag; it was the part still bothering me, too.

"Bob, I know it was a mistake. I was trying to keep Norm from losing his veterinary license permanently, and—"

"Yeah," he said. "And you didn't know it

mattered, who put the stitches in Devine's fore-head."

That the fact might've started the state homicide investigators on a line of inquiry that led to Norm, he meant.

"Bob, I'm very sorry. If I'd just spoken up, if I'd told you what Norm told me . . ."

Miss Blaine might still be alive, I was about to say. But Bob was already taking pity on me.

"Ah, forget it, Jake. I was pretty ticked off, but the truth is, it wouldn't have made a difference."

He drank some ginger ale from a plastic cup. "Norm couldn't let the old lady live no matter what you said or did, or when. So don't make yourself miserable about it."

Relief touched me. Not a lot of it, but more than I'd had in a while on this particular subject.

"In fact, he was so paranoid, he waited several days to get rid of the rest of the evidence in case he was under surveillance," said Bob.

That was what Norm had been doing at Jasper Beach, of course. Bob went on: "Meanwhile, even if you had spoken up, the state cops wouldn't have jumped right to the conclusion that Norm was hiding something."

"Sure, but . . ."

"Bottom line, he'd have killed the old lady anyway. I asked him," Bob added, "specifically about it. So I know you're not responsible for her death, Jake, you just feel like you are."

"Oh." The rest of the weight rolled off my shoulders. Bob had asked Norm this pointed question just so he could tell me the answer, I knew.

"Thank you. I mean it, Bob. And I promise, I will never again keep any secrets from—"

You, I was about to finish, but he held his hand up again.

"Never say never," he cautioned, and after a moment I decided he was probably right about that, too.

"So how about my dad knocking Norm off his motorcycle," I said, changing the subject, "was that great, or what?"

Using his new pickup truck to do it, naturally. Bob smiled. "Just what I'd have expected from him. Tough old bird."

Then another thought struck him. "I got a call from the medical examiner's office this morning. She took a second look at Toby's body after Norm and Marienbad confessed. And with what she said plus what the culprits have told anyone who'll listen, now I can pretty much figure how the whole thing went."

The musicians had been playing dinner music. Now they put away their acoustic instruments and picked up electric ones.

"Marienbad got Moose cups and chocolate

sprinkles off your shop counter," Bob added once the shriek of electronic feedback got hastily cut off and the amplifiers were repositioned.

"She did it weeks ago, long before the murder happened. Just walked in and took what she needed."

Everything . . . "Wait, you mean the shake itself wasn't one of ours?"

"Nope," Bob answered. "The night of the murder, Norm mixed what passed for a milkshake in the blender behind the bar in the Ducky, right before they did the bad deed. Milk, ice cream, and Hershey's syrup, that's all."

Another little pulse of relief went through me; I hadn't liked thinking that one of our Moose Milks had been involved.

"What exactly did the medical examiner say about the poison?" I prodded.

"Well, for one thing, that there was no poison in Toby's mouth. That meant that both the cyanide and the insecticide were added to what remained in the milkshake cup *after* Moran had drunk most of it," Bob replied.

He went on, "Norm says they used the can of Raid that Marienbad kept in the bar's utility closet."

"Okay," I said slowly. "And they did that part, put the smelly insecticide in, because . . . ?"

Bob sighed. "So people would think it was what killed Toby. Think it, I mean, just long enough for Norm to go out and silence Miss Blaine. That way, by the time the cyanide was revealed as the real method, Miss Blaine wasn't alive anymore to talk about having given any to Norm for his supposed rat infestation."

"So if he didn't drink it, how *did* the cyanide get into Toby's stomach, then?" I asked.

Bob answered grimly, "After the argument that Andy and Toby had in the Ducky, Norm slipped out the back way. He caught up with Toby on the walkway behind the Ducky, but then Andy appeared again."

I pictured it: Norm crouched in the shadows, ready to pounce, until suddenly . . .

"Couple punches got thrown, Andy missed but got slugged in the forehead, himself; then he backed off, started thinking about how not to get written up for fighting right when he's in line for a big promotion," Bob continued.

Sure, because good character was important if you wanted to rise through the ranks in the Coast Guard.

"Once Andy was gone, Norm approached Toby and offered him the milkshake, and Toby was pretty loaded that night, you know. Sweet and cold, I suppose it must've looked good to him."

Bob took a breath, watching the dancers. "No poison in it, yet; they had to be sure there wasn't any off taste to the drink at all, so Toby would be sure to swallow it right down."

So far, so fine. But I still didn't see how . . .

"Then, when Toby had nearly finished the shake," said Bob, "that's when he got stabbed in the stomach with a hypodermic needle from Norm's old veterinary practice. It's what shot the cyanide into him."

He turned to me. "Finally Norm doctored the milkshake with both poisons, and the deed was done."

"Wait a minute, the autopsy wouldn't show that the cyanide was injected?"

Bob shrugged. "Yeah, if the coroner was looking for something like that, which she wasn't, at first. It's a needle track, not a stab wound, and with cyanide in the drink and in Toby's stomach, why would she be looking for it?" he finished.

Right. "So the argument with Andy, earlier in the bar," I began.

Just then the groom danced by with his bride in his arms, looking so handsome in his uniform that it was hard to imagine him even thinking about murder.

"Had nothing to do with it," Bob said. "Handy way to put the blame on him, that's all, that he had argued with the deceased earlier in the evening."

He dropped his plastic cup into a trash bin. "But Andy didn't commit murder and that's what the state cops have told Andy's Coast Guard superiors."

So Andy's career wouldn't be ruined, after all. "Gave Norm a good scare, though, when Andy turned up at his place two minutes after Norm got home that night, himself," Bob added.

A laugh burst out of me. "I'll bet. It's a wonder he could keep his hands from shaking long enough to put the stitches in."

Bob nodded wryly, sipping his ginger ale. I went on. "What about the other syringe from the guys' camp out at the lake?" He'd interviewed those guys very extensively, I knew.

More couples danced by. "That was an old syringe they'd used for giving medicine to one of their dogs," Bob replied.

"Oh," I said weakly. "Sure." I'd forgotten the dogs until now.

"But," I went on, "then why was their business card on the steps down in the Machiasport house?"

If it hadn't been, they wouldn't have been summoned by Sally Sanborn to come and fetch me in their van. "I mean, they must've been involved somehow, because surely that wasn't some kind of a—"

"Nope," said Bob, "no coincidence. But think, now . . . you were in a *vacant* house. And those guys had what in the back of their van?"

He eyed me expectantly until I got it. "Oh . . . they had plumber's tools, didn't they? For pipes, to cut them and . . ."

"Correct," Bob said. "And you remember all those copper thefts that've been driving me nuts lately?"

I did, and I recalled that the water hadn't worked in the vacant house, either; I'd thought it had been shut off.

Bob's eyes narrowed in satisfaction. "Turns out it was our two pals doing the crimes. They won't be depriving any more innocent basements of their plumbing pipes, by the way, 'cause they're both going to jail."

It's what they'd wanted at Miss Blaine's house the night she was attacked, I supposed; to case the joint for future stripping of its valuable metal, and to make sure Ellie and I weren't there to get it all before they could.

I said as much to Bob, and his answering smile was like the one on the face of the tiger.

"Yep. As for the motorcyclist at Miss Blaine's, that part was almost like you thought. Norm McHale had told Miss Blaine he had a rat problem, talked her into giving him one of the cyanide cartridges for some traps he claimed he'd made."

"Ellie and I saw one rat down near the car barn," I recalled, "but with all those cats he has—"

"Yeah, and you wouldn't use poison around pets anyway, would you? Which he didn't, it just got used on Toby. But afterward Norm didn't want it in his possession, or for Miss Blaine to be able to say he'd had it."

"So he went out there and put the cartridge he'd used back into the box with the rest of them," I theorized.

Bob nodded. "Tiny little hole in it, he hoped nobody would ever look at the cartridge, but if they did, maybe they wouldn't notice."

"Only she caught him at it. Surprised him, maybe?"

"Yup. Not that it would've mattered. Like I said, he knew all along he'd have to kill her sooner or later. Just hadn't wanted to take that particular risk until it was necessary."

Hey, it wasn't how I'd have done it, but then, I'm not a killer so what did I know?

"Oh," I replied as George and Ellie danced past us, making the most of a slow tune that the musicians had begun playing.

"Anyway," Bob said, smiling a little as they went by, "Moran had finally pushed Marienbad too far. Drunk, slobbering all over her, then threatening her with those tax problems of hers. So with Norm's help, she finally did something about it."

Yeah, she sure had, all right. Only it seemed to me that Norm had done more than just help . . .

I got up. Those little hot dogs weren't going to taste themselves. Again, I mean.

"Oh, Jacobia," interrupted one of the wedding

guests, waving a champagne glass. "That whoopie-pie cake was completely fabulous!"

Then the bride and groom danced by. Sharon appeared rapturous, and as for Andy, if anyone ever looked more like somebody had just handed him the keys to the kingdom, I'd never witnessed it.

"Cute couple," Bob said, his face softening.

Which was when my dad came in, pausing in the church hall's entryway to peer searchingly around the room for me.

"Bob, one last thing. About that business card . . ."

His face creased into a grin. "Yeah, interesting, huh?"

But then he saw my expression, which I imagine must've been puzzlement combined with the impulse to swat someone.

"Oh, wait, you don't know how it got there yet?" he asked.

I stifled my impatience. "No, Bob, I don't. And I hardly think that card with both the copper thieves' names and a handy phone number on it got dropped there by accident. They're a pair of doofuses, those guys, but they aren't *that*—"

Dumb, self-destructive . . . whatever. At last Bob relented.

"Okay," he said, "so what happened was, one of those guys is getting a divorce."

The papers I'd seen on the counter at the guys' camp . . . "Okay," I said. "And?"

"And the wife wants custody of the kids."

The ones I'd seen swimming with the dogs out there, maybe. "Go on."

"*And* she knew that if hubby's in jail for what she knows they've been doing, and she knows where they've been doing it—"

The lightbulb went on. "Likely she'd win custody of the kids."

"Bingo. So she drove down and planted one of their business cards at the scene of one of their most recent crimes," Bob said.

"That way it would be there when the copper-pipe theft out of that house was discovered and the cops would know—"

"Who did it," Bob finished approvingly for me. "In fact, she was just about to call in an anonymous tip about it when instead all this other stuff happened."

Then he told me one more very interesting thing about Moran's murder and spread his hands. "And that's it. No big mystery, no . . ."

No coinky-dink. Just then Jenna Waldrop danced by with her curls bouncing and her bracelets clinking, wrapped in the arms of one of Andy Devine's handsome Coast Guard colleagues.

Glowering from one of the folding chairs lined up along the wall, Henrietta Waldrop sat

382

clutching her rubber-tipped cane, watching the dancers. Mrs. Waldrop's dark, glittering eyes raked the dance floor from beneath eyelids heavy and wrinkled as old draperies. Her toe, however, tapped to the music, which I regarded as a good sign.

Then my dad spotted me and gestured that I should follow him outside, and with a last glance around the room full of good cheer, good music, and delicious cake, I knew my work here was complete.

So I did go with him.

"Your mother-in-law tells me you and Ellie are still planning to close up The Chocolate Moose this week."

We were in his red pickup truck, headed out Route 190 past the bank and the hair salon. Outside was all spring-green trees, indigo water, and azure sky streaked with a few high summer clouds.

"Yeah," I said. "Money situation's a little worse than I thought, even. And if Ellie's going to make a move she wants to do it soon, she says, so that in the autumn Lee can start school where she's going to be for the rest of the year."

It was a boiled-down version of what Ellie had shared with me that morning, that they were still leaving.

"George has got a job offer now, too, over in

Bangor, with health insurance and other benefits. And you know those don't grow on trees," I added disconsolately. "He can't very well not take it."

My dad turned left onto the old Eastport Road. "Anyway, about the question you asked me earlier?"

When he came into the shop only an hour before the wedding, I'd been finishing cake decora-tions: roses and forget-me-nots, made from the kind of frosting that looks much better than it tastes but holds its shape like plaster of Paris.

So I couldn't talk with him then. But now: "You wanted to know about what Norm was burying that day, down at Jasper Beach," I said, then went on. "It was the big needle and syringe that Marienbad used on Toby Moran," I told my dad, and he turned, surprised.

"Yeah, it was her," I said. "Norm tried, took the milkshake and the cyanide-loaded syringe with him. But he chickened out."

It was the last thing Bob Arnold had told me just now. A sharp laugh burst out of my dad.

"Oh, beware the deadly female of the species," he intoned.

"Right, and you know why?" I retorted. "Thousands and thousands of years of really good motivation, that's—"

"I know, I know," he put his hands up in a

warding-off gesture, then dropped them back onto the steering wheel. Then, "So it was Marienbad," he repeated to himself. "Damn, I guess I blew up the wrong barn, then."

I turned to him. "You *what?* Dad, don't tell me you—"

Rumor around town was that Norm McHale's car barn had blown up due to faulty wiring and careless oily-rag storage, plus improper ventilation. Why it had blown up just when it did, though, was so far not being discussed much, the pair of murders having sucked up most of the conversational oxygen in town lately.

Luckily for my dad, maybe. "Never mind," he said hastily now. "It's nothing you need to be worried about at all, I was just thinking out loud."

"Well, think a little quieter," I told him. "No need to remind anyone about that."

I changed the subject. "Where are we going, anyway?"

The road we'd turned onto paralleled Route 1 but was even more narrow, twisty, and rural, running between newly placed factory-built houses, old family graveyards, and overgrown woodlots.

My dad shrugged. "I felt like going out for a drive, that's all." He paused. "Although I've got something to tell you, too, actually."

Uh-oh. Back at the house they'd have begun

wondering about us, asking one another if anyone had seen us. Any minute now my cell phone was going to start ringing.

"Dad? What is it?" All I could think of was that he was sick again, only this time with something we wouldn't be able to medicate.

He turned left again. "Well, I was down at the Waco Diner and I overheard something this morning. You know, those fellows over at the Coast Guard Station think a lot of Andy Devine."

The truck dipped into a little valley with a stream at the bottom of it, chuckling over a stone spillway. "And?" I prodded him.

His bushy eyebrows knit. "And it seems they'd got up a reward for whoever cleared Andy. You know, the whole information-leading-to bit."

I began to see where this might be going. "But, Dad—"

Because this was about the Moose, I was sure of it. He thought a lump sum award might pull the shop out of the dire straits it was in.

And then Ellie wouldn't have to go, which was the lump in my throat that I just couldn't seem to swallow no matter how I tried.

"And you two are going to get it, is what I heard. In fact," he added a little shamefacedly, "in fact, I went over and asked the guys about it, to make sure I *did* hear right. And they confirmed it."

Wonderful. But: "Dad, that's very nice and I'm

sure for Ellie especially it will come in handy. I mean, assuming it *does* happen," I said, and he nodded, accepting this.

Because in this world, as we'd all just learned yet again in our different ways, nothing is certain.

"But it's not going to be enough to—"

"Ten thousand dollars," he pronounced.

I just stared at him.

"Also," he said, ignoring my expression, "I learned one other thing while I was at it."

I half-expected him to say he'd discovered the secret to world peace; after that first bombshell, anything was possible.

"Two things, actually," he amended as we climbed out of the valley. Here the granite hills thrust sharply upward, thinly covered with soil so that grassy chunks of it sagged downhill like frosting.

"The first thing," he said, his knobby hands curved around the wheel competently, "is that according to Bob Arnold, nobody who's in any authority to do anything about it is worrying too much about why that damned barn blew. And," he added, "they're not going to be."

I turned to him. "Dad! You mean you really *did*—"

His skinny shoulders moved up and down. "Jacobia, I had to do it. I had no phone, no weapon, and with nobody else around—"

Right, I thought, it must've been pretty scary. He went on. "I couldn't very well go charging in there with just my . . . well."

He'd been about to say something rude about having something in his hand; I appreciated his restraint. But . . .

"You used explosives?" I couldn't believe it; I'd thought he'd given up the really dangerous parts of that old past life. But now I recalled the cardboard box in the truck bed that day, and understood.

"So I had a few old things lying around, so sue me," he said. "It wasn't even anything big, just maybe the size of cherry bombs was all. I wanted them off the property, anyway."

Because of the baby, he meant. "In fact, I was in the midst of getting rid of them that day when . . . well, at any rate they're all gone now, so you don't have to worry about them anymore," he finished as we rolled up onto a bluff overlooking the bay.

Gone because he'd used them. I couldn't help it; a laugh burst out of me. "Man, that barn really went up, didn't it?" I said, recalling how relieved I'd been. Like, *really* relieved, as Sam would've said.

"It sure did," my dad agreed, accepting the compliment as we drove on. Soon the road narrowed, and when we reached the water's edge where the old toll bridge's seaweed-draped remains stuck skeletally out of the water, we stopped.

"Beautiful," he said, and it was, too, the islands out in the bay showing mistily through a fog so thin that the sun still shone in it.

"Thickening up, though," he observed, turning the truck around to head back. To our south, the horizon was already cloud shrouded.

"Anyway," he said, "the other thing I learned at the Waco was—"

I was still thinking about my dad racing down to that barn of Norm's, placing whatever he'd used to create an explosive diversion and getting away uninjured.

So he could save my life. Ellie's, too, of course. "Thanks, Dad," I said, feeling all at once like everything was hilarious.

Like, *really* hilarious . . . "You're welcome," he replied gravely, but his crinkly old eyes twinkled; apparently he thought so, too.

Just not the part about Ellie leaving; at the thought I felt downcast again. And then as we turned back onto Route 190, he told me.

"Seems Andy and Sharon have changed their minds about going on a honeymoon. Instead they've decided to purchase the bakery building," he said. "And not charge any rent to the two women who, as Andy put it, saved his bacon and his new wife's, too."

I sat back in the big red truck's plush leather

passenger seat. It was heated, and had more positions than a yoga instructor.

Also, the vehicle ran powerfully and smoothly, and it handled well, with none of that swerving and swaying around that a less-well-engineered vehicle might tend to display.

"Wh-what did you say?" I managed, and then, "Are you *sure?*"

Because that would change things tremendously: a lump sum plus much less monthly overhead expense would carry us through lean spots for a couple of years at the very least.

My dad whisked us up onto the causeway toward Eastport. Tide ponds, clam flats, spruce trees, and sweetgrass fields flew by.

He drove easily and well. "I'm sure. I went and talked to him this morning before the ceremony, wanted to get it right. He signed the sales agreement, soon as he got free and heard what happened."

We rolled past the city yards, where the big orange plows were parked for the summer, lined up at the very back edge of the gravel lot. Next came the campgrounds, the power plant, and the long curve leading around into Eastport.

"And," my father said, "not only that, but it seems the Coast Guard is looking for a civilian contractor for the Eastport station. Carpentry, maintenance, general repairs . . ."

George's specialties, in other words. It would mean he needn't leave Eastport, either.

"Oh," I breathed, and moments later we pulled up outside my big old house on Key Street.

I still couldn't speak, my heart thumping with excitement and hope: could it be true? But when I looked out the truck window, there they all were, and the big smiles on their faces said that *something* wonderful had happened.

"Jake!" Ellie cried breathlessly, running down from the porch to meet me. "You're won't believe what Andy and Sharon have decided—"

So I let her tell me again, and about the reward, too, which we, of course, were going to donate part of, but still.

"Jake, it means we can stay!" she rejoiced. "I mean, for a couple of years, anyway, and by then who knows what might happen!"

From the porch rail where George leaned, grinning, I gathered he felt the same way. He'd never wanted to leave here; no one does.

And there was one final surprise. Going up the front walk, my dad stopped me before a skeptical-looking Bella could get to him.

"Listen, I thought I might just give Sam that truck," he said.

He angled his head back at the shiny red vehicle, then waved at the pile of yard-work tools that Sam had assembled. With them sat a truck ramp, a riding lawn mower, and some other yardish-looking items.

All were cleaned and repaired. "Those tools

and so on will all fit in that truck bed pretty well, don't you think?" my dad asked.

But he knew the answer, and so did Sam, who by the grin on his face as he jogged over to us had already been informed of the plan.

"I've got a customer already," he informed us happily. "That big house out on the point, with the lawns and manicured shrubberies."

He sloped off happily to join Mika and Ephraim, while Bella, finally persuaded by the smiles on all our faces, beamed down at them from the porch. Then Wade arrived, swinging into the driveway and hopping down from his own truck, making a beeline for me.

"Hey." He dropped an arm carefully around my shoulders. "How're you doing?" He'd been helping the church ladies take home the serving dishes and utensils from the wedding reception.

"Fine," I breathed, leaning against him while the rest of the bunch went inside.

It was still only mid-afternoon, but the bright day was over; cool fog drifted up the street, billowing in gauzy plumes and settling an early dusk on the town.

A foghorn honked. "So about the baby," Wade began, and I looked up; this was the only part that still didn't make sense to me.

"I talked with Tabitha," he said. "The teenaged babysitter Mika's been using?"

Right, from across the street; the one whose house we'd gone to and whose door Bob Arnold had pounded on when we were looking for the missing youngster.

"But she wasn't . . ." Home, I meant to finish. The girl had been asked about it in the days since the event.

"Well, actually she was," Wade corrected. "She's just felt too scared and guilty to say so. And I'd had a feeling about that, so . . ."

"A feeling about Tabitha?" I questioned, and he nodded firmly.

"So I went over this morning while she was outside, had a little conversation with her," he said. "Let her know that everyone here was still pretty worried, that it would help us out a lot if we just knew what happened."

"And that nobody would be mad at her," I added. Which for having that kind of a conversation, there was no one better than Wade.

"Yup. So in a little while, the story came out."

We walked slowly toward the house. "Tabitha was supposed to babysit that day, remember? Mika says the girl had arranged to take Ephraim over to her house and keep him inside the fenced area they'd set up. But when she came to our place for him, nobody was around."

Just the baby in his playpen. "So she took him, anyway."

"Uh-huh. She's done it before if Bella's upstairs

393

for a minute or whatever. So Tabby took Ephraim across the street, put him down on the blanket inside the fence, and ran inside her own house to get him a toy and her workbook for a science project she's doing at school."

I couldn't help smiling. "Really opened up about the whole thing, didn't she?"

"Yeah," Wade chuckled, "she was dying to tell, really. Scared she'd get in trouble, but—"

"So then what?" I cut in. But I'd already guessed what must've happened, just not the details. "That's when we all rushed out and finally spotted him there alone?"

"Yup. She was inside, ready to run out again, but just then her dad called, she knew from the caller ID it was him. And he's . . ."

"Needy. Demanding. A pain in the . . ."

"You got it," Wade nodded emphatically. "He's yelled at her before, she told me, when she wouldn't answer the phone. So she did, and then he didn't believe her when she said she couldn't talk right then. Guilt-tripped her and so on."

I understood. "So it took a while, and by then Bob was probably pounding on her door. So she got *more* scared and wouldn't answer?"

"Precisely," agreed Wade as a relieved sigh whooshed out of me. I *hadn't* put Ephraim in harm's way, after all.

"What did you tell Tabitha about all this?" I asked, already thinking about asking the girl to babysit again, maybe on a regular basis, so as to get Mika more involved in The Chocolate Moose.

Bella could use more time with the house all to herself, too, I thought, the way it used to be. I'd ask Mika about that, as well.

Wade put his other arm around me, squeezing gently. "I said that what she'd confessed was understandable, although, of course, it should not happen again, and she should come on over and tell you about it, too, and apologize for the fright she gave everyone."

In the thickening fog of an island summer evening in Maine, my big old house loomed whitely like a ship plowing through mist.

"And she promised she would," Wade went on. "So she felt better, and I felt better, and then I told her not to worry about it anymore, because . . ."

The porch light went on, shedding a warm glow onto the fog-swept front lawn. The baby laughed, and from Sam and Mika's room upstairs faint music began drifting.

" 'All's well that ends well,' " Wade said.

Ginger Chocolate Biscotti

The gingery heat in these biscotti gets mellowed by the rich, melty chocolate. They're knockout good, and you make them this way:

Preheat the oven to 325 degrees and get out a cookie sheet. I don't grease mine, but you know your own cookie sheets better than I do, so use your judgment. Assemble the ingredients:

1 cup flour
¾ teaspoon baking powder
½ teaspoon ground ginger
¼ cup softened butter
⅓ cup sugar
1 egg
½ teaspoon vanilla
⅓ cup crystallized ginger, very finely chopped
½ cup semisweet chocolate chips

Mix together the flour, baking powder, and ground ginger. In another, larger bowl, mix together the butter and sugar until creamy, mix in the crystallized ginger, and beat in the egg and the vanilla. Then mix the dry ingredients into the moist ones and stir until well blended. Last, mix in the chocolate chips.

Now take a large serving spoon and scoop all the batter up into it. Drop the batter from the spoon into your other hand and use both hands to form a 12-inch-long log. Place the log onto the cookie sheet.

Bake the log at 325 degrees for 25 minutes, remove from oven, cool for ten minutes, and then slice the log with a sharp knife into 12 slices, leaving the slices standing up, separate from one another on the cookie sheet. Return them to the oven for 5 minutes to dry them out a bit (or if you like them very crunchy, for up to 10 minutes).

This recipe makes a dozen.

Center Point Large Print
600 Brooks Road / PO Box 1
Thorndike, ME 04986-0001 USA

(207) 568-3717

US & Canada:
1 800 929-9108
www.centerpointlargeprint.com